SWEE[...]
COL[...]

including

LOVE IN THE FAST LANE
by Rosemary Vernon

PROMISE ME LOVE
by Jane Redish

THE PROBLEM WITH LOVE
by Rosemary Vernon

BANTAM BOOKS
TORONTO • NEW YORK • LONDON • SYDNEY • AUCKLAND

SWEET DREAMS COLLECTION
A Bantam Book

Cover photo by Pat Hill

This collection first published 1989

including

LOVE IN THE FAST LANE
A Bantam Book/July 1984
Copyright © 1984 by Rosemary Vernon and Cloverdale Press Inc.

PROMISE ME LOVE
A Bantam Book/February 1987
Copyright © 1986 by Cloverdale Press Inc.

THE PROBLEM WITH LOVE
A Bantam Book/April 1982
Copyright © 1982 by The Cloverdale Press and Rosemary Vernon

ISBN 0 553 40077 0

*Reproduced, printed and bound in Great Britain by
BPCC Hazell Books Ltd
Member of BPCC Ltd
Aylesbury, Bucks, England*

LOVE IN THE FAST LANE

Rosemary Vernon

*Special thanks to Michael and
Jon-Pierre Levesque
for their valuable information on motocross.*

Chapter One

"**H**ey, what do you think you're doing?" Alison Matlock snapped, dragging Jeff Cutler away from the open hood of the car. "Trying to kill us both?"

Jeff was about to undo the radiator cap of his overheated car without waiting for the steam to die down. His car had suddenly started to sputter and finally chugged to a stop, steam pouring out of the engine. Jeff had swaggered over and lifted the hood as though he were Mr. Mighty Mechanic.

"You obviously don't know the first thing about cars," Alison continued. It was unlike her to be so snotty, but Jeff was really too much. If there was one thing she couldn't stand, it was a know-it-all boy—especially when it came to cars. Alison had been rebuilding engines before she could even drive them, and when Jeff pretended that he was going to save helpless Alison, her patience gave out.

1

She stood with her hands on her hips, her big brown eyes narrowed, and said, "Go ahead, try fixing this car yourself and see whether you make it home by Monday morning. As for me, I'm leaving. Good night." With that she turned away from Jeff, his gaping mouth, and his steaming car and walked briskly away.

It had not been a fun evening from the start. Sure, Jeff was popular and handsome. A lot of girls would have loved to have been in Alison's shoes that night. Jeff was one of these all-around talented boys, one who had a charming smile and always won student council elections and played the leads in school musicals. He had asked Alison out only after a lot of pressure and hinting from her friend, Heather, whose brother was Jeff's best friend.

Such set-ups never worked. They always made Alison feel at a disadvantage—like some poor, lonely soul who needed help in meeting boys and going out on dates. She had never seen herself like that before. Her natural good looks and quick smile had always rewarded her with lots of friends. But after Marty, she had found herself wanting to be alone more and more, not smiling quite so often and only going through the motions of being interested in meeting people and doing things.

"Oh, Marty, I miss you," Alison whispered into the dark night as she walked toward the bus stop. How many times in the past year had she murmured the same thing?

Marty had been her first love. "Soul mates" was what everyone had called them. Ever since he had moved next door to Alison when she was in first grade and he was in third, they had been friends. Alison was adventurous, and was willing to do anything Marty did. Their friendship had blossomed into a romance when Alison began ninth grade.

Marty and Alison were exactly alike. They both loved challenges and excitement and fun. It was Marty who had taught Alison all about cars—and every boy she met after Marty seemed boring and bland by comparison.

She thought about the hours she had spent huddled under the hoods of cars with Marty. The image of his face, black with grime and grease, grinning up at her as he slid out from under a car, brought a slight smile to Alison's face. He was so happy-go-lucky and free. Marty never seemed to be afraid of anything—whether it was tackling a new problem with an engine or racing toward a challenging finish line.

Marty had been a stock-car racer—and a really good stock-car racer, too. He had won so many races that it was a wonder that his trophies meant anything at all to him. Part of Marty's success had been that he was as safe as he was fast. That was what made his last race such a shock. Marty didn't believe anything terrible could ever happen to him when he was racing—and, as a result, neither did Alison.

She wished she could know if he was afraid just before he died. There were three days of agony as he lingered in a coma, somewhere between life and death. She had put all of her energy into giving life to Marty during those three days, whispering, "Live, live, live" continuously. But Marty needed more than words to live.

Alison had lost her best friend and her only love. She kept thinking that if she hadn't been in love with Marty, she wouldn't feel so much pain now. Her friends, especially her two best friends, Heather and Julie, tried to keep her from withdrawing and building a protective shell around herself. They set her up with dates and always included her in their

4

plans. Alison had seen almost every movie that had come to town and been to lots of concerts. Heather and Julie had practically become her sisters. They came over all the time, and they made sure she stayed in the swing of things.

But in spite of their efforts, Marty was continually on Alison's mind. It had been exactly one year since he had died. She hadn't had another steady boyfriend, and her blind dates seemed absurd when she recalled Marty. They had known each other so well, had really clicked. And sometimes they seemed to know what the other was thinking without uttering a single word.

The one thing that still didn't seem absurd to Alison was working on a car. She loved to dig into a sick engine, thinking logically and mechanically to solve its problem. The results of her work were immediate and always satisfying. Cars were a part of Marty that Alison had to hang on to—all but the racing of them, that is. She had never been back to a race track. The thought of cars zooming around a track was now a nightmarish memory.

Her daydreaming was interrupted by a sudden squeal of tires and a screech of brakes.

At first she was afraid that the car pulling up next to her was Jeff's. Maybe he had fixed it and was now coming to flaunt his success as a mechanic. But instead a cheerful-looking boy with red hair stuck his head out of the open window of a pickup truck. Alison had never seen the driver before, a guy about her age who had a welcoming grin on his face.

"It's pretty late to be walking alone. Need a lift somewhere?" he asked.

Instinctively Alison refused and kept walking, her eyes on the road in front of her.

The voice said, "Your choice. Maybe some other time. Be safe, now."

Alison stared longingly after the rear lights, disappearing around the bend. It wasn't that she minded walking. It wasn't that late, and there were several couples out walking and enjoying the warmth of the April night. But there was something about that open smile and the friendly, songlike voice. She was sure she could have trusted that boy for a ride home. Just for an instant she had forgotten the misery of her evening.

Well, at least I'm not a basket-case, she thought as she boarded the bus. *Some things can still cheer me up a bit.*

* * *

"It looks as if a man is going to help you in the fulfillment of your dream," intoned Heather, running her fingers over a Tarot judgment card.

"Oh, give me a break, Heather," replied Alison. "That's what you tried to tell me about Jeff and look what happened with him. I made a total fool of myself."

Julie giggled and reached for another slice of cheesecake. The three friends all had the last period free on Fridays, and every week they would gather at Alison's to watch their favorite soap opera. Traditionally Julie would make some exotic but delicious food for the occasion. She was a great cook and constantly tried out new recipes and tested them on her friends.

Julie and Heather were opposites in almost every way possible. Julie was the practical problem solver, while Heather was more emotional and dreamy. Even physically they were opposites. Julie was short and needed to lose about fifteen pounds. Her short, curly hair matched her round body. Heather had long, blond hair, and her tall, lean body resembled a picket fence. But Heather was anything but gawky or stiff. She was devoted to modern dancing and really knew how to move what little flesh she had.

Heather always brought her Tarot cards over on Fridays to entertain her friends during the commercials. Neither Julie nor Alison believed that the cards could foretell the future. They were convinced that Heather just used the cards as an excuse to give advice. But they always pretended to take her seriously.

"Get a load of this, Alison," Heather continued, not to be put off by her friends. "This is the three of cups. You have had serious doubts about your future happiness, but never fear. Because of some effort on your part and some chance happenings, including a mysterious visitor and the help of a man, you should have a happy answer to your burning question." Heather sat back with a self-satisfied smile.

"And what question might that be?" asked Alison. "I know my problems all too well. Seems like my biggest problem is that too many people are trying to give me answers. Anyway, are you trying to tell me to sit back and twiddle my thumbs, waiting for Prince Charming to come and rescue me? So much for all your efforts at matchmaking."

They were in one of the sitting rooms in

the inn that Alison's family had bought three years before. Her parents loved the inn in the Berkshire Mountains in Massachusetts. It had been a run-down eighteenth-century farmhouse when they had bought it. Alison's mother had transformed it into a modern, comfortable living space that retained its earlier charm. Each room was individualized with the antiques that Mr. Matlock collected. It had a homey and warm atmosphere.

The friends' chatter was interrupted by the phone.

"Maybe that's your Mr. Mystery right now," chimed in Julie. Her smile was teasing.

Alison picked up the phone, trying to answer in her most casual voice but half expecting some man to claim her as his queen then and there.

It was a guest of the inn, canceling the inn's only reservations for that night.

"No problem," replied Alison. "I hope you can make it some other time."

Alison was relieved when she hung up the phone. She helped out at the inn a lot, especially during the busy months and on weekends. Usually she enjoyed the work. But she had been wanting to put a new radiator in her father's Toyota for a few weeks. The cancellation meant that she would have time before dinner to run over to the junkyard and get started on the project. She could finally spend some time with her true love, a sick car.

Chapter Two

"Hi."

Alison turned in the direction of the voice. A boy walked toward her from a pickup that had just arrived at the junkyard gate.

"Want some help?" he asked when she didn't respond.

Alison was poised under the hood of an old Chevy, disconnecting the radiator hoses. "I can do it, thanks," she replied, undoing the last bolt that held the radiator in place.

"Let me." He moved next to her, and she became aware of the mixed scents of motor oil and soap on him as he helped her hoist the radiator out of the car.

"Thanks."

"Where to?"

She pointed to the Toyota station wagon on the other side of the cyclone fence. They walked through an opening and over to the car. She spread newspapers inside the back of the Toyota so that the boy could set the radiator down.

He was tall and the large muscles in his back and upper arms showed through his blue T-shirt. He wore a blue- and white-striped cap low over his brow, shading his freckled nose and hiding his hair. There was a little white scar shaped like a bow next to his mouth, which Alison focused on.

"Are you doing this job yourself?" he asked, looking straight at her with his dark brown eyes.

Alison shivered slightly even though there was a warm breeze. "Yes. That radiator is practically new."

"So I noticed. Are you good at fixing cars?" He seemed genuinely interested.

"I'm OK," she answered and shrugged, not wanting to appear immodest.

"How'd you ever get into it?" he asked.

"My old boyfriend, Marty Willins, taught me everything I know."

"Marty Willins, the driver?" The boy seemed impressed. "I've heard of him. He's a great racer. *Was*, I should say."

Alison nodded automatically but was silent and stared at the ground.

"Sorry." He made a circle in the dust with the toe of his sneaker.

"Yeah, me, too," she said softly.

"I'm looking for an engine," he said cheerfully, changing the subject. "Do you know where there are some late-model Fords?"

Alison took in his pleasant, wide grin, the sun that was slanting across his face, and the way he shoved his hands casually into his Levi pockets. With one foot leaning on a car bumper, he waited for her reply.

"They brought in a new Ford last week," she said, smiling. "Follow me."

"I need to get my pickup fixed, my dad's getting tired of me driving his. Then I'll be able to haul my bikes around again. Hey, this one looks great." He glanced inside the red truck, then yanked up its hood. "Only seventeen thousand miles on this thing. Not bad, huh? This is exactly what I've been looking for. My troubles are over."

"How do they get the engine out?" Alison asked.

"They cut it out with a blowtorch. Then I pick it up tomorrow." He grinned at her. "By the way, my name's Billy Kendall. What's yours?"

"Alison Matlock." He extended a freckled

arm to her, and she took his hand, warmed by his firm shake.

"Ever put in an engine before?" He was twisting sideways as he leaned into the truck's engine.

"No." Alison studied his back. "But I've always thought it would be interesting."

"Would you like to help me put this one in?"

"Well, sure." Alison wondered why she felt so comfortable talking to Billy. Maybe it was because the subject of cars and engines was so familiar.

"It's a grungy, two-day job—taking out and putting in. You probably know that already," he explained.

"I've got time, and I'm not afraid of grunge," she said.

He grinned. "I believe it. You're a rare bird." His eyes followed the line of her long brown hair, which spilled loosely over her shoulders.

Together, they walked up to the office, a ramshackle shed that cast a long shadow across the crumpled bodies of cars and trucks.

"That's one good deal you've got there," the owner of the junkyard told Billy with

14

enthusiasm. "I'm charging you three-fifty for it. I just got that truck in the day before yesterday."

"Sounds OK to me," Billy said. "Still cheaper than a new car."

The radiator Alison had just removed cost her twenty-five dollars.

"Both of us made out like bandits today," Billy remarked once they were outside. "Maybe we should work together. I can help you with the radiator after I get this engine in."

"OK. This weekend?" She hoped he didn't think she was too pushy, but she was suddenly enthusiastic about the idea.

"Yeah, sounds good. I'll give you a call early tomorrow morning. Are you in the book?"

"Yes."

"OK, Alison Matlock. See you then." He hoisted himself onto the truck seat, removed his cap in imitation of a true gentleman, and bowed his head in a goodbye flourish.

And what a flourish! Spilling out from under the cap was a mass of red curls. Unmistakable big, red corkscrew curls that flew everywhere without the containment of the cap. Billy Kendall was the boy who had stopped her on the road the night before!

What a coincidence, she thought, trying to close her mouth as he drove away, waving his arm out the window. Not only had she felt comfortable with him at the junkyard, she had even felt comfortable when he stopped for two seconds to ask her if she needed a ride home.

As she slid into her father's Toyota, Alison smiled to herself. *Maybe this is Heather's mysterious visitor,* she thought.

In the rearview mirror she watched Billy turn his truck out of the rutted road onto the state highway. She kept sight of it in the rearview mirror until the pickup disappeared in the flow of traffic that sped westward across the valley.

Yes, cars were a weird pastime for a girl, she reflected, gunning her motor. But then cars had been a big part of a very special friendship. She remembered that she and Marty had planned to put a new engine in his car after the race that turned out to be his last.

Funny how things happen, she thought, suddenly aware that her loneliness had dissolved as she imagined herself working beside Billy Kendall. She'd been solo for too long. . . .

Chapter Three

Alison fixed a bowl of ice cream for dessert and went to talk to her father in his office.

"I found a radiator at the junkyard, Dad. Your car will be like new in no time at all."

Tom Matlock had short-cropped, brown hair the same shade as Alison's. His features were sharp and distinguished. He glanced up from his bookkeeping to smile at his daughter.

"You're going to need a hand with it, aren't you? Buzz Tyler might be free this weekend—"

Buzz was a friend of the family who had helped Alison with a few repairs in the past year.

"No, Dad, I won't need help. I met a guy at the junkyard who's putting in an engine this weekend. I'm helping him with that, then he'll come over, and we'll do the radiator." Alison tried not to show her excitement.

"Sounds like a great way to spend the weekend," her father said, laughing. Working on cars was not his idea of relaxation.

"Things may be busy around here this weekend, Al," said her father, thinking about the inn. "If you can't work, will you see if Heather wants to take your place?"

Alison nodded and stared at her father poring over his long columns of addition. Suddenly she felt weary as she looked at her father's tired face. As much as he loved the inn, it was still hard work to run it. Even after dinner there was a lot of work to do.

Alison was the Matlocks' only child. Marty had been almost like a son to them, but now there was just Alison. They had tried to hide their own sorrow to help Alison recover. They hoped that by keeping her busy she would start to forget about the pain that she had been through.

"Al, come here a minute, will you? I want your opinion on this wallpaper!" Alison's mother poked her head around the corner and motioned to her.

"Sure." Alison followed her mother upstairs to the room she was redecorating. Wallpaper books were spread out on the floor near a swatch of rust carpeting. Her mother

18

was kneeling on her hands and knees, experimenting with different combinations. Like Alison, Marcy Matlock was slender and of average height and had delicate features. Her blond hair was naturally curly and fell in soft swirls about her face. She was active, fun, and casual, preferring sweat pants to a skirt any day.

"Which do you like better? The floral or the checks for this room?"

"The floral," Alison said. "It goes with the French print chair."

"You're right!" her mother exclaimed. "I never thought of that. I knew you'd save the day." She kissed Alison lightly on the cheek and absently asked about her day.

"I bought a radiator," Alison said, realizing how different she was from her mother, who barely knew how to use a self-service gas pump. Yet Alison had inherited a flair for decorating from her.

"Sounds thrilling, Al," Marcy Matlock said, laughing. "It'll be nice to get that car running right again, won't it? I'm sick of the knocks and pings."

"Yeah."

"Anyone helping?"

"A boy I met at the junkyard."

"Another grease monkey, huh?" her mother asked, giggling. "Sometimes I wonder about you."

"I think it'll be fun."

"Is he cute?"

"Is that all you ever think of, Mom?"

"Sorry. It's just that I worry about you."

"He's got two left feet, a crooked nose, and ears like Dumbo."

"You're such a tease. But you understand I want the best for you, don't you? You don't seem very interested in finding a boyfriend." She stacked the wallpaper books.

"There are not very good choices out there," Alison said, sighing. "I'd rather not waste my time."

Alison went downstairs to her bedroom, a large space with windows overlooking the back woods. The room was decorated in a blue bandanna print wallpaper, with matching bedspread and curtains. Alison had taken several photos of Marty's race car, and these hung in a cluster over her dresser. A collection of antique dolls sat at the end of her four-poster brass bed. She had started collecting them years before, when she went to antique auctions and flea markets with her father.

Alison changed into a pair of designer

jeans and a soft wool sweater. She was going to the movies with Heather and Julie. Alison tried on some eyeshadow and mascara—her complexion was smooth and clear, so she needed nothing else. She hadn't worn makeup in a long time, but somehow she felt like being a little prettier that night. "Just in case you bump into Billy Kendall again, huh?"

She laughed at her own silliness, but she was surprised at the warm glow she felt at the thought of running into Billy.

Julie and Heather breezed in. "It's so windy out there! I love it!" Heather exclaimed. "We ought to go kite flying tomorrow." Heather was the athletic one of the two.

"Hey, guess what? I'm going out with Barry Saturday night." Heather gave her friends a self-satisfied smile as they walked outside to Julie's car. Barry was the tallest boy in the eleventh grade. Heather was always looking for someone taller than herself.

"Are you still his lab partner?" Alison asked as they got into the car.

"Yes. We've been rubbing shoulders in chemistry for the last six weeks, which has helped us get to know each other. We talk about everything under the sun—except chemistry, of course. I've been sort of keeping him a secret."

"So we noticed."

"But he asked me if I wanted to see the new movie at the Windsor, and of course I said yes. I'm dying to see it."

"The Windsor doesn't play new movies," Alison noted.

Heather sighed. "It's an old movie we both missed."

"How romantic." Julie stared at the red light before her.

"It's a start, anyway. At least he won't have to stand on tiptoe to kiss me good night."

Alison laughed, although she did feel sorry for her friend because she was so embarrassed about her height.

"I'm doing a piece for the newspaper on new couples on campus. Can I include you two?" Julie asked mischievously. Another of Julie's interests was writing.

"Don't you dare. At least not yet," Heather instructed. "We aren't an official *couple* yet. I mean I just told *you* girls about it, don't go telling the world."

"Did you find your radiator, Grease?" That was Julie's nickname for Alison. Both girls teased her about her interest in cars—

especially when she would join a group of boys at a party and talk about nothing else.

"Yes. I found a nearly new one at the junk-yard for twenty-five dollars. I'm really excited about it."

"It's almost as exciting as my date," Heather said and giggled.

"In a different category, I think. I'm putting it in this weekend with a boy I met at the junkyard."

Both girls' eyes widened in curiosity. "Who?" they asked as a chorus.

"I've never seen him before. He must go to another school," Alison replied quickly, knowing they were trying to picture who he was. She didn't want to tell them too much just yet—the coincidences surrounding their meeting; the little somersault of her heart—it was still too soon to be talked about. "I'm helping him put in an engine this weekend, too."

"Wow. Just like that?" Heather asked.

"He's easy to talk to. A nice guy," Alison found herself saying defensively.

"Is this one of those love-at-first-sight things?" Julie wanted to know.

"What did I tell you yesterday, Al? This is your mysterious visitor," Heather cried jubilantly, clapping her hands. "It's amazing."

"OK, you guys. There is no love involved—except for maybe a love of grease and getting cars running," Alison told them loftily and was glad the night was dark so they couldn't see her blush. "I've never put in an engine, and although that sounds incredibly boring to you, it's not to me. It's going to be fun."

"Yeah, I suppose it will be. You were going to put in an engine with—" Julie stopped in mid-sentence. "Gee, sorry, Al."

"It's OK. I know—with Marty," Alison finished for her. "It'll be good for me. Even you guys would probably order some cure like that for me."

"Yeah, you're right. Except that it's not the sort of activity that we think of first," Heather added practically.

"Hey, Al, what's this guy's name?" Julie asked.

"Billy—Billy Kendall."

Alison thought his name had a nice ring to it when she said it out loud, but she didn't mention anything more to her friends. Her thoughts of Billy were brushed away as they pulled into the parking lot of the movie theater.

In the deli where they stopped on the way

home, the three girls studied the patrons as though they were characters in the spy thriller they had just seen.

Julie hunched down in the booth, narrowing her eyes to slits.

"Julie, you look crazy," Alison said, giggling. "Before you know it, someone's going to arrest you for escaping the loony bin."

"The question is—is that man in the denim jacket involved in some Mafia scheme?" Julie asked with a mock French accent.

"Actually, I think this restaurant is a Mafia front. Look at how suspicious the waiters act," observed Heather. "They seem anxious to get us out of here."

"I wonder why," said Alison. "Could it be that we're taking up the space of full-paying customers and only ordered Cokes?"

"You *would* think of that." Julie shook her head. "What are you, a double agent or something?"

Alison got up to leave. "C'mon. Let's go see if there's some food at my place."

Sure enough, there were a couple of apple pies cooling on the counter when they walked in.

Alison considered herself pretty lucky.

She loved her home—it was unusual, but it suited her family so well. She liked how it could be a very private place, but at the same time it offered room for many people.

Her friends loved it for their own reasons. Julie's parents were divorced, so that meant she spent only every other weekend with her father and the rest of the time with her mom. The inn was solid and welcoming for her. Heather was the oldest in a family of six kids, and she loved the peace and adult atmosphere of Alison's home.

"I can come over and not worry about tripping over a toy or finding a banana peel under the rug," she explained.

"My dad wants to know if you'll work this weekend," Alison asked Heather while she cut a pie.

"Sure," Heather replied. "While you're off putting in an engine?"

"Yes."

"Hey, Al, you never told us what this mysterious Billy Kendall looks like. His name sounds awfully familiar."

"Probably because it's so common," Alison guessed. "He's got red hair and freckles and is kind of cute."

The girls laughed. "Any other distinguishing qualities?"

"Well, he's got a great smile, a soft way of speaking, and he's just comfortable. That's all I can say."

Heather and Julie exchanged glances. "That, my dear, is a pretty good start," Heather announced dramatically.

"We can see already that he doesn't blend into the woodwork," added Julie.

"Oh, you say that about all boys."

Heather took a large bite of pie. "Mmmm, great. By the way, did you sign up for the float committee, Al?"

"Yes. When do we get together?"

"In about a week."

The float committee had been formed to decorate the "royal float" for the May Day parade. It had to be set up so that there was a special throne for the May Day queen and her court. This year the junior class was in charge of it. Alison had signed up to work on the committee because she wanted to keep herself busy. It was one thing her friends had insisted on after Marty had died, and she hadn't stopped since then. Now, she was starting to enjoy class activities and looked forward to the float.

Alison shook her head at the thought. "What would I do without my social directors?"

Julie held up her hands. "Who knows, my friend!" she exclaimed.

Heather winked. "You know, Julie, I'm not sure we're needed anymore. She seems to be managing quite well by herself these days. Soon we might let her out on her own."

"On a leash," Julie added, and the girls burst into hysterical laughter.

Chapter Four

"I didn't realize your family ran an inn, Alison," Billy said when he phoned early the next morning.

At the sound of his voice, Alison felt her breath catch in her throat. It was like jumping off the high dive or flipping on a trampoline.

"You'll have to see it," she replied.

"I will, when I pick you up. I've already got the engine so I'll be there in fifteen minutes, around ten. OK?"

"OK, see you soon." Alison's heart was beating quickly as she hung up the phone.

Alison settled into the torn seat of the truck. It was the same pickup that had pulled up beside her the other evening. She wondered if he knew it had been she on the road.

"What school do you go to?" she asked, watching him mash the blue and white cap down over his forehead.

It felt strange and a little awkward finding out bits of information about a new person. Alison had always known all there was to know about Marty; so there was never any need to ask all these silly questions.

"I go to Bradley. And you must go to Lee."

She smiled and nodded.

"First, we're going to the car wash to clean the grunge off the engine," Billy said, winking at her.

Alison was struck again by the ease that she felt with Billy. One phone conversation and a meeting at a junkyard were hardly grounds for friendship, yet she experienced an unmistakable warmth when she was with him.

Billy pulled into the car wash and jumped out of the truck. His springy energy caused Alison's heart to take a small leap—as if she expected him to hop away.

She got out, too. "I can help or watch," she said.

"Watching's help," Billy said, dropping the gate on the pickup to hose down the engine. "Of course, you should expect to get dirty, but that comes later. No need to be unrecognizable yet."

Alison laughed. "Is that grease already?"

She pointed to the bluish-black smudge on his forehead.

"No. That's a bruise I got yesterday, fooling around," he said quickly, but abruptly his expression turned mischievous. "Have you been swimming yet this year, Alison?" he asked with mock innocence.

Before she could reply, he turned the hose on her.

"Billy!"

Alison looked down at her drenched T-shirt. The purple ribbon she'd used to tie her hair back clung to it like a dead snake.

"Couldn't resist," Billy said, chuckling. "I knew you'd look so cute."

"Wet is a better description." She couldn't stop herself from bursting into laughter. "Do I spend the rest of the day squelching around in these sneakers?"

"No. I'll lend you some dry ones, although they might not be as fancy as those you're wearing."

They both looked down at Alison's old ripped shoes and started laughing. Absently Billy handed her the hose. She took the opportunity to give him a dose of his own medicine.

"Ahhh!" Billy tried to ward off the blast of water with his arms. His hair formed damp

31

ringlets across his forehead, and when he looked at Alison, his eyes were bright. "I deserved that, didn't I?"

"Afraid so. You look cute," she added, mimicking him. He made a face at her.

"Let's stop for doughnuts, and then we've got to get to work. Did I tell you I work part-time at Whoppin' Donuts?"

"No. Do you get a discount?"

"Yeah—on day-olds."

Billy hopped into the truck, dripping water over the seat and the floor. The two of them giggled so hard on the way to his house that he could barely keep his eyes on the road.

Billy's house was a brown clapboard with a sun deck extending from one side. It was located near one of Lenox's old abandoned estates.

"I used to play over there as a kid," he told Alison, pointing out the stone gateposts that marked the estate driveway.

"My parents looked at some of these estates when they wanted to buy an inn," said Alison. "But most of them are too big."

"They're not good for anything these days, and definitely too expensive and too big to live in."

When Billy opened the garage door, Alison

saw the other truck, which needed the new engine. She also saw two motorcycles, one bigger than the other. Fresh mud was trapped in the tire treads; so she guessed they'd been ridden recently. She remembered Billy had mentioned needing to overhaul his engine so he could transport bikes.

"Those are yours?" she asked.

"Yeah. Both of them," he said. He got out the come-a-long and hooked it onto the elm tree branch that hung over the driveway. "OK, now we'll push my truck up to the tree so that the engine's underneath the come-a-long."

The come-a-long was essential to their work. It was a sort of pulley contraption that Alison had seen before but had never used. They had to hook it to the old engine in order to remove it, and then they would use it again to lower the new engine in place.

"Now we've got to disconnect the radiator hoses," Billy said.

At the mention of the radiator, Alison was reminded of her date with Jeff. *What a creep compared to Billy*, she thought as Billy's expert hands moved confidently in the machine.

"Hey," Alison said out loud as she put a bucket under the truck to catch the drainage from the radiator. "The night before we met at the junkyard, I was walking on Old Mill Road. Was that you who stopped and asked me if I needed a ride?"

Billy looked up, leaning his elbows on the side of the truck. "That was you?" he asked, then hooted. "When I saw you in the junkyard, I thought your profile looked familiar, but I wasn't sure enough to say anything."

Alison went on to explain just why she had been walking at that hour. She left out the part about how she had almost accepted a ride from him, just telling him how mad she had been at Jeff. "You're different," she concluded, all of a sudden feeling shy. "You don't seem threatened because a girl knows about cars."

Alison hadn't really planned on telling Billy all the details, but the words had come so easily. She felt good telling him what she thought. Billy seemed to like the story, and he laughed at the image of Jeff's bumbling under the hood of a car.

Standing on either side of the truck, they were disconnecting the electrical wires now.

"And next"—Billy flipped his wrench in the air and caught it with the same hand—

"we're going to unbolt the engine from the bell housing."

Alison struggled with a sticky bolt that seemed to be rusted in place. She remembered how Marty used to call her "Jell-O-wrists" because she could barely turn bolts that he could undo in a second.

"Are you one of those people who has trouble with mayonnaise jar lids?" Billy asked, noticing her concentrated effort.

"No," she said. "I'll get it—see?" With one final thrust the bolt moved.

"Bravo. Next step—unbolting the motor mounts. But first, let's have some lunch. Mom and Dad are out for the day; so I'll have to make it."

Hours had flown by, but at the mention of lunch Alison realized that she had worked up an appetite. She poured lemonade while Billy made fantastic hero sandwiches on onion rolls. The kitchen was wide, filled with hanging copper pans and pots. It opened into a spacious dining area, where they sat down for lunch.

"I can't get over it. I've never worked on cars with a girl before," Billy remarked after they had finished the heroes. "You're really good."

"Don't tell me you're a macho-Jeff under-neath the surface," Alison said, knowing it was far from the truth. "As for me, I've never eaten such a good hero sandwich."

"Are you suggesting we've got a case of role reversal here?"

She shrugged. "I just don't like to be put in a box. People shouldn't be so strict about what boys can do and what girls can do. It has more to do with what you're capable of."

"Well said," he added and grinned. "Here, try one of my chocolate-chip cookies. I made them especially for you." He handed her a plastic container.

Alison viewed him with surprise. She wondered at his last remark. Had he looked forward to this day as much as she had? She masked her surprise by replying, "You *are* domestic, aren't you?"

"Try to be." Billy winked at her. "But I still have my wild side."

Intrigued by that comment, Alison fol-lowed Billy out to the driveway. It was time to get back to work.

Under his direction, she helped bolt a chain to the sides of the engine; the chain was then hooked to the come-a-long.

"OK, grab the other side of the chain,

Alison. We're pulling it forward now, off the bell housing shaft. That's it—great. Now let's pull it up."

"It's swinging!" Alison cried as the heavy engine started swaying out of control above the truck.

"OK, OK." They both strained to steady the engine. "Easy. Now there, we've got it." Billy wiped the back of his arm along his sweaty brow, leaving a streak of oil. "Whew. Let's dump this and quit. Tomorrow, it's this same process, only we put the new one in."

As they washed up at the outside faucet, Alison asked, "Do you want to come over and take a tour of the inn?"

Billy nodded. "Yeah, sounds great. Can I take a quick shower first?"

Alison wandered around the garage while she waited for him, noting that one whole section of the workbench was filled with parts for motorcycles. She guessed they were dirt bikes. Marty had once thought about racing dirt bikes. Billy looked like the kind of guy who would own them just for fun. There were plenty of trails through the woods to ride on, she thought, poking at a curl of dried mud on one of the tires.

*   *   *

"Pleased to meet you." Alison's father shook Billy's hand firmly. "How's the truck going?"

"We're making progress," Billy said. "Alison's a great worker."

"We never thought she'd turn out to be a mechanic," her father said and chuckled.

"She does have strange interests, but you get used to her after a while," her mother put in jokingly.

"Mother!" Alison groaned in embarrassment.

Billy looked up at the beamed ceiling. "This is a great house. How old is it?"

"About a hundred and fifty years," Mr. Matlock said.

"Let me give you the guided tour that I promised," Alison suggested, touching Billy's arm lightly.

He grinned at her. "I've seen this place from the road so many times and always wondered what it was like inside."

"Actually, we live in a small part of the house," Alison explained, leading the way through the monstrous kitchen, which was equipped like that of a small restaurant. Then she showed him the sitting room, decorated with Persian rugs, antiques, and a grand piano.

"I love the stone fireplace," Billy said. "Wouldn't it be fun to curl up next to it on a cold winter's night?"

"It is—with hot chocolate." Alison's gaze met his, then she moved quickly ahead of him toward her room. "And this is my hangout."

Billy walked quietly from one wall to the next, surveying Alison's collection of pictures. His eyes settled on a group of trophies on the bookcase. "These were Marty's?" he asked quietly.

"Yes."

"The guy was a star, wasn't he?" Billy fingered a gold trophy, then moved on to a photo of Marty's silver racer.

"He was." Alison's throat tightened, and she swallowed hard. She glanced out the window at the garden, which was now full of daffodils.

"I had a good time with you today, Alison," Billy commented, coming up behind her.

She could feel his breath at the back of her neck, ruffling her hair. "Me, too. It was fun," she told him, without turning around.

"You're a great mechanic."

She laughed. "So are you."

"It might be too early to tell, but I think we make a good team."

"Maybe." A blush crept into Alison's cheeks.

She led him out through the bar, where a few guests were gathered. At the door Billy turned to her. "I'll be by for you tomorrow morning at nine, OK?"

"OK."

"You've got grease on your face." Affectionately he rubbed her cheek with his thumb, then turned toward the driveway.

Alison watched him walk toward his father's truck, her hand on the cheek he had just touched.

The process of putting in the new engine was simply the same as taking the old one out, in reverse. The engine had to be lowered from the elm tree toward the truck cavity, then pushed toward the bell housing and carefully placed in. The difficult part was keeping the engine straight and not allowing it to sway.

When they finally had it in place and were busy bolting in the parts, Billy said, "You're a lot of fun to work with, Alison. You sure you never did this before—with Marty?"

"No, we never put in an engine. We were going to . . ." She explained about the accident.

"Sorry—didn't mean to bring up a bad memory." He studied her for a moment, ready for her tears.

"Billy, I'm not an eggshell. I won't break if you talk about Marty. It's been a year, and I'm used to him not being around. Of course, I miss him. We grew up together. He was my first boyfriend." She shrugged, not entirely satisfied that she had convinced him that she could handle herself.

"OK. But I guess I expected you to be more sensitive, you know, burst into tears or something if I said the wrong thing. You're not like that, I'm beginning to see." His gaze met hers, and Alison's heart wavered.

He cleared his throat. "We can work on your radiator tomorrow after school if you like."

"OK. Let's see how the engine works." She got in the driver's seat and started it.

Billy cheered as the engine roared to life.

Billy's parents invited Alison to stay for dinner. After dinner Billy drove her home. It was one of those balmy spring nights with a full moon that casts a yellow glow over the

41

road. Alison sat close to Billy, while he concentrated on the smooth purr of his new engine.

"Sounds good, Billy," Alison said, feeling pleased that she was part of its success.

"Doesn't it?" Billy's hand closed over hers. She was filled with warmth at his touch. He started singing an old song she hadn't heard in years, and she hummed along, harmonizing.

Alison felt so good with him that she was disappointed when the pickup pulled into her driveway.

As she started to get out of the truck, Billy leaned over, and Alison thought he was going to kiss her. Instead, he tickled her. She doubled over, laughing, and ran to the front door.

That night, as she lay in bed, Billy's face filled her thoughts, and his laughter rang in her ears. She pored over every detail of the day as though each were a treasure. She felt as though the rusty bolts in her head had suddenly been loosened and freed.

Chapter Five

"So how'd your weekend go?" Heather asked anxiously Monday morning as the three girls piled into Julie's car.

"Great. We're doing my radiator after school," Alison informed her friends.

Julie shrieked. "That's not the answer we're expecting, Al! Something romantic, please."

"I never meant to be attracted to Billy," Alison reflected dreamily. The truth was, she hadn't thought of anything but Billy all weekend. She kept rolling his image around in her mind. Now she was remembering his brown eyes meeting hers in that mischievous way of his—as though a joke were on the tip of his tongue. She realized how she'd been drawn to him from the first day she saw that red hair.

"Do you think you and Billy are up for inclusion in my article on campus couples?" Julie wanted to know as she swung into the school parking lot. "Nearly everyone in school has been dating the same person for eons, and we need new blood."

Lee High School was a box-shaped brick structure surrounded by a sweeping lawn. The tennis courts, pool, and gyms were hidden behind a row of birch trees.

"She sounds like a vampire, doesn't she?" Heather said, joking.

"You know how popular these articles are," Julie went on, ignoring Heather. "But I'm so desperate for material that I'm ready to make something up."

"How about making up an interview with Mick Jagger?" Heather suggested.

"You guys are a great help." Julie sighed. "We still want to know about your weekend, Al."

"I was hoping you'd forgotten," Alison said and grinned. "But if you have to know: first, we went to the car wash to clean the engine Billy bought for his truck—"

Both girls groaned.

"Spare us the grimy details, Grease," Heather complained.

"What we really want to know is, did he kiss you?" Julie asked bluntly.

"No—we don't know each other that well,

44

Julie. Aren't you rushing things?" Alison felt hot with embarrassment. Just the thought of kissing Billy made her very warm.

"Just trying to see how far this relationship has progressed."

"Yes, well, knowing that whatever I say may end up in the school newspaper makes me a little nervous," Alison told her, hoisting a stack of books under one arm. "I've got to run—I've got PE first period. Catch you later."

"Real cute getaway, Al," Heather called after her. "See you."

Alison ran toward the gym. She knew she wouldn't be able to avoid her friends' curiosity about Billy much longer. They were hot on her tail to know all the details, and she couldn't blame them. The fact that Billy went to another school meant that they were doubly curious. The usual channels of gossip couldn't touch Billy and Alison because no one could observe them together during the day.

The weekend with Billy stood out in Alison's mind as something special. Neither of her friends could understand what it was like to grow close to somebody while putting in an engine. Of course, they knew all about her relationship with Marty, but there had been few surprises with him. She and Marty had

45

been buddies long before they became romantically involved, and then the romance was so slow moving that Alison wasn't quite sure when it had begun. There had been no anniversary and no particular day or event that stood out in her mind. . . .

And just why was she thinking this way? She remembered how Billy had looked, leaning toward her, and wondered if he was thinking about kissing her. She tried to imagine what his lips would feel like, his arms closing around her back, and she trembled.

Billy and Alison had put in her radiator that evening. They tested her car by driving to a cafe.

"When I first saw you at the junkyard, I didn't expect that you'd be like you are," Billy told Alison. They had chosen a corner table where they were away from the bustle and glaring lights. Soft music cushioned the room.

"What did you expect?" Alison questioned, spooning the whipped cream off the top of her cocoa. That night her heart almost stopped in anticipation. She couldn't imagine what he would say next, and everything he said seemed so meaningful.

"You're different. I mean, most of the girls I know who work on cars aren't as pretty as you," he said, his blush deepening.

"That could be a sexist remark, Billy." Alison pretended to frown.

"I didn't mean it that way. I just meant, we seem to get along well. I don't want to get together only when we need to fix a car."

Alison laughed. "Yeah—I do like to do other things."

"Like dance?" Billy grinned, offering her his hand.

"Sure."

They danced slowly to a melancholy love song. They were the only couple dancing, but it didn't matter to Alison. She closed her eyes and enjoyed the tingling warmth of Billy's hand on the small of her back, guiding her movements. She rested her cheek on his red-checkered shirt and breathed in the mingled scents of cologne and motor oil, memorizing the way he felt ncxt to her. His breath against her ear sent tremors down her spine, and she wanted the moment to last forever.

When the song was over, Billy led Alison back to their table, his arm dropping to her waist.

"We'd better get home," he said, checking

his watch. "You said you had to be back by eleven."

"You don't want to risk my turning into a pumpkin," she quipped.

"Or worse, your car."

Billy and Alison walked out to her car, and Billy climbed into the passenger seat. He stroked her hair as she started the car. "Your hair is so pretty—like a waterfall," he murmured, smiling at her in the dark.

Alison didn't know what to say; she was glad she was driving so she could stare straight ahead. Marty hadn't complimented her very often, and she felt shy and awkward now. She supposed that with Marty a lot had been taken for granted, even though they were devoted to each other.

"Have you gone out much since Marty died?" Billy asked suddenly.

"Do you mean, 'out' as in leaving the house or as in dating?"

"As in dating."

"No. But my friends have kept me from sitting home. For a while they fixed me up with anyone they could find, just to keep me busy. It got to be embarrassing, though. Nobody likes a set-up."

"I would have," he said quietly, "if it had been with you."

For the rest of the ride, he kept his hand resting lightly on the back of her neck. She turned the car into her driveway so Billy could pick up his truck.

Knowing that she wanted him to kiss her, Alison cleared her throat, remained seated, and kept both hands on the steering wheel. "Thanks for helping me with my car," she said.

"You're welcome." Then Billy touched her hair again and pulled her gently toward him, covering her lips with his. Alison melted at his touch—she might have been a snowflake disappearing against warm skin.

"I like everything I know about you, Alison Matlock," Billy whispered into her hair, and she smiled.

"Will I see you this week?" she asked, not wanting the day or the magic to end.

"How about Saturday? This week I have to work Tuesday, Wednesday, and Thursday, and I've got to spend some time catching up on my classes. And on Friday I've—got other plans. But Saturday would be great."

Alison looked up and smiled. Again, his mouth met hers. She was caught up in the

49

power of his kiss surging over her, making her feel suddenly reckless. It felt good to let go a little bit after a year of thinking about someone who would never kiss her again. Now Alison wanted to experience Billy, let herself feel what she hadn't been able to feel in a long time. . . .

"I can tell by the look in your eyes that you've kissed him," Julie announced triumphantly.

The three girls were sitting in Julie's bedroom on Friday afternoon. Her house was actually a converted barn, and Julie's room was a loft, reached by a spiral staircase.

"Julie, you make me feel like I have to keep my love life under lock and key." Alison sighed. Although she had told her friends about her date with Billy Monday night, she hadn't told them about his kissing her; she wasn't ready to talk about it.

Julie handed her a plate of chocolate cupcakes. "I promise I won't take notes. Come on, I'm almost done with that article, anyway. You can trust Jules."

Yes, Alison could trust her. Sometimes she trusted her friends more than she trusted herself.

After Billy had driven off on Monday

night, Alison's head started swirling. It wasn't just the dizziness caused by their first kiss that sent her reeling—something was nagging at her. Part of it was the memory of Marty. She knew she couldn't remain faithful to Marty forever, but she felt a little guilty about how quickly she had fallen for Billy. When she had gone into her room, she had taken Marty's picture and stared at it for a long time, trying to sort out her thoughts.

She was also bothered by a slight feeling of dread, as though she were afraid of falling in love again. The pain that she had felt from Marty's death made her never want to get that close to anyone ever again, just in case he would leave her empty, too.

Julie's curiosity didn't help either, even though Alison knew that her friend would probably be able to sort through her mess in a second. She had that kind of mind. It was still too soon to talk about it, though. Alison wouldn't even know where to begin explaining the chaos that she felt.

Julie broke through and interrupted her deep thoughts. "Hey, Ted told me that there's a big motocross race today; in fact, right now. His friend Steve is competing." Ted was her brother, who was home from college for spring vacation. He had been heavily involved in motorcycles when he was in high school. "Shall we go and see what it's like?"

Alison frowned. She still felt queasy just thinking about races. Julie was looking steadily at her, trying to determine whether she should talk Alison into going.

"Come on, Al. It'll be fun. Besides, it's only dirt bikes. You won't know any of the riders. It may even be good for you." Julie's practical mind was persuasive, and Alison started to think about the excitement of a race. She remembered how few things gave her the same thrill as a good race.

Maybe Julie was right—because it was motorcycles and not cars, it wouldn't be scary or upsetting to her. It would just be exciting, like the old days. Maybe now was the time to face some of her fears—Billy had already taught her that much. She had to go on living.

She took a deep breath. "Sure, I'll go," she finally said. Julie silently took her shoulder and gave her a good squeeze.

Chapter Six

Sandwiched between Julie and Heather, with Ted next to Julie, Alison absorbed the sights and sounds of the track.

The motocross track was different from what Alison was used to with stock-car racing. The dirt track was covered with S-curves and hills, sometimes one after another. Ted said they were called whoop-de-dos.

"There's Steve!" Ted exclaimed, pointing to the mass of bikers below. "Number twenty-eight."

Alison picked him out, hunched close to his handlebars, headed for the slotted gate, where each bike waited for the starting signal.

When the gates opened, the bikes sprang forward, spewing trails of dirt from their rear wheels.

"It's just a two-lap race," Ted explained, before he turned his attention to the track. It

53

was obvious nobody would get much more information from him until the race was over.

The bikes churned and plowed up the hills, some of them tipping over, the riders struggling to right themselves. Mechanics rushed on and off the track, helping those who had engine trouble or had to be pulled out of the stream of oncoming bikes.

Alison watched as gloved hands twisted throttles on handlebars, expertly sending the bikes around the bends and over the curves. One in particular, number eighty-one, had a familiar stance. She was instantly reminded of Marty. But why? There was no reason to think of him now, here, unless it was just being at the track that triggered the memory.

"How're you doing, Alison?" Heather shouted above the din.

"Fine, just fine." Actually, Alison was pleased with how well she was holding up. She was under control, not the trembly, nervous person she thought she might be at a track. Maybe it was Billy's influence, she thought, smiling to herself. He had changed her life a little, just in the short time they'd known each other. He was special.

"I knew it would be good for you to see this race, Al," Julie said, not taking her eyes from the track. "I mean, it's not so dangerous. Steve is a real pro. The more professional someone is, the less chance there is of getting hurt."

"I know."

"Oh, sure, I know you know. I forgot." She looked apologetic.

"Steve's moving up front. Look—he's closing in on the leader!"

"Who's that lead bike? Number eighty-one?"

"He's holding position really well."

"Oh, no—look!" Alison jumped to her feet. A rider had been flipped off his bike: the scene before her revived old images of another accident. The rider lay on the track in the path of flying bikes, and one landed on him. Medics rushed over the fence toward the fallen rider, and somewhere an ambulance screamed to life.

"No, Alison—don't look." Heather's fingers pressed into her upper arm, pulling her back to her seat.

"About three people get pulled off the track with injuries every meet," Ted announced casually. "It's really a safe sport."

"You can say both those things in the

same breath?" Alison questioned, but Ted wasn't listening.

The driver was heaped onto a stretcher. Alison wondered if he had a girlfriend. It would be better if he didn't, she thought. She was very relieved she didn't know any of the riders.

A few minutes later, Ted, Julie, and Heather jumped up and screamed as Steve tore through the finish, taking second place.

"I'm going down to congratulate him," Ted said, hugging everyone he knew along the way down the bleachers.

"C'mon, Alison," Julie said and followed her brother. "Let's go congratulate Steve. He's been dying to meet you ever since I told him you used to go with Marty."

Alison knew Steve had a case of hero worship where Marty was concerned. She wished she could tell him not to. She wanted to say, "Go idolize a rock star or a baseball player—not Marty. It might be dangerous to your health."

Yet Alison knew she couldn't do that. The minute she met Steve she realized he had his heart set on racing. He was a fresh-faced, gangly boy with buckteeth and a wide grin. His expression was jubilant.

56

"Congratulations, Steve. I've heard a lot about you," Alison told him.

"Yeah? Really? Well, I think I've heard more about you, and Marty Willins. I mean . . ." He blushed, obviously at a loss for words.

Alison saved him from embarrassment. "It's OK. I'm used to it by now. Marty was a great racer, but that was cars. You're showing great promise on bikes."

"Thanks. Coming from you, that's a compliment." He shook her hand vigorously. "Well, I've got to go. The mechanic's checking my bike out now."

"Good luck—though you don't seem to need it."

"I think that, besides taking second in that heat, meeting you made his day," Heather said.

They settled down to watch the next heat in which Steve was entered. The bikes bucked out of the gate as before. Dirt and gravel crackled under the tires. The roar of the crowd caused Alison's skin to rise up in goose bumps. Why was it that the excitement thrilled through her veins even though she was scared? What was it about racing that so absorbed her? It seemed crazy; yet she reminded herself that she had loved racing before it took Marty away.

She saw Steve roaring along the outside, catching up to number eighty-one, whom she had not really watched during the first heat. An S-curve put number eighty-one in front, and the rider took a series of hills with relative ease, rising off the seat, crouching over his bike in perfect form. The other riders tried to follow his lead.

"Look how he takes those whoop-de-dos," Ted said admiringly.

"Steve's moving in on number eighty-one, isn't he? Who is that rider?" Alison asked.

"I don't know. But he rode a different bike in the first heat."

Alison listened to this conversation with one ear, her mind and body tuned into the engines' roar, the flying dirt, the well-timed movements of the riders before her.

Then Steve dropped back, his bike falling over on an S-curve. Number eighty-one surged ahead. Steve struggled up from under his bike, and a mechanic helped him move to the side of the track.

"What a bummer!" Ted wailed.

Number eighty-one skidded across the finish. The checkered flag came down with a fluttery swoop. The crowd's cheers accompanied the roar of the following bikes.

Wondering about poor Steve, Alison asked, "What happened to Steve?"

"He's OK. Looks like he'll finish about tenth," reported Ted, pointing him out. Sure enough, Steve had joined the other riders, whose cycles screamed past the finish line.

Alison's gaze then fell on the winner's circle. The bright yellow bike was straddled by a boy in a blue and gold driving suit. He was watching his points tallied while fans congratulated him. Then he turned toward the crowd and yanked off his helmet.

For a moment Alison's heart seemed to stop beating. She heard herself gasp as the familiar red hair tumbled out from under the helmet. "Billy!" The unmistakable, triumphant grin that had gotten her attention at the junkyard now filled her with a gripping fear.

"Billy," she whispered again, oblivious to everyone around her.

"That's Billy Kendall?" Julie and Heather said in chorus.

"That's him, all right," Ted informed them excitedly. "One of the best riders you'll ever see. You should see all his trophies."

Billy's face blurred before Alison's eyes.

"I didn't know," she mumbled, stumbling down the bleachers and away from the dusty track and the bikes. She wanted to be as far away from the heady, intoxicating wave of triumph as she could get.

Chapter Seven

"Alison, wait up!"

Heather raced along the planked bleachers, trying to catch up to Alison. "Alison!"

"For crying out loud, stop, will you?" Julie puffed along, bringing up the rear.

Alison stopped below the bleachers and turned to face them.

"You didn't know Billy raced motocross?" Heather took her friend by the shoulders and stared into her sorrowful eyes, immediately knowing the answer to her question. "He should have told you, Al."

"Maybe he knew how you would react," Julie guessed.

"It's not fair, though. He should've said something. Given me some warning, you know." Alison was choking back tears.

"Yes, but how was he supposed to tell you? You wouldn't want anything to do with him if you knew. He didn't want to take that chance, I bet."

"So he didn't bother to think about what the deception might do to me?" she demanded. "Doesn't he know what I've been through?"

"Sure, he understands, but this isn't the same thing. Marty had a freak accident. You know yourself, it's rare that people are killed in stock-car races."

"People still get hurt," Alison insisted and kicked at the dirt in anger.

"People get hurt lots of ways, Al. You can slip in the shower and break your neck," Julie said.

"The question is, Al, can you go on with this relationship?" Heather asked philosophically.

"Sounds like a question from a women's magazine article," Alison said bitterly.

"It's a question you've got to ask, Al," Julie put in. "You've gone through one bad scene with Marty. Chances are slim that you'd have a repeat performance with Billy, but it might be too hard to handle if you did."

"Don't you think I realize that? I thought I did a good job of shielding myself from being hurt again—up until now."

"You did. But you can't predict being attracted to somebody," Heather said.

"Yes, I wish I had a crystal ball," Alison lamented.

"Well, it wouldn't do any good," insisted Julie. "Come on, let's get a Coke and talk about this some more."

They bought Cokes at the concession stand. Alison sipped hers without tasting it. If only Billy weren't into racing, it would be so easy. Why hadn't he said something?

"Alison?"

The surprised voice belonged to Billy. The three girls turned around.

"Oh, you must be Billy," Heather remarked.

"That's right, and you must be—?"

Alison suddenly realized she hadn't told Billy too much about her friends. Julie helped her through the introductions.

"Congratulations," Heather and Julie said together.

"Thanks." Billy grinned and winked at Alison. She managed a small smile.

"Well, we're going to watch Steve in the next race," Heather said. "Nice to meet you, Billy."

"Same here."

The girls walked away, leaving Alison and Billy alone. Alison knew she was staring at him, her eyes shimmering with unshed tears. She didn't want to speak, but her words came tumbling out: "You didn't tell me you raced."

"Would it have made a difference?" he asked softly, stroking her cold, trembling hand.

"I might not have gotten to know you so well."

"That would have been a shame." He smiled, lifting her chin so that her eyes met his. "Can't you guess why I didn't tell you?"

"Yes, but I think it was unfair, under the circumstances. You should've told me," she said in an injured tone.

"Sorry. I didn't mean to hurt you." Billy kicked a rock across the dirt, and Alison watched until it stopped at the root of a poplar tree.

"Did you always hate racing so much, Alison?" Billy asked.

She felt suddenly distant from Billy, set apart from the whole scene, as if she were watching it from the top of the bleachers. The two experiences, Marty and now Billy, hung together in her mind, and there seemed to be no way of separating them. "I used to love

64

racing. I loved it so much," she said. Then she focused on Billy. "I was enjoying the race today, until I found out that you were in it," she admitted.

"I understand," Billy told her regretfully. "But you have to understand me, too."

If Billy only knew the nightmares that she had. She challenged him. "Have you ever lost anyone in a race?"

"No, but I've seen plenty of accidents. Everybody gets up and rides again. Once in a while somebody gets badly hurt, but it's usually from inexperience or foolishness. It's no big deal. This isn't considered a dangerous sport, you know."

"That's what everyone said about stock-car racing."

"I'm not going to argue with you. You're not someone I'd try to convince, Alison. You're speaking from a different experience. But from the driver's seat, it doesn't look bad." Billy's eyebrows rose as if he were asking for Alison's approval.

"I hope it never is bad for you, Billy," Alison told him.

"It won't be." He was so confident, so sunny. *Just like Marty,* she reflected. *Marty would've said something like that.* She felt suddenly chilled.

"Are we still going out tomorrow?" Billy asked as though he'd been reading her thoughts.

Alison wished she'd never met Billy. She wished she could roll back her life and start over. But Billy had jumped into her heart.

It hurt to talk to him like this—it hurt to talk to him at all. "I don't think so, Billy. I'll see you, OK?" she said, her voice quivering. She started to turn away.

He wasn't easily put off, and he grabbed her arm. "Is that a 'seeya' as in, 'seeya today or tomorrow,' or as in 'I don't want to seeya anymore'?"

Alison tried for something in between, something neutral. "I don't want to see you for a bit, please."

"For real?" He looked stunned, hurt. His eyes didn't have a trace of their usual gleam.

Her heart ached. "For real. I need to think, Billy." She scarcely recognized her own voice.

He shrugged, managing a half-smile. "Think happy," he said almost as a question.

She turned and left him standing alone, knowing that to watch him walk away from her would be more painful. She told herself she could forget him. She could forget all about him and get back to that safe place she was in before she met him.

"You're not going to forget him—zap—like that," Heather announced emphatically. "You can't go backward, Alison."

Julie, Heather, and Alison were making flowers for the May Day float. Alison twisted a length of green crepe paper around a pipe cleaner to make a stem.

"Sure I can, Heather," she insisted. "Come on, I've only known Billy a short time. We don't have a history like Marty and I had."

Heather reached for more pipe cleaners.

Heather's room was done in lavender and blue. The carpeting was a luscious, thick blue pile that you could sink your toes into. Along one wall was a ballet bar and mirror for dance practice.

Julie, ever conscious of her weight, sucked in her stomach in front of the mirror. She was on another diet.

"The thing is, he didn't try to hurt you on purpose, Al. It looks to me like he's been trying to protect you from getting upset," she said.

"He didn't do me any favors," Alison replied. "Besides, I think it makes a lot more sense for me to get out of this before I fall in love with Billy."

"Before? Aren't you in love already?" Heather questioned, her eyes zeroing in on Alison.

"Of course not," Alison snapped in denial.

"I suppose it depends on what your definition of 'love' is," Julie put in. "I think sometimes it's good to write a list to see if you *are* in love. You know, an examination of your feelings. I mean, people are all different. For example, from my interviews, I've found that some people can't eat when they're in love. Woody Allen gets nauseous when he falls in love."

"I didn't know you interviewed Woody Allen," Alison said, giggling. "Look, I'm not nauseous, I eat fine, and I know I'm not in love. It doesn't feel like it did with Marty."

But she remembered Billy's kiss. The heat of it had lingered on her lips, warming her for a long time afterward. It was unlike any kiss she had ever had—even from Marty.

"That's because you're more mature," Heather insisted sagely. "Love matures, people mature—"

"I just love the way you two have analyzed my condition. I really think you should go into

68

business—J. Merritt and H. Chadwick, Psychologists," Alison interrupted.

"We're not often wrong. Mark my words— you, Alison Matlock, are already in love." Heather stated this with utmost confidence.

Alison's paper flower trembled on the end of its pipe cleaner stalk. She fiddled with its petals, trying to make it look at least partly real.

"No, I'm not," Alison retorted, realizing that she sounded like a pouting child. Heather and Julie exchanged glances.

"The question is, Al, can you handle it?" Heather got to the heart of the matter.

Alison shivered. Her friends really knew her well. No, she knew she couldn't handle it. Suddenly she felt awfully frail.

"I'm not prepared to lose two people. I think it's over between Billy and me," she said slowly and quietly. But she was already miserable with her decision.

Alison was grateful for a busy week. She ran around arranging details for the float committee and studied for two tests. She didn't have to think about what was lying just under the surface of her mind.

After her conversation with Heather and

Julie, she had realized that she couldn't live with the fear she felt whenever she thought of Billy racing. It was too much.

She also knew that she couldn't demand that Billy give up racing. After all, they had only known each other for a very short time. But even if they had known each other for their whole lives, she couldn't ask that of him.

She realized that Billy just wasn't right for her: she had gotten carried away and had let her imagination get the best of her. Heather's cards had told her she was going to have a mysterious visitor who was going to solve all her problems. Then Billy had appeared. She was angry at herself for being so suggestible.

"I think Mother Nature looks like an Egyptian mummy," Julie said. The five girls on the float committee were in the gym huddled over a mound of papier-mâché that looked worse the more they tried to improve it. They were trying to make a figure of Mother Nature that would be placed in a forest setting. It was pouring rain outside, and all the crepe paper had gotten soaked when they had brought it from the car. The colors had run together into one sad, faded hue, and every time they touched the paper, dye came off on their hands.

"Here's the tape. Let's try to shape her up a bit." Beth tossed the tape to Alison, who wasn't very quick to catch.

She remembered Billy tossing her a wrench. She had missed it by a mile, and he'd ribbed her about it: "So you're not a star out-fielder, huh?"

"Could be—if you gave me a mitt," she had said, laughing.

The memory pinched her face into a frown. She wished she could just forget him—there was no reason to think of Billy now. She figured that they could be friends, but it might be easier if a little time passed first.

It had been over a week since she'd seen him at the track, and she was torn between relief and disappointment that he hadn't tried to contact her.

Alison hung up the damp crepe paper streamers to dry. She had no idea how to hide the water spots, but everyone was so cheerful about the project, it was bound to turn out OK.

Chloe Parker surveyed the mound of papier-mâché that was Mother Nature and clicked her tongue. "I just hope that whoever gets picked as May Queen is prettier than Mother Nature. Heather, maybe if you model for us—" And without waiting for Heather's reply, Chloe started draping strips of crepe paper around Heather's thin frame. The rest of the girls quickly joined in, muffling her giggles by tying crepe paper around her mouth.

"Look! Her neck!" Julie pointed to the torn neckline where Heather was trying to free herself of her wrappings. "She's coming to life!"

Heather staggered toward the others in an imitation of a mummy, while Julie did a mock radio announcement:

"It appears that a mummy from the Egyptian Museum has gotten loose and is prowling about the city. All citizens be on the alert— lock your doors and stay inside. This is a warning—"

She signed off with a muffled scream as Heather's palm clamped over her mouth.

"What happened to that nice Billy Kendall?" Marcy Matlock asked her daughter. "He hasn't been by for a while."

"I asked him not to, Mom," Alison said. Her mother glanced up with a sharp, questioning look, but Alison didn't offer further information.

"I suppose you know best. I just thought he was nice," Mrs. Matlock mumbled.

Alison was helping set the tables for a banquet that Friday evening. Each time the phone rang, and it rang often in the inn, she leaned toward the sound, hoping it was Billy.

But why? Did she just want the opportunity to tell him again that she didn't want to see him?

In any case he hadn't called. Maybe he was afraid she would tell him off. Maybe he was treading lightly for fear of hurting her. Maybe he was giving her time to think about everything, in the hope that she would change her mind. Or, he could have decided that she wasn't worth his time—too sensitive, too hung up on Marty. . . .

Alison toyed with these ideas as she set the tables, taking comfort in the familiar positions of the utensils and the crisp folds of the cloth napkins. A fire blazed in the stone hearth, sending flickering shadows across the beamed ceiling and the white tablecloths. Her father's bent figure, darkly silhouetted in his office, filled her with a sudden warmth. She wanted to hide in his arms, the way she had as a child. She wanted his strong arms to take away all her problems.

Just then, a bicycle touring group began arriving. The group came every year, and Alison always enjoyed their fun and energetic company.

"So how're you doing, Alison?" Mick, the leader of the bike group, asked when the group had all gathered. He dropped a kiss on the end of her nose.

Alison blushed as the other riders chuckled. Mick's girlfriend, Kit, shook her hand warmly.

"Still working on cars?" Kit wanted to know. She did all her own repairs on her bicycle.

"Yup. There's always something to fix." Alison smiled. Mick ruffled her hair playfully and introduced her to some new members of the group.

The cheerful bustle continued as everyone lounged around waiting for dinner. "Hey, let's play some volleyball," Alison suggested, and most of the guests followed her out to the net on the big front lawn.

The evening was warm, and the setting sun still provided enough light so they could see the ball. The highly spirited bicyclists were good players, and Alison was soon concentrating on serves and spikes. It was Mick's turn to serve. Winking at Alison on the other side of the net, he cried, "Get ready for the grand slam, Ally, baby."

And a grand slam it was. The ball came at her so fast that she barely had time to raise her arms. She was all ready for the disappointment of a missed shot when she saw the ball sail back across the net, right back to Mick. There was no one behind her. Who had saved the shot?

She whirled around with the joy of victory on her face, ready to congratulate the quick thinking of her teammates.

"Billy, what are you doing here?" gasped Alison, her expression having instantly changed to one of shock.

"Helping you win your volleyball game," he said lightly. "Hey, keep your eye on the ball."

With a thud the ball fell at her feet.

"Looks like you need me on your team," said Billy.

Alison looked around in embarrassment. She thought she should leave the game and not even speak to Billy, but the group of eager players was hard to resist, and the ball was already being handed to Billy for the next serve.

Alison didn't have to face Billy one-on-one until the dinner bell sounded and the guests sprinted toward the dining room. Billy and Alison lingered on the lawn.

"I brought you something," Billy said, and they walked over to his truck. He leaned in the window, and Alison's eyes fell fondly on his strong back. He handed her a wooden gearshift knob.

"Oh, thanks, Billy. It's just what I wanted."

He laughed. "Do you realize how crazy that sounds? Most girls would rather have a diamond."

"I'm not most girls," Alison reminded him.

He studied her for a moment. "I know. I think that's why I came over tonight."

She blushed, not knowing what to say. His words stunned her. Suddenly she wanted to throw herself into his arms. But she just stood in silence, not knowing how to deal with all her conflicting emotions.

Billy broke the silence by reaching back into his car. This time he handed her a bouquet of tiny lavender roses. "Just so you don't think I forgot the other part of you."

"Oh, they're beautiful, Billy. Thank you. They're my favorite color. How'd you know?"

"Lavender just seems to suit you."

Another awkward moment of silence followed. Alison kept the bouquet of roses over her mouth, pretending to smell them but mostly trying to hide her trembling lips.

Finally Billy said, "I don't know how to say this to you, Alison. So, I guess I'll just say it." For a moment he stared across the wide lawn at the setting sun. Then he turned to face her. "I understand how you must feel about me, but I want you to know I don't want to lose your friendship."

Alison frowned. Friendship? Did Billy think of her just as a friend? If that was the case, what difference did all this make to her? She felt confused, light-headed. Ever since the race she'd been on edge, and now seeing him and hearing his words made her even more tense. "Thank you," she told him stiffly.

"I wouldn't want to hurt you, Alison," he continued. "But I have this crazy idea that maybe, through me, you can overcome your fears."

Fears. The word shot through Alison's head. Yes, she was afraid, and not only of racing. She was afraid of opening herself to love.

"Aren't you expecting a lot, Billy?" she questioned him. "Don't forget who you're talking to. I didn't have any fears until Marty's accident. I thought racing was all fun. I thought nothing bad could possibly happen."

"Marty was unlucky. You know the statistics," Billy said matter-of-factly.

"Marty became a statistic," she said, thinking, *What do I do if you're unlucky, Billy? What do I do if I lose you to a race?*

"I'm not heartless." Billy tapped his chest with two fingers. "Just because I don't agree with you—"

"I know that."

"I'm racing Sunday. Do you want to go? I can get you a ticket."

Alison shook her head, the hurt building to a bursting level. His presence upset her. "I don't think I can, Billy. I don't think I can watch you race at all."

He shrugged. "OK, just no hard feelings, huh? I do other things besides race, you know—just so you don't think I'm an accident looking for a place to happen."

Alison smiled.

"Do you want to go out tonight?"

Billy's brilliant grin and the laughter in his blue eyes loosened something inside Alison. She laughed. "OK, let's go out. We'd have to make it later, though. I have to help serve dinner."

"That's OK. I have to work tonight till nine, anyway. I asked for an hour off so that I could come over here, and I've got to get back. Would you mind meeting me at Whoppin' Donuts?"

"No, I wouldn't mind. I'll see you at nine." Even as she spoke the words, she wondered what had made her agree to go out with him again. How could she do it to herself? She knew she couldn't see him without growing closer to him, and getting close to him meant danger.

He pulled her to him before turning to leave, brushing his lips against her hair and stroking her cheek fondly.

"Don't be afraid, Alison. I mean it. Everything's going to be OK," he said softly, and then he let her go before she could reply.

There was something irresistible about

him. With a twinge of fear, she suspected it might be the same "something" that had bound her to Marty—that unquenchable spirit.

Chapter Eight

At every stoplight Alison considered turning the car around and going back home. But she found herself pulling into the parking lot of Whoppin' Donuts, almost numb to the fact that she was going out with Billy. Hadn't she decided not to see him again? Her parents had always joked that they should have named her Rhino because she was so tough, but now she felt like a jellyfish. Nothing seemed more important than being with Billy.

Alison still wondered if he just wanted to be friends with her. As she caught a glimpse of him through the plate glass window of the doughnut shop, she knew that her pounding heart was definitely more than a friendly reaction. If he just wanted to be her friend, she would have to cool herself down a lot.

As she pushed open the heavy door, she was greeted by Billy's grin.

"Hi, Alison. Can you wait a couple of minutes while we finish cleaning up?"

"Sure." Alison perched on a bar stool and watched the clean-up process. Soon Billy was through and had changed into Levis and a striped T-shirt.

Suddenly something flew through the air and hit Billy smack on the head.

"Oh, no, you guys—not the doughnut holes!" Billy groaned. But he couldn't resist returning the shot. He grabbed a handful of doughnut holes and threw them at the guy nearest him.

"You'll never finish the clean-up," cried Alison, but she had barely completed her sentence when two doughnut holes landed on her lap.

"Catch," said a boy, who started juggling three doughnut holes over the freshly wiped counter. Crumbs were spilling everywhere, and the air was filled with laughter and whooping war cries.

"I'm leaving before this place is totally wrecked," announced Billy, charging for the door.

"Oh, yeah?"

"Hey, I'm going on a date. Try and keep me here one minute longer." Billy caught the three doughnut holes that came spinning toward him. Then he grabbed Alison's hand, and they escaped under heavy doughnut fire.

Outside, Alison burst into laughter. "What a bunch of crazies!"

"I thought they'd gag us with doughnut holes before we got out of there." Billy shook his head.

Alison dusted off her blouse. "Now I'm covered with sugar."

Billy grinned and kissed the sugary tip of her nose. "Makes you even sweeter than you already are. Easier to get stuck to."

Alison groaned but couldn't help laughing. She wiped the sugar granules off his cheek. "You're pretty sweet, yourself."

They drove in Alison's car to the movie theater, where they saw an Eddie Murphy movie. Alison laughed so hard her stomach ached.

"Let's get something to eat," Billy suggested as they were leaving the theater.

"If my poor stomach can handle it."

"All those jokes can be dangerous to your health."

Billy laced his fingers through hers. The movie had put them both in good moods.

"Eddie Murphy sure does great impersonations. He's like a split personality," commented Billy.

"Well, he sure split my sides," replied Alison.

"Hey! Let's get banana splits. It'll fit in with the rest of our evening."

They lingered at the ice-cream parlor, recalling some of the funnier scenes of the movie. As they drove back to Whoppin' Donuts, where Billy's truck was parked, Alison was glad the conversation hadn't turned to racing. If they didn't talk about it, she could pretend it didn't exist.

Of course, she knew it was foolish to think that way. She wanted to enjoy Billy—not a hard thing to do—without any gnawing fears. If only things were different. . . .

Alison stopped her car in the parking lot. He turned to her. For the first time that evening, his face was serious. He traced her lips with his finger and casually moved it along her cheekbone to stroke her long hair.

He cleared his throat, and Alison knew he was going to say something important. Perhaps he would tell her he didn't think they should see each other again—there were too many conflicts. That night they had avoided any topics that could bring these conflicts to the surface. But Alison knew they existed, and she knew Billy knew. She couldn't help but worry.

"I think I love you, Alison."

Her heart stopped. She wasn't ready to hear that. She had been expecting to hear "Let's be friends" or "Sorry, it just won't work." It was too unbelievable that he would love her.

"You do?" she responded, licking her lips to soothe the sudden dryness in her mouth.

"Does that surprise you?" He wrapped a length of her silken hair around his little finger. "How do you feel about me?"

His eyes searched hers, and her flesh quivered under his stare. How did she feel, besides scared? "I think I do—too."

He read her thoughts. "Are you afraid to say 'love'?" he questioned.

Alison was silent for a moment. "I'm just plain afraid."

"I know. But maybe after a time, it won't be so scary." He kissed her forehead, and they sat in silence for a long time. Alison was afraid to look at Billy but kept his hand in hers, playing with his long, slender fingers and staring out into the darkness.

Billy broke the silence. "Hey, Al, the

antique car show opens tomorrow. I have to work in the morning but I thought I'd go in the afternoon. Do you want to come?"

She wondered if she should go. Hadn't she told herself to cool it? But that was when she thought he just wanted to be her friend. Now she knew he loved her. But that didn't help her; she still felt confused and torn. Part of her knew that she could be hurt badly, just the way she had been hurt by Marty. She should protect herself from a similar experience. But her heart yearned for the warmth and fun of Billy. She wanted to let herself fall head over heels.

"How about it, Alison? Is it a date?" Billy's brown eyes met her own, prompting her.

"Yes, it's a date. I'd like to go."

"Good. I'll pick you up around one."

"I see Billy's around again," Alison's father said the next morning at breakfast. "How's his racing going?"

"Racing?" snapped Alison. "Why ask about his racing? There's more to Billy than racing, you know. He likes to design parts and work on engines, too. I don't think he's a fanatic, or anything."

"I'm sorry," replied her father, giving

Alison a knowing look. "I just asked a simple question. You don't have to jump down my throat."

Then he squeezed her shoulder gently. "I don't want you getting hurt, honey. You're not as tough as you sometimes seem. I suppose you're too old now to be protected, but when you told us that Billy races—"

"Mr. Matlock, excuse me." It was Ellie, the chambermaid. "There are some guests here asking for rooms."

"I'll see you later, Dad," Alison told him as he hurried off.

"Have a good time," he called over his shoulder.

Her father's words swirled in her head. She knew he meant well, but she did not need to hear his worries. They were too much like her own, and she didn't want to face the issue of racing just yet.

"Are you free as a bird this afternoon?" Billy asked Alison when he arrived.

She climbed onto the seat next to him. "Not quite. I have to be back to help with dinner. We have twenty people coming tonight."

"Don't worry—we'll be home on time."

As they drove along the highway, Alison's

tensions disappeared. The day was beautiful, the sun poured through the young blossoms on the trees, crops were springing up in the brown fields, and a scent of new-mown hay was in the air.

And Billy was beside her—that was the best part. She really did love him. She and Billy together were something special—what was she worrying about?

Billy knew a lot about old cars. He could guess the model and the year of practically every car at the show.

"One of these days I'd like to collect old cars and bikes." He was looking at a white '57 Chevy.

"What a beaut," he said and whistled. "You can almost see the saddle shoes and hear the doo-wap of Elvis." He started snapping his fingers to an imaginary song.

"You know the words to those old songs?" she asked teasingly.

"Yeah, don't tell anybody, but I'm really kind of old-fashioned. I still believe in Chevys, rock 'n' roll, and love." He kissed her on the lips, right in front of the judge's stand. Two boys leaning against a Model T whistled.

Alison blushed, but she couldn't help giggling at their reactions.

Billy sang fifties songs all the way home. Alison hummed along with him, listening to the words. All the songs were about love.

"If someone landed here from outer space, they'd think we earthlings had one-track minds," observed Alison.

"We do," Billy said. "We want what's hardest to find."

She studied the curve of Billy's neck. Then her gaze traveled to where his eyebrows met his thick curls.

Without thinking, she reached over and squeezed the back of his neck. He smiled at her, his lips slightly parted.

Alison thought about what Billy had said—"We want what's hardest to find." Well, she had wanted to find somebody to help her get over Marty. Now it looked like she had someone. But would he help her get over Marty? Or would he repeat that old nightmare for her, making the pain even worse? If she could put in an order for the perfect boyfriend, he would be a Billy without the racing.

Maybe love wasn't made to order, she considered. But as Billy's hand moved toward hers, she wondered what she was complaining about. If she wanted it, she had, at her fingertips, what was hardest to find.

Chapter Nine

In the dream Alison was weightless. She floated a few inches above the bleachers at the track. She wanted to clutch the metal railing, but her fingers couldn't reach it, and all she could feel was the wind sifting through them.

Marty was in the lineup, tucked into his car away from her view. The sun reflected off the car's silver finish, blinding her. The crowd's roar was like a living force that, combined with the heavy air, choked Alison. Suddenly a feeling of horror sent her earthward, groping for her seat and gasping for air.

The starting gun sounded. Marty's car shot from the lineup as though from a cannon, and dust billowed around him. Alison thrilled at the sight, and the deafening roar made her skin rise in goose bumps.

She raised her binoculars to see Marty go around the first curve. Cars screeched around it, and one turned over and over. The driver emerged, unhurt. Alison could see he'd taken the turn wrong. At least Marty knew how to take turns, he never made mistakes. . . .

There was a sudden shriek of tires. A car was out of control, hitting the guardrail, flipping onto its roof. Another car charged into it, spinning it like a top. The crowd's screams mingled with her own. "Marty, Marty, Marty," echoed in her head.

Then the suffocating odor of smoke filled her lungs. Alison wished with all her might that it wasn't Marty under the rubble.

She ran while medics dragged Marty's body from the wreckage. She couldn't get to him; her legs would only carry her—it was as if she were running in slow motion. A blast of foam hit the flaming car, extinguishing the blaze and her view. She was running, crying, trying to reach him, her feet were as heavy as lead. She felt as if she were running through water. . . .

Alison awoke to the sound of the phone ringing.

"Al, are you coming with us today?" It was Julie.

"Where to?" Alison blinked sleep from her eyes, the image of Marty's accident still fresh in her mind. She couldn't remember making any definite plans.

"It's Sunday. The race—Billy's race. Aren't you going?" she questioned. "We're watching Steve again."

The news was like a splash of cold water. Billy had mentioned his Sunday race, but she had wanted to change the subject and had completely put it out of her mind.

"Didn't you and Billy talk about it? I mean, you two spent the entire weekend together practically, since Friday night. I thought you'd get free passes."

"He told me Friday evening, Julie, but I forgot. I guess I didn't really want to know about it."

"Oh, Al." Julie heaved a sigh. "I'm sorry."

"Well, don't be." Alison felt awful. She had awakened to another nightmare.

"You're getting along with him OK, aren't you?" Julie asked.

"Yeah. Too well, if you ask me. Maybe it would be easier if we didn't get along."

"Don't be silly, Al. He's just your type. Cheer up about him, will you? Listen, Heather and I are coming over. When we get there, you can decide whether or not you want to go."

Alison hauled herself out of bed and

stared in the mirror before taking a shower. *If you're going to love Billy,* she told her reflection, *you're going to have to separate yourself from his racing. It's not going to be easy, but it's the only way.*

When Heather and Julie came over, Alison fixed coffee and bagels. They sat out on the porch and talked about the weekend.

"Billy and I discussed his racing, and I said I didn't think I could watch him again," Alison said.

"Are you just going to ignore the fact that he races?" Heather asked.

"I don't know whether that's possible," Julie added.

"Well, he does understand how I feel, Julie. I just have to keep my cool about the whole thing." Alison ran her finger along the rim of her coffee cup. "We had such a good time this weekend." She told them about the car show on Saturday and the movie Friday night.

"We told you so. You *are* in love!"

"Come on, you guys," Alison protested and smiled in spite of herself. She didn't mention the fact that Billy had said he loved her. That was a little nugget of gold that she wanted to keep secret.

"If you aren't in love," Julie insisted, "then you've got the worst case of blushes I've ever seen."

"Isn't anyone going to ask me about my weekend?" Heather demanded.

"How was it with Barry?" Alison gladly turned the focus of conversation to her friend.

"Just wonderful. The only thing that bothers me is that he still doesn't kiss very well."

"Give him time," Alison said.

"True love overlooks all flaws," Julie said.

"Just think if he complained about your bony elbows, Heather," Alison said, knowing how Heather felt about her elbows.

"Oh, let's not talk about my elbows!" She moaned. "Do you really think they're ugly, Al? Really?"

Julie and Alison cracked up.

"You guys are mean," Heather decided. "By the way, tomorrow after school we'll consult the cards again. I want to find out about Barry."

"Yeah, and while you're at it, I want to know something. I thought the cards said my mysterious visitor would solve all my problems," challenged Alison. "It seems like Billy has *caused* all my problems."

"Well, are you going to wait for an answer from the cards before you make up your mind about the race today?" Julie brought them back to reality. "Come on, we're going to be late. You coming, Al?"

Alison drew a deep breath and shook her head. "No. Maybe someday I can watch, but not yet."

"Is this the same thick-skinned person we used to know?" Heather quipped.

"I'm sorry to be such a party pooper," replied Alison, and then she tried to lighten things up a bit. "But keep an eye on Billy for me. I don't want him smiling at too many cute girls." She strolled outside with them to examine a new dent in the side of Julie's car. "I don't know, Jules. It's pretty bad, but I can try banging it out with a hammer. Drop it off when you get back from the race."

"See you later, Al." Heather tucked her long legs into the passenger seat.

"Yeah. Let me know who wins," she called out. A lump formed in her throat as she waved goodbye.

It was impossible for Alison not to think of Billy. She prepared breakfast for a few guests who were late risers and then went outside.

She needed to keep busy, and her father had told her there were some flats of pansies that needed to be planted. She picked up a spade and began the task of putting the flowers in the ground.

Strains of a Mozart piano concerto drifted out from her father's office. Alison loved her father's music. They favored the same measured, ordered pieces. Somehow the music helped her organize her chaotic feelings and made her feel calmer and more in control.

But really, everything flowed perfectly with Billy. Julie and Heather would be surprised if they knew just how well she got along with Billy. He was so understanding—not like the other boys she had briefly dated. They had all seemed afraid of her. Either they were afraid because she knew more about cars than they did, or they were afraid to touch her in case the memory of Marty should come surging out like a bursting dam. Billy understood the pain that Alison felt, but he didn't treat her like a china doll. He treated her like an adult who knew how to take care of herself.

There was one thing that she was quite sure Billy did not know. And that was how frequently she thought of him. Marty's face was becoming a blur to her, and in its place was Billy's image.

Is it OK to be so adaptable? Alison asked herself, feeling slightly guilty.

Her mother rode the lawnmower over to where Alison was working and switched off the engine.

"How's it going?" she asked, shading her eyes from the midday sun with her hand.

"Fine."

"Where's Billy today?"

"Racing." Alison pronounced the word without emotion.

"And you're not watching?" Her mother's eyebrows arched in surprise.

"No."

"I can understand why you don't want to watch, Allie," Mrs. Matlock said sympathetically. "I just wonder how it's going to work out between the two of you."

"We get along fine."

"So I noticed. And your father and I also noticed that you are living again. That's nice to see." She hesitated for a moment, examining her fingernails. "Sometimes it can be painful, but there's a certain amount of risk taking in life."

"So I'm finding out."

97

Marcy Matlock smiled, her slender, tanned arms reaching for the steering wheel. "I'm here if you need me."

"Thanks," Alison said as her mother drove away. And she meant it.

Alison finished smoothing earth around the young plants, then carried the empty plastic containers up to the garden shed and went inside to wash the grit from her hands.

The phone rang as Alison entered the kitchen.

"Alison." It was Heather. She spoke her name with finality, but her voice was small, unsure.

"Yes. What is it, Heather?"

There was a pause as Heather took a deep breath. "Billy's hurt. They don't know how bad it is, but he's going to the hospital now."

Alison closed her eyes and tried to breathe to clear the sudden dizziness that swamped her head.

"Al, are you still there?"

Barely, she thought. She nodded, then realized that Heather couldn't see her. "Yes. Is he—?" She couldn't bring herself to ask too many questions. She wanted to know everything, but she also didn't want to know anything. The dream of the night before hung in front of her eyes, and she blinked to clear it.

"He's unconscious, Al."

Unconscious, that means he's not dead. It also means that he's badly hurt. Alison swallowed hard, but her throat was dry. Her tongue stuck to the roof of her mouth. "I'm going to the hospital," she managed to say.

"Want me to pick you up?"

"No, I'll go right now from here. Which hospital?" The rushing in her ears made Heather's reply almost inaudible.

"Brentwood."

When Alison got off the phone, her father was standing next to her, waiting.

"Billy's hurt," Alison announced, although she needn't have bothered. He knew from her expression. Perhaps she already knew, too. Perhaps the dream was an omen. The driver in her dream had been Marty, but it could just as easily have been Billy. She should have stopped him. She could have tried.

Her mother appeared in the doorway. She had seen her daughter like this before and instantly knew something was wrong.

"I'm going to the hospital," Alison announced stiffly.

"We'll drive you, Al. You're in no shape to drive." Her father's quiet insistence offered some comfort. Like a little child, Alison took his hand, while her mother went off to gather car keys and pocketbook.

The sterile odor of the hospital filled Alison's senses, making her stomach churn. She hated that smell, and she hated the memories that came with it: the smell of burning rubber, the crackle of flames, the image of Marty, lifeless.

The ride to the hospital had felt so strangely familiar. At one point she had wanted the car to stop so that she could get out. She wanted to go back to the garden, hide, forget. But she couldn't change a thing. She felt so helpless, sitting in the car while the world whizzed by. Her legs were heavy and still, like in the dream. She remembered whispering in Marty's ear, the words tumbling out of her mouth as if in a rush to get said before . . .

Her arms felt empty—the same feeling she had had after Marty died. As she walked into the waiting room and saw Billy's parents there, she thought of Marty's sobbing mother.

Trembling, Alison sat down next to Billy's

mother. Mrs. Kendall explained what had happened.

"Billy crashed into a tree after another kid swerved into him. He's broken his ankle, and he's damaged a kidney. They're operating on it right now."

Mrs. Kendall's fingers, lightly covering Alison's, were ice-cold. She wore a floral print skirt, and her hair was pulled back into a bun.

"Were you at the race?" Billy's father asked. He wore faded blue jeans and tortoise-shell framed glasses perched on his nose.

"Uh, no, I wasn't," Alison said quickly. She didn't want to explain herself to Billy's parents. They probably didn't know about Marty, and it wouldn't make them feel any better to know that she had been through this before, and that the last time her boyfriend had died.

She closed her eyes, a rush of images filling the darkness—Billy's crazy grin, his freckled nose, the way he wore a cap pulled down over his brow . . .

Her father brought her a cup of coffee. He had to hold it for her while she sipped because her hands trembled so.

Alison recalled Billy saying that people wanted what was hardest to find. *When we finally find it, is it always taken away?* she wondered. *When I find somebody to love, is he always going to disappear?*

Two hours passed. The waiting seemed like an eternity, but finally Billy's doctor emerged from the operating room.

"The operation was a success," he told Billy's parents. "We've oversewn the laceration, and Billy is resting comfortably now."

"Will he be all right?" Mrs. Kendall asked. Her voice quivered.

Alison was thinking of Marty and how serious the doctor had looked when asked that same question.

"It will take him a while to recuperate, but he should be fine," the doctor said. "You can see him now."

"Come on," Mr. Kendall whispered in Alison's ear. "You can come, too."

The nurse frowned at him, but he tugged at Alison's elbow. Dutifully, she followed him.

Billy was still asleep. He lay in a sea of white, hooked up to IVs, his usually vibrant, sun-browned face now a pale, sickly color. His hair was rumpled with sweat against the pillow. His hand lay upturned on the top of the sheet. Alison thought he looked like a little boy.

She loved him. And, she realized, as tears leaked out the corners of her eyes, that she didn't want to.

Chapter Ten

Alison moved like a sleepwalker through the next hours. She went home and tried to rest, but she waited anxiously for news about Billy. Heather came over and insisted on going with Alison to the hospital that evening, saying she'd wait outside in the corridor.

Alison quietly entered Billy's room. He was still groggy and could only manage a weak "hi."

She did all the talking. It reminded her so much of when Marty had been lying in a coma. At least Billy was conscious.

She tried to seem cheerful and confident. She talked about the float the committee was building.

"We've got this huge blob of papier-mâché that's supposed to look like Mother Nature, but it just looks like blobs of papier-mâché. We're going to take it to an art class to see what can be done with it. Otherwise, it's not

104

going to be featured in the parade. I mean, who wants a blobby Mother Nature?"

Billy's mouth turned up slightly in a smile. He looked awfully weak. The nurse came in and told Alison she had three or four more minutes, and then she would have to leave.

"Then we have a flowered canopy where the queen will sit. I hope you'll be better by then, so you can see it," she said, smoothing damp curls off his forehead.

He smiled again and squeezed her hand.

"It's time to go, Alison. Billy has to rest now," the nurse told her.

Alison stopped her nervous chatter. Gently she said, "See you tomorrow, Billy." Alison leaned over and kissed his forehead, which felt cool.

"How'd it go?" Heather asked when Alison came out into the corridor.

"He's weak, but he can smile and talk a little. The nurse says he'll be much better tomorrow, after the painkillers wear off a bit. It's just a relief to see his eyes open."

Heather squeezed her hand. "He'll be fine, Al, don't worry. You know, I talked to him before the race. He said he wished you had come."

"I bet he doesn't wish that now." She sighed.

"Are you up for getting something to eat? It might be good for you," Heather said.

"I'm not really hungry, but I'll go with you. You eat, I'll watch."

At the restaurant Alison sipped on a Coke and tried to keep up a conversation with Heather, but her mind never strayed far from Billy.

The next afternoon after school she drove to the hospital. Billy had been moved to another more cheerful room, next to a window. Flowers filled the nightstand.

Billy looked better. There was a little color in his cheeks, and he smiled more readily when she entered the room.

"How're you feeling?" she asked, leaning over to kiss him.

"Better, but not exactly normal." He grinned at her. His voice was still weak, missing its familiar ring of laughter.

"I'm so relieved you're going to be OK," Alison said, sitting down at his side, her heart beating fast.

"I know." He moved his fingers along the sheet to grasp hers. "I'm glad you're here."

"I love you, Billy." Those words came out

106

so easily now. Yet she ached inside. She didn't feel she could ever go through this pain again. When he was well, she planned to tell him she couldn't go on loving him. She couldn't bear to see him hurt. If there had been any doubt before, there was none now—she knew she couldn't love a racer.

Not attending his races wouldn't solve the problem. He could get hurt whether or not she was there. She couldn't go on ignoring Billy's racing; it was part of him, important to him. Alison knew that she was up against something that would eventually come between their love for each other.

Billy's hand closed around hers and squeezed tightly. His grip was still strong and made her tingle. "Alison, I've been doing some thinking."

Alison held her breath. Was he going to tell her not to love him anymore? Was he going to tell her to forget about him?

"The doctors told me this morning that I damaged a kidney. It's fixed now, but if I bounce it around much more, I could permanently damage it. I can't afford that. Breaking an ankle is one thing, but I can't abuse myself to the point of no repair." He paused and cleared his throat. "I'm quitting motocross, Alison."

Alison blinked hard, not sure if she'd heard him right. "Are you sure?"

"I'm positive. I have to. And it's not as if I don't have other things to do. Safe things. I can keep my foot in the door building and designing bikes. I love doing those things, and I can always watch the races from the bleachers." He grinned.

Alison wanted to melt with relief. "Billy, I hate to see your body banged up like this. And if it's really as serious as you say—"

"It is. I can still ride, but I can't smash myself up like this by racing. It made you awfully nervous, anyway, so maybe it's for the best."

"That's strictly my problem, Billy."

"Yeah, but I can't stop you from feeling how you do, and I think eventually it would've divided us. I love you, Alison. And there shouldn't be anything pulling us apart."

She kissed him tenderly, shivering at his words. She felt totally unafraid right then. It seemed that nothing could take Billy away from her now.

"Guess what! I've been nominated for May Day queen!" Heather announced ecstatically the next day.

The three girls were sitting in the quad, eating lunch. Julie grimaced at her yogurt and carrot sticks, enviously eying slim Heather as she pulled the wrapper off a candy bar.

"There are ten others nominated, so I may not make the finals. They choose only four princesses and one queen from the bunch," Heather went on. "But it's still an honor."

"We have a celebrity in our midst, Al. Can you believe it?" Julie nibbled daintily on a carrot.

"Congratulations, Heather. I knew those bony elbows were OK!" Alison gave her friend a huge hug.

"You look better today, Alison," Julie noted, "now that you know Billy's going to be OK."

Alison had gone back to the hospital the evening before, then had had to do a lot of homework, so, other than telling her friends that Billy would be all right, she hadn't had time to tell them what had happened. "I am. But Billy had a close call. The doctors don't think he should race anymore. He says he's quitting."

"Seriously?"

"He suffered some kidney damage," she

explained. "But they say he'll be fine as long as he doesn't race."

"Does this solve all your problems, or what?" Heather stated. "The cards were right after all," she joked.

Alison felt drained. Yes, it did seem as if her troubles were over. But it made her feel a little sick that a serious accident had to happen to make her dreams come true.

"I guess my problems are solved," she said aloud. "Except that I never wanted Billy to get hurt. I was just beginning to try to work things out for myself."

"Hey, I've got an idea." Julie threw her empty yogurt container into the trash bin. "Let's have a get-well party for Billy after he gets home from the hospital. How long will he be in there?"

"I think about a week."

"Perfect. We'll plan it for the weekend after. Talk to his mom and see what she says, and then it's full speed ahead!"

The party was held at the inn. Alison's closest friends as well as many of Billy's were there.

Julie had insisted on being in charge of the food. She had prepared a beautiful buffet

110

of cheeses, cold cuts, vegetables with dips, and homemade breads. She had even baked a huge chocolate cake.

Billy sat on a chair, his crutches beside him, and a group stood around him, waiting to sign his cast.

"You sure you don't want me to sign autographs?" Billy joked, waving his pen in the air.

"Who wants your autograph, Kendall?" his friend Joe called out. "You lost your last race!"

"He's a hero 'cause he came out of it in one piece," someone else said.

"Almost one piece." Billy grinned.

Alison caught his eye, and he winked at her. She was across the room, serving lemonade.

"Hey, didn't you used to be Marty Willins's girlfriend?" a tall boy with the beginnings of a mustache asked her.

"Yes."

"I heard about him. Sorry," he said sincerely.

"It's OK. It was a year ago."

"How do you know Billy?" he wanted to know.

111

"We met at the junkyard," she told him. "I work on cars."

His eyes lit up. "No kidding?"

Some of the couples started dancing. Billy hobbled over to Alison's side.

"I'd dance with you, Alison, but I'm feeling clumsy tonight," he teased.

"Uh, thanks anyway, Billy. If you stepped on my toes, I might need a cast, too."

"Sounds romantic," replied Billy. "We could play great footsies together."

Julie and Heather breezed by to say hello.

"Congratulations, Heather," Billy said. "I hear you might be joining beautiful Mother Nature on the float."

Heather pointed to Billy's cast. "Save my autograph! It might be a collector's item someday."

"How's the float coming?"

"We think it's afloat," Julie said, and everyone groaned.

"Billy, when's your next race?" his friend Joe asked.

Alison dropped her smile. She'd known someone was going to ask this question and had been dreading the moment.

"Never, Joe. I'm giving up racing," Billy replied, his voice firm and steady.

"Is that right? This is a goodbye party then?"

"No, I'll still be around."

"Sounds like you're afraid," Joe baited him.

"I'm afraid, yeah. With good reason."

Alison detected the annoyance in Billy's voice. She wished Joe would stop testing him.

"Billy, you're so good. Why do you want to quit?" someone else joined in.

"Doctor's orders, Sam. My kidney was damaged."

"Really?" Sam clicked his tongue. "Man, nothing short of World War Three could keep me off the track. I thought you were pretty crazy about motocross, too."

"Sure, I'm crazy about motocross, but I'm not crazy. I'd have to be to keep racing after what happened to me."

"Yeah?" Joe and Sam didn't look convinced.

"That's right," Billy said. "I'll keep up with things by fixing and building bikes. Maybe I'll even design some parts."

"You always were good at that," Joe offered.

"And I can get better at it, too." Billy's grin warmed Alison. "Maybe Al and I will even go

113

into business together." He slid his arm around her waist, and the other boys wandered away.

"I'm glad we're together," he said, squeezing her hard. "I think we're good for each other."

"Me, too." She was so relieved to hear Billy stick up for his decision.

"They don't understand," Billy said; "because they've never been badly hurt. I didn't really understand either, until it happened to me."

You don't know how glad that makes me, Alison said to herself. Now, she didn't have to be afraid of losing him. She was suddenly free—free enough to love him.

Chapter Eleven

"I think this float's just about ready to roll," Julie said as she and two other girls twisted crepe paper around the base of the truck bed. "Isn't it beautiful?"

"Yeah. I just hope it looks this good once it's out in daylight," Beth said. "We might notice all the flaws."

With the help of the art class, Mother Nature had been vastly improved. She actually looked human, and the wide crepe paper drapings gave her dress a fairylike look that everyone thought was suitable. She was placed opposite the arch where the May Day queen would sit.

"Tomorrow's the big day, isn't it, Heather? But now that Mother Nature looks so good, you have really stiff competition for the queen."

"I'm not going to sleep a wink. I'll probably have huge bags under my eyes tomorrow."

"Hey, it's early," Chloe noticed. "We didn't plan to be finished so soon. Want to celebrate with ice cream?"

"I'm meeting Billy at the track. He's watching a friend try out a new part on his bike," Alison said. "I'm heading over there now." Then she added, "Good luck, Heather. I'll be thinking of you."

"Won't we all!" cried Julie.

Alison left the barn where the float was being assembled, glad that it was finished. The past week had been hectic. She hadn't seen much of Billy.

She pulled onto the grounds surrounding the practice track. In the distance bikes roared over hills, their riders looking like tiny black insects on a leafy background. One of them lagged far behind, obviously not part of the practice competition.

Alison stood behind two boys who leaned against the metal railing. They talked loudly over the roar of engines.

"Since the accident, he's been scared. Says he's not racing again," said one.

"Billy? Not race? You're joking!" The other boy was shorter, with black curly hair and a bandaged elbow.

"No, it's true. Doctor's orders, he says.

116

But a lot of people think it just scared him to death. His girlfriend used to go out with Marty Willins, the stock-car racer."

"Oh, yeah. Bet she's scared, too —probably threw a temper tantrum until he promised to quit."

It took all of Alison's self-control to keep from butting in to the conversation. She didn't want people thinking she was responsible for Billy's quitting! But, she supposed, it was only natural that they would think that after what had happened to Marty. Still, it made her furious.

"Look, there he is!" The taller boy pointed to the track.

Alison moved away from them so that she could watch and wait for Billy in peace. She glanced in the direction the boy pointed.

The boys' attention was fixed on the slow rider. He chugged along, driving around the jumps instead of taking them.

Alison saw the below-the-knee cast. It was definitely Billy. *Why is he out here? He was supposed to be watching a friend try out a new part.*

As if in reply to her question, the other boy said, "He must be racing this weekend.

Guess he's not listening to the doctor after all."

So, Billy couldn't resist. He was practicing for a race. *If I hadn't arrived early,* Alison thought, *I would never have found out. He could race and deceive me for a little longer.*

I should never have believed that he would quit. Alison's anger and disappointment were building. *He likes racing too much to give it up. It doesn't matter what the doctor's orders were. It doesn't matter what I want.*

The track blurred in front of her. Alison wiped at her sudden hot tears as she ran back to her car. She certainly couldn't face Billy now.

It rained that night, and the inn was quiet. All the guests were in their rooms. Alison went to get wood for a fire. As she was putting the first log in place, her mother called, "Billy's on the phone!"

Alison started at the mention of his name. She picked up the downstairs phone.

"Why didn't you come down to the track? I waited hours for you, Alison. Did something come up?" he asked.

"I was there, Billy."

118

"Where? Are you invisible? I looked all over." He chuckled.

"No, I was there. I saw you on the track, and I left." She pronounced this with finality. "I saw you riding, and some boys standing in front of me said you were practicing for a race. I guess you decided to disobey the doctor."

"I wasn't practicing!" he cried.

Alison felt very far away from him. "Billy," she said coldly, "I don't want you to have to make excuses or tell me some story just to save me the pain."

"Alison, you're not listening to me! Do you really think I'm going to race with a broken ankle and a screwed-up kidney, for crying out loud?" His voice had risen an octave. She moved the receiver away from her ear.

"I don't know, Billy. I don't ever know what you're going to do next. That's up to you. I just know I can't handle this whole thing. I thought your health would be enough of a reason to quit racing, but now it looks like it isn't. Goodbye, Billy."

Alison hung up before she could hear further protests and before she burst into tears. Feeling small, cold, and alone, she wrapped herself in an afghan and sat in front of the fire.

119

Chapter Twelve

"Congratulations, Queenie," Alison told Heather, giving her a kiss on her flushed cheek.

Heather was wearing the flowered crown of the May Day queen and a long, pale blue dress that made her thin figure look full and feminine. Her voice bubbled with joy. "Did you bring your flowers and costume, Al?"

"Got the flowers, got the costume." Alison produced a wicker basket full of paper flowers, which she was to throw from Heather's float. Her costume was a pink jumpsuit, and she had braided pink and yellow ribbons in her hair.

The restroom where they were changing was a madhouse. All of the princesses were busy with last-minute details. They wore long pastel dresses. Every sink was littered with makeup and brushes and combs. Stray ribbons and flowers littered the counters.

One girl tried frantically to repair a snag in her stocking, and two other girls were fixing a shoe strap with a safety pin. The teacher in charge of the parade kept everyone jumping by calling out the time. "Five more minutes, girls. Now hurry."

"You think anyone will notice my shoe?" Delia asked.

"We can always bury it in crepe paper," Beth said, trying to calm her.

"Three more minutes!" screamed the teacher.

The excitement was growing, and Alison and Julie gathered around Heather. "You look fantastic, kid," said Julie. "I think I'll go on a starvation diet tomorrow. You're quite an inspiration."

"Even Mother Nature came out looking OK," said Alison, getting caught up in the bubbling energy. "Now if only my ribbons didn't look like seaweed in a monster's hair," she said. But despite her jokes she kept thinking about how rude she had been to Billy the night before.

After she had hung up on him, Alison worried about what she had done. Maybe she should have given him more of a chance to explain himself, instead of jumping to conclusions. But she couldn't hide her disappointment and anger. The old chaos of her feelings had just swamped her. She had felt out of control again.

If Billy chose to go ahead and disobey his doctor, then what could Alison do? She couldn't dictate to him. She would just have to forget Billy—it obviously wasn't working out.

The float looked beautiful. A flowered arbor made up of every spring blossom imaginable formed an arch behind Heather, who stood on a small raised platform. Her princesses stood around her, holding small bouquets.

Alison stood on the far end of the float and tossed flowers to the crowd as the parade moved slowly through the street. It was hard to smile so much, but the perfect weather and the enthusiastic crowd lifted her spirits.

Alison saw her parents standing next to Heather's. Her father whistled loudly, and her mother waved. Alison threw them extra flowers, which they tried to catch over the bobbing heads in front of them.

Suddenly she saw Billy. Alison was surprised to see him catch a flower and place it between his teeth, like a performer in a nightclub. He looked so funny—leaning on crutches with a paper peony in his mouth. She had to laugh.

"Is that Billy?" Chloe whispered to her, continuing to smile and wave at the audience. "He's so cute."

"That's him."

"How's he doing? He's not sick anymore?"

"He's fine as long as he doesn't race, Chloe. As you can see, he's still got a broken ankle."

"Can you believe it? Some kids are crazy enough to keep racing after an accident like that. Mike Mitchell . . ."

Mechanically, Alison kept throwing flowers while Chloe told her about Mike Mitchell, who apparently had been in critical condition for weeks and went back to motocross as soon as he could walk again.

"Just like Evel Knievel, who's broken every bone in his body," finished Chloe.

Finally the parade was over. Floats clustered in the supermarket parking lot, and friends and parents crowded around them. Alison jumped off her float.

"Hey, you almost jumped on my feet."

Billy appeared in front of her. He waved his paper flower in front of her and smiled

123

uncertainly. "You want my other foot in a cast?"

Alison groped for words, and Billy spoke before she could say a word. "Can we talk?"

Families moved in around the queen and princesses. Everyone was occupied. Alison figured this was as good a time as any.

"OK."

They strolled away from the float, and Billy started talking.

"I know why you're upset with me. I guess you must think I'm going to start racing again, after I told you I wouldn't."

"That's right."

"Well, I'm not racing again. I can't. I'm not stupid, Alison. But I can ride a bike to test it out, which was what I was doing yesterday. I designed a new type of shock absorber for rear tires, which I want to sell to Johnnie's Cycle Shop."

"But you're not supposed to ride at all, are you? What about your kidney?" She hoped she didn't sound too dramatic.

He shook his head. "Do you want to talk to my doctor? I can ride, just not compete. I can't ride over jumps. You know, the rough stuff. But I can hang around the track all I want."

"Those guys at the track—"

"They're all good racers, and they're anxious to see me go back in full force. They don't know what I've been through."

Alison surveyed his sincere expression. Clearly he was being honest with her. She was wrong—wrong for doubting him, wrong for thinking he would lie to her, wrong for thinking that he wasn't strong enough to resist the thrill of racing.

"I thought that because you loved racing so much, you would go back to it eventually. Most racers are pretty addicted to the track." Alison tried to explain herself. "I've been around racing long enough to know that if you can't take the danger, you have to get out of it. I would never want to change you, Billy, you must know that. Then you'd be somebody else, and I love who you are."

"I know you'd never try to change me. That's one of the things I love about you." He fingered the ribbons in her hair. "And I also know that if it wasn't for Marty, you wouldn't feel this way about racing. Believe me, I don't want to change anything about you, either."

He leaned forward and brushed his lips across hers. "Your hair looks almost as good

125

in ribbons as it does with car grease in it. Did I tell you, you looked beautiful on the float—better than the queen and princesses?"

"No—but don't tell them that." Alison giggled, thinking how horrified Heather would be by that comment.

Billy threaded the paper flower into her long hair and kissed her again. Alison's doubts and fears vanished as his arms closed around her.

Chapter Thirteen

"Can you hand me that wrench, Alison?" Billy called from under the hood of his truck.

"Sure, boss." Smiling, Alison handed him the tool. He was adjusting the carburetor on the truck. She had her eye on his slender form leaning over the fender, and she wanted to reach out and hug him.

She was deliriously happy. Billy was happy working on motorcycles. The people at Johnnie's Cycle Shop liked his ideas and were going to buy some of his designs. After that good news, he had told Alison, "I feel as thrilled now as I used to when I would do a good jump at a race."

Alison also noticed a change in herself. She was forgetting about Marty. Not forgetting, exactly, but his memory was taking a backseat to Billy now.

She had spent an afternoon one weekend cleaning out her closet. She took all the memorabilia from her days with Marty and piled it in the center of the room—trophies, photos, play programs, a pressed carnation he'd given her for the spring prom. She kept two pictures on her bureau, just to refer to once in a while, but the rest she put into an empty boot box, which she placed in a corner at the top of her closet.

"I think that's it." Billy straightened up and wiped his hands on his jeans. There was a streak of oil on his nose. "Let's test-run this thing."

As Alison hopped into the truck beside him, she was slightly nervous about whether or not the engine would run smoothly. Lately, there had been some problems with the engine that she and Billy had put in together, and they had been spending their free time getting it to work perfectly. Now they would see if their work had been successful.

That first date, putting the engine in with Billy, seemed ages ago as Alison took in his familiar profile—the cap pulled down over his brow, the firm mouth that generally wore a hint of a smile. And she recognized his expression of concentration as he listened to every sound of his engine.

They drove in silence until they were both satisfied that the truck sounded right.

"The truck's fine," said Billy. Alison let out a whooping cheer.

"In fact," continued Billy, "I can tell this truck is very happy by the direction it's headed."

"And what direction is that?"

"To Mickey's Ice-Cream Parlor. See? It's got a mind of its own. It's turning into the shopping center, and now it has even found its own parking place." Billy slid out and offered Alison his hand. "Here, m'lady."

"Why, thank you, sir."

They ordered ice cream and sat outside on the curb, happily licking their cones. Billy's cast stretched out on the blacktop, and Alison read her signature on it: "To Billy, the bravest guy I know. Love, A."

She glanced up to find Billy looking at her. He wrapped a strand of her hair around his little finger.

"Let me taste your butter pecan," he said.

Alison held out her cone, but his mouth moved past it. Suddenly he was kissing her.

"Hmm, tastes good." He laughed at her surprise. "Want to try the chocolate chip?" Expecting another kiss, she raised her lips.

This time Billy handed her his cone. Always the unexpected with him, she thought fondly. As she went to taste it, she noticed a flattened surface on the double scoop. Inscribed in melting letters were the words, "I LUV U."

Alison laughed and with her pinky finger scrawled on her own cone, "ME 2."

PROMISE ME LOVE

Jane Redish

For Bob, who introduced me to
modern technology

Chapter One

My whole life started to change in March of my sophomore year, just as Two Penny Farm headed into its busiest season. Until then I'd never really had a boyfriend, at least no special boy. Whenever I went out on a date it was with Paul Stern, a boy who boarded his horse at my father's stable. Paul was OK until he started to talk about computers—then he became a real bore. But he was someone to go with to the movies and school dances. Eventually I learned to tune him out whenever he used words like microprocessor and dual disc drive. It was either that or sit at home; no one else ever asked me out.

My life would have been a lot different if I'd looked more like my best friend, Diane Cummings. She had a terrific body—round in all the right places. Diane never had any trouble attracting boys. But I'm built more like a boy

1

myself, flat-chested—well, *almost*—and narrow-hipped. I also have the great misfortune of being short, so I look a lot younger than sixteen.

With those two strikes against me it didn't matter that I have, in Diane's opinion, expressive blue eyes and beautiful auburn hair. Few boys ever bothered to look that close, and certainly not Chad Harris, a junior at Hamilton High. He didn't even know I was alive.

Only Dancer, my junior show horse, noticed me when I was around. He whinnied expectantly whenever I walked into the barn and nuzzled me fondly when I stopped by his stall. Dancer always appreciated me, which was one of the reasons I spent so much time at the stables. The other reason was that I worked there after school and on weekends.

Three years ago, when all my friends began babysitting for their spending money, I asked my father to let me work in the stables. I thought it would be a much better way to earn money, and I knew my brother Ken—who already worked there—could use the help. Fortunately, my father agreed with me, and I was hired to help the grooms. I fetched brushes and cleaned tack, rolled bandages, held fussy horses, and walked others to cool them down. When Ken went away to college, I started exercising the horses, and I even trained some if my father was too busy.

With all my responsibilities at the stable, I didn't have much free time. But I didn't mind, working at the farm was better than sitting at home while most of my friends were out on dates. It also helped me take my mind off the fact that Chad, the one boy I was crazy about, would probably never notice me.

My parents were concerned about the amount of time I spent at the stables. I'd even heard them talking about it. My mother didn't like the idea of my being around the grooms so much. They were all a lot older than I was; she wanted me to spend more time with kids my own age.

I figured that sooner or later they were going to confront me about it. A couple of times my mother had suggested that I cut back on the number of days I worked, but I shrugged off the suggestion. Still I wasn't ready for what happened one evening while we were all sitting around the den.

I was sprawled out on the floor, my head propped up on my hand, thumbing through the latest issue of *Glamour* magazine.

My father cleared his throat and put down his newspaper.

"I've decided to hire an extra hand at the farm," he said. "A teenager to help with the horses."

My chin almost hit the floor. I looked across the room at my parents. They were both seated on the sofa, my mother knitting.

"Why *now*?" I demanded, sitting up straight and glaring at them. "Haven't I been doing a good enough job?"

My father nodded. "Of course you have, Julie. It's just that spring is almost here, and things will be getting a lot busier."

It was true. With the warm weather approaching, many owners who had stayed away during the winter months would be coming back to ride. That always meant more work for everyone. Horses would have to be groomed daily in order to be ready at a moment's notice, and the number of lessons my father taught would probably double as riders prepared for the upcoming show season.

"Could you put a help-wanted ad on the school bulletin board?" my mother asked. She didn't even look up from the sweater she was working on. And while her question sounded very innocent, I knew that my mother never said anything without carefully thinking it out. It looked as if she had decided that the only way I would spend more time with kids

4

my own age was if they worked at the farm.

"What's wrong with the local newspaper?" I asked, scowling in protest. I didn't object to my parents hiring someone to work with me, but I didn't want to have to get involved.

"I think we'd get a better response advertising at school," my father answered. As if on cue, my mother put her knitting down and smiled at me.

"I'm sure there are plenty of kids at Hamilton High looking for part-time work," she added. I could tell by the tone of her voice that there was no point in arguing. If I continued to protest, we would end up in a shouting match, with me bursting into tears.

"OK, if you insist," I conceded. My father moved over to his desk and took out a piece of Two Penny Farm stationery.

"How's this?" he asked, holding up the paper a few minutes later. With a black felt-tip marker he had neatly printed a sign.

PART-TIME HELP WANTED
AT
TWO PENNY FARM
MUST LIKE HORSES AND BE WILLING TO
WORK HARD
Call Steve Peterson - owner
742-6880

"Fine," I said, sighing as he handed it to me. "I'll hang it up before homeroom tomorrow."

The next morning, instead of waiting for Diane as I usually did, I went directly to my locker, then on to my homeroom to drop off my books. I was glad that Betty Comden was too busy finishing up her homework to look up because I didn't want to stop and chat. If I could get the notice hung up before the warning bell sounded, I could avoid being trampled in the last minute rush to classes.

The bulletin board was located on the first floor. On it were notices for everything from Drama Club tryouts to an ice skate sale. Miss Crystal, the principal's assistant, was in charge of keeping everything on the board up-to-date, but she almost always fell behind.

I took the two old notices down and was reaching up to tack one corner of my father's advertisement to the bulletin board when a group of laughing, talking students bumped into me. I dropped the ad and the thumbtacks, and when I bent down to retrieve them, a white leather sneaker came down on my fingers.

"Ouch!" I yelped, snatching my hand back.

"Sorry!" said an apologetic voice I vaguely recognized. I glanced up in time to see Chad Harris standing before me.

My mouth fell open as I gasped—not from pain, but from surprise. I had first seen Chad at a horse show two years earlier and had a secret crush on him ever since. He was at the center of all my dreams and now he was reaching out to take my hand. A tingling sensation in the pit of my stomach felt a little like nerves, but I knew it was really from happiness.

Maybe now he'll notice me, I thought. I let my eyes wander over him while he examined my fingers. He was lean, but he had broad shoulders. The sunshine pouring in from the high hallway windows cast golden streaks in his light brown hair.

"I don't think anything is broken," Chad said, looking at me. For a moment I couldn't answer, all I could do was stare into his green eyes. Only they weren't exactly green, they looked more aquamarine to me, which might have been because he was wearing a turquoise shirt.

"Me, neither," I finally managed to mumble. He released my hand and we stood face to face. Although I knew that other kids were

7

clattering down the hallway around us, I didn't really see nor hear anyone except Chad Harris.

I continued to stand there with my heart pounding, hoping he would say something—*anything*—to let me know he knew my name or had seen me around. But not once in the few moments we were together did his eyes show even a flicker of recognition. Silently he picked up the notice and helped me tack it up.

I quickly dropped my gaze to the floor to hide my disappointment. It was hopeless. Chad Harris would never look at me; boys just weren't interested in girls with slim figures. They went crazy over girls with well-rounded curves—like Cheryl Williams. In fact, Chad used to go out with Cheryl. I sighed.

"See the nurse if your hand starts to swell," Chad told me as the warning bell sounded. He then scooped his books up from the floor, tucked them under one arm, and took off down the wide corridor.

I twisted around to watch him disappear, telling myself to give up on him. I was hardly aware that I'd started walking toward the staircase until I heard a voice calling to me.

"Julie! Julie, wait up!"

I whirled around and saw Diane jogging down the hall, waving one hand in the air.

"Guess what!" she said, even before she had caught her breath. "It happened. It *finally* happened. Doug Fisher asked me out for a date Saturday night!"

"How'd you manage that?" I gasped as we walked toward the steps together. We'd both known Doug for years, but Diane had only recently discovered how cute he was. She swore she was in love with him.

"Believe me, it wasn't easy. I had to work on him for a *week* just to get him to notice me. Then once that happened, I just let love take its course. It worked!" she declared.

I tried to smile even though deep inside I was a little jealous. I'd been trying for *years* to get Chad to notice me, but nothing I did seemed to work.

"I think he's taking me to a party," Diane continued. I didn't have the heart to tell her to stop.

Diane and I had been best friends practically all our lives. We shared secrets and heartaches, but as I fixed my eyes on the steps, counting each one, I knew she had no idea what I was feeling just then. She had so many dates that she even tried fixing me up with the boys she didn't want. Finally, I asked her to stop trying. After all, I wanted to be asked out by someone who liked *me*.

9

"What do you think I should wear?" Diane asked once we had reached the second floor landing.

"Wear?"

"To the party on Saturday," she said, giving me an impatient look.

"What kind of a party is it?" I asked, trying to keep my voice steady.

"Haven't you been listening to a word I've said?" Diane asked in exasperation.

I can't help it, I wanted to scream at her. *Right now I'm feeling very unattractive and unwanted, and I don't want to hear about your date on Saturday.* Fortunately I was saved from having to say anything else by the final bell signaling homeroom.

We had to dash to our room then, and I was glad for the opportunity to get control of myself. I knew I wasn't being fair to Diane. If a boy had asked *me* out, she would have been thrilled and helped me plan my whole wardrobe. Thinking about clothes gave me an idea.

Just last week Diane had admired my new pink sweater. To make up for my lack of interest in her date, I scribbled her a brief note, saying she could borrow the sweater to wear with her rose-colored jeans. I folded the note in half, wrote "Diane" on top, and slipped it to Joel Berg in the next row. Passing notes during class is something we have down to a science.

"Are you sure you don't mind?" she asked as we headed to our English class. "You've only worn it once."

"No problem," I reassured her. After all, that's what friends were for.

"Well, anytime you have a *special* date and want to borrow something of mine, you just let me know," Diane said warmly.

"Chad *will* notice you, someday," Diane reassured me, taking hold of my arm. "Just give him time."

I had heard that line from her before—a thousand times before—and I didn't believe it any more now than I had then. But I said nothing. It would take a miracle for Chad to notice me, and I didn't believe in miracles.

Chapter Two

When I got on the school bus after school, I deliberately chose a seat by a window. That way I could look out at the scenery and not have to talk to anyone. I wasn't really in the mood to carry on a conversation; I was still trying to accept the fact that I would never attract Chad Harris.

Face it, Julie, I said to myself, looking at my reflection in the school bus window. *You may be cute, but no boy is going to notice you as long as girls like Cheryl Williams are around.*

And it was true. I could never compete with her. Cheryl and Chad had dated for a while.

I continued staring out the window as the rows of neatly kept houses became more and more spread out until the bus finally pulled up in front of the familiar white gates leading to Two Penny Farm. I jumped out and went through the gates, heading down the wide lane that led to our white Victorian farmhouse. The barn where the horses were stabled was to the left of the wide lane. It was a long, white barn surrounded by paddocks and rings.

"Is that you, Julie?" my mother called out as I let myself in the front door.

The house smelled of apples and nutmeg, so I knew she was baking. I hung my coat up in the front closet and went straight into the kitchen.

"Smells good," I said, dropping my books on the large round table. I hadn't had much of an appetite all day. Still, when I peeked into the oven and saw a large apple pie browning on the top rack, I felt very hungry.

"Want a piece?" my mother asked, pointing to a second pie cooling on the counter. She had to know it was a silly question. The only time I had ever turned down apple pie was when I'd been so sick I couldn't swallow anything solid.

I nodded, and she cut me a slice. Going over to the refrigerator, I took out a container of milk. I quietly poured some into a tall glass. I hadn't noticed my mother watching me until I sat down at the table.

"Did something happen in school today?"

she asked, sitting down across from me. "You're awfully quiet."

My mouth suddenly went dry as I remembered what had happened with Chad that morning. I took a big gulp of milk to compose myself before I answered her.

"I just had a bad day," I mumbled. "Mr. Simpson sprang a surprise quiz on us, and I had trouble opening my gym locker and was late for class. Uh—and when I put up Dad's notice, I dropped it and someone stepped on my fingers."

I ached to tell her who that "someone" was, but I knew that would only make me feel worse. I wasn't sure I could talk about Chad without giving away my feelings for him, and I didn't want my mother to know I had a crush on him. Only Diane knew about my crush, and she was sworn to secrecy.

My mother nodded sympathetically. I was pretty sure that she knew I wasn't telling her everything, but she didn't press me further. Instead she changed the subject.

"I went to the bank this morning. There are still some papers to sign, but they approved our loan. Now we'll have the money we need to paint the barn."

"That's great, Mom," I said halfheartedly.

My mother ran the business side of the

farm, and any other day I would have listened with interest to the other things she planned on doing with the loan money. But that day my mind was elsewhere. I must have looked as if I were paying attention because she kept talking about her day until I reminded her I was scheduled to work.

"I'm supposed to exercise the new junior show horse," I told her. Placing my dishes in the sink, I scooped my books up from the table. Then I dashed upstairs to my room before she could object.

I changed into my "uniform" as my mom called it. It consisted of riding breeches, one of Ken's old flannel shirts, and my navy blue down vest. Then I tucked my hair up under a black hunt cap and turned to examine myself in the mirror that hung on my closet door. What I saw was no different from the me I looked at any other time. I still had the same boyish figure with very few curves; those I did have were well hidden under the oversized shirt and vest.

I wished, briefly, that I were the kind of girl who could get away with stuffing my bra with tissues. *But I'm not,* I thought. It would be too uncomfortable. But I did put on some blusher and lip gloss before heading for the stables.

Dancer, my horse, was alone, busily eating grass in the small paddock as I made my way down the lane. I whistled, and he lifted his head and turned to look at me with his ears pointing forward.

"Hello, boy," I called out from where I stood by the fence. He trotted over to me. Dancer was a handsome horse with a dark silver gray coat patterned with round, pale dapples and a silver mane and tail.

He nuzzled me affectionately when I patted his nose. Then he stretched his neck over the top railing and tried to reach inside my vest pocket for the lump of sugar that he knew I always carried. It was a game we played.

"Don't be so greedy," I said, taking the sugar out of my pocket. I offered it to him with a flat palm.

Dancer ate it eagerly, then nuzzled me for more.

"Later," I told him, scratching behind his ears. He snorted as if he understood me. Then he followed me around the edge of the fence toward the barn.

The door was open, so I unhooked the paddock gate and led Dancer inside by his halter. On either side of the aisle were huge box stalls paneled in light wood, and inside most were blanketed horses. Many of them were hack horses, ridden mostly for pleasure. But some were first-class show horses whose owners boarded them at our farm in southern New Jersey because of my father's reputation. He had been a professional rider before he retired from the circuit. Now he helped train other riders and their horses.

I walked Dancer down the aisle to the stall with his nameplate on the door. After I put him in the stall, I pulled a soft body brush from the wooden box of grooming tools fastened to the wall. I got to work, and it wasn't long before his coat was gleaming. Exchanging the soft brush for a harder one, I began working on his legs.

When I was finished, I rubbed his soft muzzle with my fingertips. "Let me check with Dad to see if I have time to take you out for a ride today," I told him in a low voice. Then I hurried down the aisle to the office at the far end of the barn.

My father wasn't in the office, so I walked across it to the large windows that looked out over the farm to see if I could spot him. Then I crossed back down the aisle to main doors, and that was when I saw Chad Harris. He had just gotten out of a beige Honda and was walking toward the barn with his head down and his hands shoved inside his ski parka pockets.

A tingling sensation swept through me as I stood there staring at him. Chad Harris at Two Penny Farm—I was stunned.

"Hi, there," Chad said, walking into the barn. He smiled, and I thought I would faint. My knees felt rubbery, and my heart began to beat so loudly that I was sure he could hear it.

"Hi," I managed to answer. I thought my voice sounded odd. "What are you doing here?"

"I came to speak to your father," Chad answered.

"My father?" I asked, my mind still spinning. I never dreamed that Chad would even know who I was.

He nodded. "About the part-time job—remember the notice I helped you tack up on the bulletin board this morning?"

"Oh, yes—sure!" I blurted out as a sudden rush of blood warmed my cheeks. Only Chad Harris could have had that effect on me.

"Is he around?" Chad asked when I didn't say anything else.

"Somewhere," I answered. The instant the words were out I wanted to die. What a stupid thing to say! Of course my father was around. I should have offered to go look for him, but all I could do was stand rooted to the spot, staring at Chad.

I was just about to do that when my father walked into the barn. He glanced at Chad, then at me, and I noticed a puzzled look on his face. "D-Dad," I said, trying to keep my voice steady. "This is Chad Harris. He's here about the part-time job."

"Glad to meet you, son," my father said, smiling as he reached out to shake Chad's hand. "I got the message that you were coming."

I wondered when Chad had called and decided it must have been during lunch. I hadn't seen him at his usual table when Diane and I walked into the cafeteria. I had noticed because I looked for him every day. But he had been there by the time the bell rang later. It didn't really matter anyway. What mattered was the fact that he was here now.

"Why don't we go sit in the office?" my father asked, moving down the aisle. "You, too, Julie. Just in case you want to add something."

I nodded silently and followed behind.

"Why do you think you'd like to work here?" my father asked after we were settled in his office. Chad looked thoughtful for a moment. I was worried. My father liked simple, honest answers.

"Well, sir," Chad answered. "I'm trying to pay off a car loan. And I've always loved being around horses—and I think horses are comfortable around me."

My father smiled. "Well, horses do have a way of sensing if a person's nervous." He paused for a moment. "So, what kind of schedule do you have? Are you out for any spring sports?"

I was having a little trouble sitting still, but I sat up at that one. Chad would have to work both mornings and afternoons, as the rest of the employees did. I usually just worked the afternoons.

"Not this year. I could handle just about any schedule. My weekends are pretty free, too—I guess it depends on how much you need me," Chad answered.

How does twenty-four hours a day sound? I thought. I tore my eyes away from Chad and looked at my father. He had his hands folded in front of him, and he was still smiling at Chad. I knew that he liked him.

Then came the final question, the one that I knew was the most critical.

"Have you had any experience with horses?" my father asked pointedly. For a moment I felt my heart stop.

I knew Chad could ride because when I

first saw him he had been at a local horse show riding the Bennetts' champion hunter. But that didn't mean he knew how to *care* for a horse. Many of the people who boarded their horses at Two Penny Farm didn't know the first thing about caring for them. All they knew was how to ride.

I held myself rigid. Then Chad said, "My sister and I were members of a Four-H pony club." I didn't need to hear anything else. I knew it was all right and let myself relax. All 4-H members had to take care of their own horses. It was a requirement of the club.

Joy seeped through every part of me. I imagined how wonderful it would be to spend part of every day with Chad Harris. It didn't matter that we wouldn't always be working together or that some days we might not even be able to say more than hello. Just knowing he was nearby would be enough. And maybe—just *maybe* he might get interested in me.

My heart began to beat frantically as my father leaned back in his chair and began tapping his desk with a pen.

"What do you think about starting work tomorrow?" he finally asked. When I saw Chad nod, it was all I could do to keep from jumping off the sofa.

I was so excited I wanted to laugh and cry

at the same time. My father had made me the happiest girl in the world, and I wanted to apologize for being so difficult when he and my mom had suggested hiring someone else. I'd gladly promise never to doubt their judgment again. Instead, I just sat there with a foolish grin on my face until my father suggested I get back to my chores. He said he was going to show Chad around the farm.

Just then I remembered the reason I'd come to his office in the first place and asked if there would be time for me to exercise Dancer then. My father thought for a minute, then nodded his approval.

"Just don't keep him out too long," he said as I stood up to leave. "I should be ready to help you with Baxter in an hour."

"No problem," I said, glancing over at Chad one last time. Then I left them and practically skipped off down the aisle.

Work was the furthest thing from my mind as I led Dancer out of the barn. But once I was in the outdoor ring, I managed to pull my thoughts together. The cool late-afternoon air felt good against my face as Dancer cantered around the ring. I took him over the jumps I'd set up. Before I knew it an hour had passed and it was time to get Baxter, the junior show horse I was helping my father train.

Baxter was a small horse, and he was very inexperienced. But as I started to work him in the indoor ring, he moved well. After a while I decided to try to pop him over a few low rails that were set up in the center of the ring. That's when I caught sight of my father and Chad coming into the enclosure.

I was used to my father watching me, but it made me nervous to have Chad there while I schooled Baxter. He was still such a green horse and couldn't be counted on to perform properly. The last thing I wanted was for Chad to see me tossed to the ground.

"How's he behaving today?" my father called from the side where he and Chad stood.

"OK, so far," I replied, shrugging to hide my nervousness. "I was just going to take him over the low rails."

"Go ahead," my dad said. I turned Baxter toward the first jump and mumbled in his ear that if he did anything to embarrass me, he would never get another lump of sugar as long as he lived.

But Baxter didn't seem to care. He took the first two jumps well but refused the third one, which almost made me fall forward over his ears. When I finally did get him to take the fence by keeping my legs pressed firmly against his side and his head pointed directly at the railing, he barely scrambled over.

"Keep taking him over those railings until he gets it right," my father said when I looked over to see his reaction. I was short of breath and totally embarrassed, but my father seemed pleased with my efforts. Chad was even grinning at me.

It was one of those wide grins that can warm your heart. Unfortunately, it also warmed my face, so I had to turn away. I didn't want Chad to know he'd made me blush.

I put Baxter at the jump again and for the next half hour forced myself to concentrate while my father called out instructions. It wasn't easy with Chad standing there, but after the fifteenth try I finally got Baxter to take all the jumps without hesitation.

"He still needs a lot of work," my father said when I pulled up in front of the gate. It was clear that the schooling session was over for the day.

Relieved, I patted Baxter on the neck and slipped down from the saddle and ran up the stirrups. Normally I would have walked him until he cooled down, brushed him, and put him back in his stall. But this time my dad called one of the grooms to do it. Then he motioned for me to follow him and Chad back to the office.

Chapter Three

We had just entered the stable portion of the barn through the breezeway that connected it to the indoor ring and were making our way down the aisle when my father turned to Chad. "Why don't you join us for dinner? Julie's mother is a great cook, and it will give us a chance to talk some more," he said.

"Sounds fine with me," Chad said. He reached out to pat one of the horses as we walked by. "But I better call home."

My father merely nodded and told Chad to use the office phone while he collected some papers to work on at the house. I was far too excited to wait for them, so I suggested that I go on ahead and tell my mom that there would be company for dinner. My dad agreed.

It was dark out, and a crisp March wind was blowing. But I hardly noticed the chill as I raced toward the house. I couldn't believe my father had actually asked Chad to stay for dinner. He rarely invited grooms or trainers to eat with us. Most of his business meetings took place in his office over morning coffee, before things became too hectic.

I went in through the back door and into the mud room, which led into the kitchen. I could see my mother through the open door placing a lid over a large saucepan on the stove.

"Chad's coming to dinner," I called out excitedly as I pulled off my boots. "Dad invited him to eat with us."

My mother paused to glance at me and laughed. "That's nice, but who is Chad?"

The question caught me by surprise. I hadn't stopped to think that my mother couldn't possibly know who Chad was since I had been very careful never to mention his name around the house. Even that afternoon, when I'd told her about someone standing on my fingers, I hadn't said Chad's name.

"He's the new part-time help," I told her. I tried to keep my voice steady while I made a big show of straightening out my boots. It was a rule in our house that anyone coming in from the stables had to remove their boots in the mud room.

"Is he a friend from school?" she asked

when I finally stepped into the kitchen in my stocking feet.

He's more than that, Mom—much more, I ached to admit. But I swallowed my words and shrugged instead.

"Not really. I've seen Chad around school a couple of times. But he's a junior so we don't have any classes together," I told her.

Before she had a chance to ask any more questions, I asked if there was time for me to wash up and change.

"You go ahead," my mother said. She gave me one of her knowing smiles before turning to check something in the oven. "I'll set the table tonight."

Nodding gratefully, I ran up to my room, and began rummaging through my closet for something to wear. I wanted to look my best at dinner without appearing too dressed up. Finally I decided on a pair of navy corduroy jeans and a blue and white striped blouse. I carefully laid them across my bed, then headed into the bathroom to wash up.

As I pulled off my dirty clothes, I thought of how much I'd have liked to have taken a shower and shampooed my hair. But there wasn't enough time, so I settled for scrubbing my face and hands with a washcloth. Then I splashed a light cologne my aunt gave me as a present for my last birthday. I brushed my hair until it glimmered before pulling it off my face with two combs. Usually I just put it in a ponytail or shoved it behind my ears.

After that, I put on a fresh coat of lip gloss and reached for the mascara. For years people had been telling me that my eyes were my best feature, and I wanted them to look outstanding—especially if Chad was going to be sitting across the table from me. I applied a thin, even coat.

A tightening in my stomach—nerves—took hold of me as I slipped into my clothes. I wasn't used to having boys stay for dinner and hoped I looked OK.

I didn't.

Glancing in the mirror, I knew that I looked more as if I were dressed for a date than for dinner in my own home. I quickly discarded the blouse and pulled a baggy purple sweater over my head. To my relief, it made me look much more casual. It also brought out the color of my eyes.

"Much better," I said. I wished I could quiet my nerves as I could my footsteps on the carpeted stairs.

Chad and my father were in the den. I longed to join them, but I figured I'd better help my mother in the kitchen first. She had already set the kitchen table for four and was getting ready to serve dinner. I was glad she hadn't felt it necessary to eat in the dining room because I preferred the coziness of the kitchen to any other room in the house.

Our kitchen looked like a country kitchen, with colored tiles on the walls above the butcher block countertops and pots and pans hanging from a grid above the stove. On the sill of the bay window that overlooked the farm were a variety of ferns, each planted in a ceramic pot.

"I'm glad I baked those pies today," my mother said as she placed the food on the table.

I was glad, too. A warm slice of pie would top off the chicken dinner perfectly.

Everything about the dinner was wonderful, except that Chad, who was sitting across from me, never once looked my way even when I asked him to pass the salt. It made me wonder why I had bothered to change my clothes.

Instead of talking to me, Chad spent the entire meal talking with my parents. He asked all the right questions about the farm, which won him points with my father. But it was his compliment to my mother that scored the highest.

"This chicken is the greatest!" Chad said as he accepted a second piece. "Could you give me the recipe?"

My mother laughed. "Why don't you have your mother call me?" she asked.

"It's not for her," Chad said, glancing up. For a moment he seemed embarrassed. "My parents are divorced, and since my mom has to work crazy hours, my sister Kate and I are usually on our own when it comes to dinner.

"You mean, *you* cook?" my mother asked, trying to hide her surprise.

"A little," Chad said and shrugged. "Kate's really a lot better at it than I am."

He didn't seem to mind admitting that he knew how to cook, and I wondered if other boys would be so casual under the same circumstances.

But before I could say anything, Chad turned back to my father and began asking more questions about the farm. Since he still hadn't acknowledged my presence, I couldn't decide whether to continue to sit there or run up to my room and cry.

My mother must have sensed that I felt awkward because she suggested I start clearing the table. Chad, who had finished his dinner, jumped up to help.

"It's the least I can do," he said when he saw me look at him in surprise. "At home I usually get stuck washing the dishes."

"That won't be necessary here," my mother told him. "We have a dishwasher."

Chad grinned. "I know. It's one of the first things I noticed." My parents laughed appreciatively as they carried their coffee to the den.

Then Chad turned toward me, and it was suddenly very difficult to breathe. I searched around frantically for something to do while Chad carried the dishes over to the sink where I was standing. He stacked them neatly so it was easy for me to rinse them before I loaded them into the dishwasher.

"Watch out for your eyes," he cautioned when I was washing the pots and a spray of soapy water squirted up from the sink and landed on my cheek.

I tried to wipe away the soap with the back of my hand.

"Let me," Chad said, picking up a dish towel. Before I could protest, he dabbed it against my cheek. We were only inches apart.

"You know, you've got nice eyes," he said.

"You really mean that?" I blurted out, stunned by his compliment.

"Sure, hasn't anyone ever told you that before?"

Many times, I wanted to tell him. *But it's never really meant anything until now.* Instead I just shrugged and somehow managed to continue loading the dishwasher.

Was this really happening, or was I living a dream? All this time I thought Chad Harris hadn't known I was a member of the human race, and now he was telling me I had nice eyes!

"You also look a lot different with your hair pinned back," he said, giving me a lopsided grin.

I almost dropped the glass serving dish that I was placing in the drying rack. With those few words he had started my heart racing so fast I was almost dizzy with excitement. I knew immediately that nothing would ever be the same again. Emotions I hadn't dreamed existed were churning inside me.

Chad helped me wipe off the table, then watched as I cut each of us a piece of mother's apple pie. We ate standing up at the counter and talked a little. He mentioned how glad he was to have seen the notice. "But I am sorry about your hand."

I waved my fork with the injured hand. "It's as good as new," I said. "See."

We finished our pie, and Chad said he had to leave. Reluctantly, I showed him into the den so he could say good night to my parents.

"I'll be here bright and early tomorrow morning," he said as he shook my father's hand. Then he turned to me and smiled.

"See you later, Julie."

I watched as my father walked him to the back door. Then I told my mother I had homework to do and ran upstairs where I could be alone and relive the entire afternoon and evening. Chad had touched my day with magic. Sitting on my bed, I hugged my pillow and wondered if he, too, would think of that day as special.

Don't be a fool, Julie Peterson, I cautioned myself. *Chad was just being friendly. He's got no idea how crazy you are about him.*

Still, it was hard for me to stop thinking about him. He was on my mind when I did my French homework and when I read a chapter in my history book. He was even on my mind when I washed up and brushed my teeth, which was probably why I squeezed too much toothpaste on my toothbrush.

Even when I got into bed and closed my eyes, every detail of Chad—how he looked sitting across the kitchen table from me, how his hair curled around his ears, how his eyes lit up when he laughed—was still fresh in my mind and sent wonderful, dizzy, tingling feelings through me. Even though I knew it was silly to think about him so much, he was at the center of my thoughts as I drifted off to sleep.

Chapter Four

My alarm went off, jarring me from my warm cocoon of sleep. I reached out to silence the clock, then snuggled back under my covers. I was never at my best during those first moments in the morning. I always took my time getting out of bed. Once I was up and about, I was fine. It was just that first move that I found so difficult.

I turned over on my stomach, deciding to grab five more minutes of sleep. But as soon as I closed my eyes I remembered that something special was going to happen that day. A moment later it came to me.

Chad.

I bounded out of bed, ignoring the chill in my room, and raced into the bathroom to splash cold water on my face. I wanted to wake up quickly, so I could hurry up and get to the stables to see Chad.

35

Every morning I stopped by the barn before school to find out my afternoon schedule. I usually stayed for only a minute or two, but I was determined to be there extra early on Chad's first day.

Within moments I was out of the bathroom and dressed in a pair of soft, faded jeans and a navy turtleneck. I pulled the same baggy sweater I had worn the night before over my shirt, simply because it was handy. Then, picking up my brush, I ran it quickly through my hair. I started to walk away, but then went back to the dresser and pulled my hair back in the combs again. Then I stuffed my feet into socks and sneakers, grabbed my books, and dashed downstairs.

"You're up early this morning," my mother said as I bounded into the kitchen and dumped my books onto the counter. My mother and my father always got up at five o'clock because my dad liked to be at the barn by six.

"Yes, I know," I answered as I reached for a cereal bowl with one hand and a spoon with the other.

I filled the bowl with cold cereal, and a hearty splash of milk. Then, without bothering to sit down, I began shoveling spoonfuls of cereal into my mouth.

My mother eyed me critically from behind

her newspaper, but she refrained from saying anything until I had placed the empty bowl in the sink and grabbed my ski parka.

"Is that all you're having for breakfast?" she asked.

"Sorry, Mom. I don't have time for anything else," I answered. "I'll grab some cocoa at the barn." Before she could protest, I had grabbed my books and dashed out of the house.

At first the only sound I heard as I started toward the stables was the noise my sneakers made on the frost-covered lane. As I got closer to the barn, however, the morning stillness was broken by the stamping of restless horses and the rumbling of feeding carts being rolled down the aisles. Although the sun hadn't risen above the treetops yet, the day at Two Penny Farm had already begun.

I went into the stable area through the office doorway and immediately spotted Chad by Dancer's stall. He was checking to see if the water bucket needed filling. Looking at his lean, handsome face, I couldn't help but smile.

Chad looked terrific. His hair fell in an easy wave across his forehead, and he was wearing jeans and a faded orange sweatshirt under a jean jacket with a thick white pile lining.

37

"Hi, there," he called when he spotted me coming toward him. "What are you doing here?"

"I-I have to get my schedule for this afternoon," I answered a little too quickly. I felt myself blush.

"Why so early?" Chad asked, catching me off guard. It hadn't occurred to me that showing up at the stable so early might seem strange to him.

"The bus!" I blurted out. "I'm one of the first stops in the morning."

"What a drag," Chad said. He reached over to turn on the faucet that was recessed beside Dancer's stall.

Every stall had its own faucet, complete with a short hose. This made it possible to fill each bucket without having to haul water.

"Hey! I have an idea," Chad said once the bucket was filled. "Why don't I drive you to school? Then you won't have to leave so early."

It took a minute for what he said to sink in. When it did, I almost didn't believe it. The thought of driving to school with Chad was too exciting for words.

"Well?" he asked. He stopped working when I didn't answer him.

"Sure. I—I mean, that sounds great!" I stammered.

38

He had his back to me and was struggling with a short hose attached to one of the recessed faucets. It looked as if it had sprung a leak, and Chad was trying to fill the bucket without getting himself soaked.

I stood there waiting for him to say something else, but he didn't. I decided it was up to me to talk. I knew I couldn't stand there much longer without feeling foolish.

"Would you like some help filling the rest of the buckets?" I asked when Chad turned off the faucet.

"Is that an offer?"

"Yes," I answered.

Chad gave me one of his lopsided grins. "OK," he said. "You can finish filling the water buckets in this aisle while I start on the next."

I felt as though I had been punched in the stomach. I had only offered to help because I'd assumed that we would work *together.*

My shoulders sagged as I watched him disappear. *You set yourself up for it this time,* I thought as I began checking and filling the rest of the water buckets. Fortunately, none of them had to be scrubbed so it didn't take me long. When Chad returned a short while later, I was standing by Dancer's stall watching him pull at wisps of fresh hay.

"That's it for the water buckets," he said. He came to stand beside me. "Thanks for your help."

I simply smiled. I was just trying to think of something to say when the intercom crackled.

"Julie and Chad, you're wanted in the large tack room," my father's voice boomed from the loudspeakers hooked up around the barn.

I moaned and pushed myself away from Dancer's stall.

"He wants us to attend the scheduling meeting," I told Chad. "They're held every morning at seven-thirty after the grooms finish feeding the horses."

"So? What's the big deal?" Chad asked.

"Bo-o-oring!" I grimaced.

"Come on," he said, teasing. "It can't be that bad."

"Want to bet?"

I never attended the meetings because I had to catch the school bus. Now I'd lost my excuse.

The four male and two female grooms were already in the tack room when Chad and I arrived. A couple of them were standing beside the table that had a pot of coffee and a pot of hot cocoa on it; the others sat perched on wooden chairs with their steaming cups

and doughnuts. My father bought fresh doughnuts every day, and the sight of them reminded me that I hadn't eaten much for
breakfast.

"Help yourself," I told Chad. I watched him
scoop up two plain doughnuts and pour himself a cup of hot cocoa.

I did the same. Then we both walked to the
back of the room.

The hot cocoa tasted so good going down
that before I knew it I had drained my cup.
But that left me with nothing to wash down
my second doughnut, and I was too self-
conscious to get up for more cocoa in the
middle of the meeting.

I turned to see if Chad had finished his
cocoa and found him watching me. I suppose
I should have felt embarrased, but I didn't,
because I spotted a brown mustache of cocoa
on his upper lip. It curled up on either end
like a devil's horn and instead of wondering
why he'd been watching me, I giggled.

"What's so funny?" he whispered when I
put my hands up to cover my mouth.

"You," I said, pointing to the mustache.

Chad used his napkin to wipe away the
telltale cocoa. Then he glanced at me again
and grinned. "Better?" he asked.

I nodded. I was finally feeling more natural around him.

"Now, how about if we make a deal?" Chad said. He held out his cocoa. "I'll share the rest of this with you if you give me half of that doughnut."

I looked down at the doughnut on my lap, then back up at Chad.

"Deal," I told him.

A few minutes later the meeting was over and the grooms filed out to go back to work. Chad and I, however, stayed in the tack room. We polished off two more doughnuts before leaving for school.

Chapter Five

I was glad Chad's little Honda had bucket seats. I didn't have to wonder if I was sitting too close to him or if it looked as though I was leaning against the door.

The car was spotlessly clean, inside and out. Although it must have been eight or nine years old, it started up the minute Chad turned the key.

"Pretty good for an old heap, don't you think?" he said proudly as the engine continued to purr smoothly. It was obvious to me that the Honda was Chad's pride and joy.

I leaned back against the seat and smiled as we waited for the motor to warm up. Chad had turned the radio on, and the voice of Bruce Springsteen, my favorite singer, filled the car. At that moment, there wasn't a place on earth I would rather have been.

"You buckled up?" Chad asked. And when

I nodded, he shifted into reverse, accidentally brushing his hand against my left thigh. The contact sent a shiver through my body.

I tried to pretend nothing had happened, but Chad noticed. He asked if I was cold, and I lied by nodding yes.

"No problem," he said and turned on the heater. Before long, the car was toasty warm. I wished I could think of something clever to say. But everything that came to my mind sounded so stupid that I decided I'd be better off just being quiet.

When I had woken up that morning, I had never dreamed that I would be riding to school in Chad's car. Even now, I found it hard to believe.

Usually I was standing by the front entrance with Diane when Chad pulled into his parking spot. He arrived at the same time every day, and he was always alone.

I imagined the look on Diane's face when she saw us pull up together. She'd be so surprised! No one ever paid attention to the students who took the bus or walked to school. But everyone noticed the ones with cars.

I glanced at the students who were already standing around as Chad turned into the driveway. Some were in the parking lot, and others stood in groups by the school entrance.

Diane, however, wasn't in our usual meeting place, and I assumed it was because she hadn't seen me get off the bus. She probably figured I wasn't coming to school that day.

Just wait, I thought. I swallowed hard. The last thing I wanted was to appear to be gloating when I got out of Chad's car, but my smile just wouldn't go away. Still, I wanted to look as if it were perfectly natural for us to be together.

"Thanks for the lift," I said over the hood after he parked the car and we had both gotten out. "It sure beats taking the bus."

"Anytime," Chad called as he headed off to join a group of boys gathered around a nearby car.

I followed a few steps behind him, wondering if he had meant it seriously or whether it was just a figure of speech. It would be wonderful to ride to school with Chad every morning, and not just because I was crazy about him. If I rode with Chad I wouldn't have to put up with the younger kids on the bus anymore—the ones who still threw spit balls at one another.

I was still trying to figure out if he had been serious when a familiar voice broke into my thoughts. I recognized it as Peter's, one of Chad's friends.

"Hey, Harris," he said loudly. "Got yourself a new girl?"

"Cut it out," Chad growled, playfully shoving him against the car. "I just gave her a lift."

"Really?" another of his friends teased.

"Look, I'm working at her father's stable. She needed a ride so I drove her to school this morning. Don't make a big deal out of it," Chad told them.

I picked up my pace as I passed the boys, hoping they would think the deep shade of my face was from the cold and not from embarrassment. It was bad enough that they knew I had overheard their comments. I didn't want them to think I cared.

Another group of students stood laughing and talking as I got closer to the entrance, and I planned to ask if they had seen Diane. But before I could, she suddenly appeared before me, bundled up in her oversized tweed jacket and carrying an armload of books.

"Did I just see you get out of Chad Harris's car?" she demanded, grabbing me by the elbow and leading me away from the crowd.

For a moment I wasn't sure what to say. Chad's comments to his friends had taken away some of my joy. Then I caught the look on Diane's face. And I knew I was all right.

Nothing Chad nor any of his friends said could change the fact that I *had* ridden to school with him.

"It was me," I said and smiled at her.

"Are you going to tell me how it happened or do I have to drag it out of you?" Diane asked.

"Well," I began slowly. "Remember I told you how Chad helped me hang the help-wanted ad on the bulletin board yesterday? At the time I didn't think he had bothered to read it, but he must have because he showed up at the farm after school. I almost passed out when I saw him walk into my father's office. My heart stopped, and I just stood there staring at him like an idiot."

"Did he get the job?" Diane asked, her grip on my elbow tightening.

"Not only that," I nodded smugly. "He also ate dinner at my house."

"He didn't!" she said, stunned. "You must have died!"

I drew in a deep breath and closed my eyes in order to recall every word that had been spoken. "You could say that," I said after a few moments. "Chad helped me load the dishwasher, and he even told me I had nice eyes."

"Julie! Do you know what that means?" Diane exclaimed. She tossed her head to dislodge a strand of hair that had blown across her face.

I nodded and lapsed into silence. It meant nothing. I might be crazy about Chad but it was obvious that as far as he was concerned I was just a friend. So what if he told me I had nice eyes? It was no big deal. He probably paid compliments to all the girls he knew.

"What else happened? Tell me everything," Diane urged.

"Nothing, really," I said, and it was true. I wished there had been more to tell her. But other than Chad's driving me to school, that was it. Nothing else had happened except the schedule meeting. Suddenly, I giggled, remembering the chocolate mustache.

"All right, tell me. What have you been holding back?"

I wasn't sure I wanted to share those few moments with Diane. They had been very special to me, and I was afraid telling her about them might make them seem silly.

"It's just crazy. That's all," I said, and shrugged. "When my parents first mentioned the idea of putting a help-wanted ad in school, I was against it. I didn't think we needed any help and was afraid I'd get stuck working with someone like Daryl Fishbinder or one of the Stanford twins. I never dreamed that Chad would apply for the job."

Diane smiled at me, and I knew she understood. But whatever she was about to reply was cut off by the sound of the warning bell. We had to hurry into school, and then we were separated in the crush at the door. It wasn't until we were near our lockers that Diane caught up with me again.

"He must like you a little," she insisted as we both turned the combinations on our locks. "After all, he *did* drive you to school."

I didn't answer her. If only I could believe what she had said was true. But I'd already spent two years waiting for Chad to notice me, and it didn't seem possible that overnight he would discover that he liked me. Of course, it would be a dream come true if it did happen that way.

As I sat in the cafeteria eating my lunch later that day, I reminded myself that dreams don't usually come true. I knew I was being a real pessimist, but I was also afraid to get my hopes up.

Diane and I always sat at the same table with three of our friends. We didn't have assigned seats or anything. We just liked that particular table because it gave us a good view of the lunchroom, and it was far enough away from the cafeteria line so we didn't get bumped by students carrying trays.

Chad's usual table was against the windows. From where we sat, I could watch him without his ever realizing it. That day, when I first spotted him, he was leaning back casually in his seat, laughing hilariously at something one of his friends had said. When he wasn't talking to the girls at the next table, he was glancing around the lunchroom. Yet, not once in the entire forty-minute lunch period did he look my way.

There's no hope, I thought as Diane and I gathered up our books. We usually tried to leave the cafeteria before the bell rang, so we could stop by the girls' room to comb our hair. But when I stood up, Diane grabbed my wrist and held it in an iron grip.

"Don't look now," she said from behind me. "But I think Chad is coming over to talk to you."

A feeling of panic ran through me. *How do I look?* I thought frantically as I spotted him making his way through the crowd of students.

Obviously, there was no time to check my appearance in the small pocket mirror I always carried, so I closed my eyes for a moment. I hoped that my hair hadn't become stringy and that I still had *some* blusher left on my cheeks.

"Hi, Julie," Chad said as he reached our table. I hastily introduced Diane. But his eyes were fixed on me, and the intensity of his gaze sent a little shock up my spine. "I thought, since I'm driving directly to the farm after school, you might like a ride."

"A ride sounds good," I managed to answer. I was overwhelmed by the idea that Chad would offer to drive me home, too. I mean, a ride *to* school was great enough, but home as well? "Where should I meet you?"

"How about the parking lot?" Chad answered. His warm voice reached into the depths of my heart.

It took several moments for me to calm down after Chad left the cafeteria. Neither Diane nor I could stop smiling. All sorts of wonderful emotions were rippling through me, and I didn't know how I was going to make it through the rest of the day.

"I think I've died and gone to heaven," I finally whispered to Diane. Then we glided out of the cafeteria.

Chapter Six

That same happiness continued throughout most of the weekend, even though Chad and I weren't able to spend a lot of time together. But just hearing his voice in the next aisle or catching a quick glimpse of him bringing a horse in from the paddock was enough. There was only one bleak spot in my weekend, and that was on Saturday after I had finished exercising Dancer.

Chad had been extremely busy all day—one minute he was helping someone up onto a horse, the next minute he was cleaning tack. When I walked into the tack room around noon, holding Dancer's saddle and bridle in my arms, he jumped up from his work and took the saddle from me.

"Don't leave it there," I told Chad when he tossed the saddle over the sawhorse. "My father's pretty fussy when it comes to putting

52

the tack away." Every horse had its own saddle and bridle, and every saddle and bridle had a carefully labeled placed in the tack room where it belonged when it wasn't on the horse or being cleaned.

"It won't be there long," he said, turning back to the saddle he'd been working on.

Chad looked busy, so even though I had other chores to do, I said, "Look, if you want, I'll just clean the saddle myself."

"I can do it, just hang on," Chad answered without looking up.

"But you should do—" I started. Chad glanced sharply at me.

"Stop worrying, will you? I said I would take care of it, and I will," he said in a low, tension-filled voice.

I felt as if I'd been slapped. "Forget it!" I flung at him before I even realized what I was saying. "I'll take care of it myself after I settle Dancer in his stall."

"Suit yourself," Chad said, stiffening. "I was only trying to help."

I realized that Chad was right as I led Dancer into his stall and closed the door. But it didn't ease the horrible thoughts that were crowding into my mind. How could I have spoken so harshly to him? What if he never spoke to me again? What if he quit his job? I knew I had to apologize before it was too late, only I didn't know what to say. It was the first argument I'd ever had with a boy, other than my brother. I couldn't just walk into the tack room and blurt out, "Hey, Chad, I'm sorry." Or could I?

I tried to convince myself I was making a big deal out of nothing. Maybe Chad had already shrugged off the incident and returned my saddle to its peg. But deep inside, I knew that was only wishful thinking. If I cared at all about Chad and wanted to make things right between us again, I would have to go and apologize, no matter how hard it was.

I took a deep breath and tried to find the courage to return to the tack room. There wasn't any point in delaying what had to be done. But as I moved down the long aisle, I was so nervous my heart was thudding against my ribs.

The first thing I saw when I went in the tack room was my saddle, still sitting on the sawhorse—untouched. I just stared at it until Chad realized I was there and looked up. Our eyes met for an instant, but he didn't make any attempt to speak and neither did I. I couldn't get myself to say anything.

To my relief, Sandy, one of the female grooms, came in just then. After pouring some coffee, she took out a sandwich wrapped in foil from the refrigerator. There was no set lunch hour for the grooms. They just ate whenever they had a few minutes to spare.

"Anyone care to join me?" she asked, pulling a chair up to the small, square table in the corner.

"Sure," I murmured. I took my own lunch out of the refrigerator. I wasn't particularly hungry, but I felt awkward just standing around. Eating would give me something to do.

For the next few minutes I pretended to be very busy setting my lunch out on the table. I was surprised to find two tuna fish sandwiches, along with some cut-up raw vegetables and a bunch of chocolate chip cookies. But I was too preoccupied to give it much thought. I left the extra sandwich and the cookies in the bag.

"How about you, Chad?" Sandy asked. He had glanced our way but made no move to join us.

He shrugged his shoulders. "Thanks, anyway. But I didn't bring any lunch."

My head shot up, and I suddenly realized why my mother had packed the extra sandwich. She had obviously worried that Chad might forget to bring a sandwich on his first full day. I made a note to myself to kiss her when I got home. Now I had the perfect excuse to break the silence between Chad and me.

"You can share my lunch," I said softly, holding out the bag.

"Are you sure?" he asked. I nodded. What I really wanted to do was reach over and hug him and say, *I'm sorry, Chad. It was all a mistake, and I didn't mean to snap at you. Please forgive me, and let's forget this ever happened.* Only I didn't do any of that.

"I think my mother thought you might forget to bring your lunch," I admitted instead. "She's never packed two sandwiches before."

Chad seemed to accept the peace offering and pulled up a chair. He straddled it with his arms folded across the back. Some of the tension between us had eased, but not all of it. There was still a thin wall there that I knew wouldn't come down until I apologized. We ate in silence.

Finally Sandy left to go back to work. We were alone in the tack room, and I forced aside the lump in my throat. "I'm sorry for snapping at you, Chad," I said.

His expression changed then, and he looked over at me. "Are you always so touchy about your saddle?"

"Not usually," I said. I even managed a smile. "It's just that I really don't want you to get in trouble with my father the very first week on the job."

The explanation made him laugh, and I felt myself relax a little. The nervousness in my stomach went away, and my head no longer felt as though it were being squeezed by a tight rubber band.

"I wouldn't risk getting into trouble, you know," Chad said. He aimed the sandwich paper he had crumpled up at the large wastebasket in the corner and tossed it in with one easy motion. "I just wanted to finish what I was doing before wiping down your saddle. Then after you left, I was afraid that if I so much as touched it you'd have me fired or something."

I stared at him then, too stunned to speak. *Me, have Chad fired?*

"A *lot* you know!" I exclaimed.

"You mean you're not the spoiled little rich girl that I thought you were?"

I saw the teasing glint in his eyes, but I answered him seriously. "No, I'm not!" I said. I twisted my entire body around to face him. "My father may own Two Penny Farm, but that doesn't mean we're as well off as some of the people who board their horses here. As

57

for my being spoiled," I went on, "I work because I *have* to in order to pay for Dancer's upkeep, and— " Then I stopped.

Chad continued to look at me after I'd stopped talking, and I felt my face grow warm. I knew I had overreacted and was sure I had blown it that time. Then I saw a smile begin tugging at his lips. "In that case, what do you say we both get back to work?"

"Why not?" I said. We looked at each other and smiled.

Everything was easy and natural between us after that. Chad and I worked together wiping down Dancer's saddle. Then I helped him bring some horses in from the paddock and put the others out. At one point my father came by, watched us for a few moments, then left without a word.

Sunday was pretty much the same. I was busy schooling two junior horses when he first came. But in the late afternoon we were both given horses to walk and were able to spend half an hour together in the paddock.

"It sounds as if you and Chad are getting along pretty well," Diane said. Her voice bubbled with excitement as we walked to our homeroom class on Monday morning. "It shouldn't take long now."

I turned to her and stared. "What are you talking about?"

"You and Chad," Diane announced. "I bet he'll ask you for a date soon."

"Come on, Diane. Get your head out of the clouds." I forced my voice to sound light. "The only reason Chad's being nice to me is because my father owns Two Penny Farm. He happens to need the job and figures it can't hurt to be friendly."

"You're amazing, Julie!" Diane protested. "I don't understand why you can't accept the fact that he actually might *like* you."

I'm afraid to, I wanted to say. *I'm afraid that if I let myself believe something could develop between Chad and me, I'd just be setting myself up for a terrible fall.* But I couldn't say that to anyone, not even Diane.

Chad could date any girl in the school. And although I had never actually seen him with anyone since he and Cheryl broke up after Christmas, I was sure he dated a lot.

It didn't stop me from caring about him. Nothing could do that. It just helped me accept the fact that Chad and I could be friends, but nothing more.

At three o'clock the dismissal bell rang and I hurried out of school to catch the bus. I was a little disappointed that Chad wouldn't be driving me home, but the stables were closed on Monday and he deserved the day off.

I felt lonely at the thought of spending an afternoon without Chad nearby, so I tried to think of happier things while I changed into my breeches and down vest. I always looked forward to Mondays because no one came to ride. The grooms used the day to catch up on odds and ends, but I spent Monday afternoons schooling Dancer. And usually I had the entire outdoor ring to myself.

When I got to the barn, I began wrapping his legs in bandages and bell boots to protect them during the workout. Dancer was used to the procedure and stood still while I worked, so it didn't take long.

I had already finished his second foreleg when a shadow fell over my left shoulder. "How's it look?" I asked, thinking it was my father.

"Looks fine to me," a familiar voice said. But it wasn't my father talking—it was Chad.

I turned around, amazed to see him standing behind me with his hands jammed into the pockets of his jeans. "Hi," he said. He smiled as I stood up.

I wished I had thought to put on makeup and something more flattering than the sweatshirt my brother had brought me from college. It wasn't in the best of shape and didn't really look good with a vest.

"W-what are you doing h-here? I thought you had the afternoon off," I managed to stammer.

Chad laughed. "I do. But your father said it was OK if I wanted to stop by and hang around. Need any help?" he asked.

I looked at him and shrugged. Chad knew perfectly well that I didn't need help, but he stood there waiting for me to give him something to do anyway.

"You can saddle Dancer for me while I finish wrapping his legs," I said, hoping my voice wouldn't crack. Chad always had that effect on me.

"Sure thing," he said. He moved down the aisle toward the tack room. A moment later he reappeared with Dancer's bridle slung over one shoulder, holding the saddle tightly with both hands.

He seemed glad to be doing something useful. I didn't even have to remind him to smooth Dancer's coat with a soft brush before he placed the saddle on the horse's back.

"Heads up," he called before letting the girth slide down; I automatically passed it to him under Dancer's belly. Our hands touched and an unfamiliar feeling rippled through me. It increased when, instead of letting go, Chad's grip grew stronger, and he began yanking gently on my hand.

It was a playful gesture and we both laughed, but I didn't pull back. I was feeling so wonderful I didn't want the moment to end.

I lifted my head to find Chad looking at me from under Dancer's belly. "Anything wrong?" he asked innocently.

"Only my hand," I murmured and gazed at his fingers wrapped around mine like steel bands. "It seems to be caught."

His eyes followed the direction of my gaze, and he smiled. "So it is," he said, releasing his grip and letting my hand drop. "Is that better?"

I swallowed in spite of the lump in my throat and nodded. "Yes, thanks." Then I returned to fastening Dancer's bell boot; I needed something to do with my hands. At that moment I didn't trust myself to speak.

From then on, the afternoon that I had thought would be boring and lonely was filled with wonder. Dancer lowered his head for the bridle, making it easier for me to slip on the head piece. Then Chad followed us outside where he helped adjust the jumps for me while I put Dancer through his paces.

Every so often Chad would point out a mistake when we finished a round of jumps. But since his comments were valid, I didn't mind. Chad noticed when I let Dancer come in too close to a jump or if he didn't tuck his forelegs up high enough. He was also very generous with his compliments whenever we had a perfect round.

I found myself enjoying the session even though a crisp, cool wind was blowing across the open ring. I wasn't self-conscious in front of Chad. In fact, I was thrilled that he'd insisted on staying outside, even after I suggested he watch from the office window.

"You don't look very comfortable," I had said when I caught him hunching his shoulders against the wind. "I don't mind if you go inside."

"I can't help you with the jumps from in there," he said, shrugging off the suggestion. The joy I felt at his willingness to stay and help me brought a wide grin to my face.

Chapter Seven

I remained on cloud nine for the rest of the week. Not only had Chad promised to come to the farm the following Monday to help me school Dancer, but he continued to drive me to and from school every day. Those few minutes in the car with him were always very special. Chad was open and friendly, and we talked a lot about TV shows, new rock groups, and the farm.

I didn't feel awkward being alone with him, either. I looked forward to the rides. For one thing, it was the only time we were ever *really* alone. When we saw each other in school, Chad was always surrounded by friends. And at the farm, there was always someone nearby. So the only time I could depend on being alone with Chad was when we were in his car.

As soon as the dismissal bell rang each

afternoon, I would dash out of class and down the hall to my locker. I was usually one of the first ones out of school, and I would sit on the front bumper of Chad's car waiting for him.

On Friday, however, I was late leaving my last class because my science teacher, Mr. Simpson, decided to give us back our test papers just as the bell rang. We had to stay in our seats until he called our names, and since the papers were arranged in alphabetical order, I was near the end. It seemed to take him forever to get to the *P*'s, and by the time I got my coat out of the locker and made my way to the front door, the entrance was jammed with people.

"Excuse me," I kept repeating as I elbowed my way through the crowd. Several friends tried to stop me to talk, but I shook my head, explaining I had to get to work right away.

Chad was leaning against his car with his arms folded across his chest when I finally made it down the steps. I waved, and he straightened up when he saw me coming. He flashed a grin at me that made me want to laugh aloud with relief.

"Sorry I'm late," I said as soon as I reached the car. We faced each other over the hood, and I was amazed again at how handsome he looked with his jacket collar turned up. I didn't pay any attention to the group of students gathering around a car that had just pulled up behind us.

"Hey, Harris! Come have a look at this!" someone called just as Chad was reaching into the pocket of his jeans for the car keys.

We both turned around at the same time to see Chad's friend Ben waving him over to a shiny new Porsche. The driver of the car was a senior whose name I didn't know, but seated beside him was Cheryl Williams.

Her long, silky blond hair fell gracefully over her shoulders, and her deep blue eyes surveyed the crowd of people around her. No matter how hard I tried, it was impossible not to feel jealous of Cheryl. Maybe I wouldn't have felt that way if Cheryl hadn't once been Chad's girlfriend. But I couldn't seem to forget that there *had* been something between them, and that maybe there still was.

"Hello, Chad," Cheryl said in her most flirtatious voice. He walked over to the car. Her eyes followed him as he silently admired the car's smooth lines.

"Pretty sporty," she purred. Chad had finished his inspection and went over to lean in the open window to check out the interior.

"Dan's parents just gave it to him for a birth-day present," Cheryl added.

Chad still said nothing, and because his back was to me, I couldn't get a look at his face. But there was no mistaking Cheryl's warm smile directed at him, and it made my heart sink.

She sat there like a queen holding court. Occasionally she would wave to friends who passed by. The last thing I wanted to do was go over and join her and her friends, but I had no choice. Chad's car was locked so I couldn't sit inside it and pretend to be doing my homework, and I was beginning to feel foolish standing there by myself.

I kept my chin up and pasted a smile on my face as I stepped out from between the parked cars. Cheryl and I might not have spoken to each other in three years, but it wasn't as though we were strangers. We used to take riding lessons together every week-end, and she still boarded her horse, Jupiter, at Two Penny Farm.

Her eyes flickered over me curiously as I approached the Porsche, and for just an in-stant I thought she looked surprised. Then her expression changed to indifference. "Hello, Cheryl," I said.

"Hello, Julie," she responded. The words barely made it past her lips.

I sucked in my breath and tried to keep the smile on my face. There was something about her that made me cringe inside, and it wasn't just her stunning good looks or her terrific figure. It was the knowledge that behind that beautiful face was a spoiled and snobby person who seemed to enjoy making other people uncomfortable.

Cheryl ignored me while she laughed and chatted with Chad and the others who were gathered around the car. It reminded me of when I'd first started working at the stables three years before. Until then, Cheryl and I had been casual friends. But the minute I started working, everything changed. Cheryl and the other girls who rode at our stables were there to have fun. They didn't understand that I had to work and I took my job seriously. I couldn't give them—or their horses—special treatment. So they dropped me. They began to act as if they didn't even know who I was.

At first their cold-shoulder treatment hurt, then it made me furious. It wasn't until Ken convinced me they weren't worth worrying about that I was able to stop caring.

"Chad, don't you think we'd better get

going?" I asked expectantly a few moments later. A relieved look crossed his face. It was almost as though he'd been waiting for me to say something.

"Why the rush?" Cheryl called out as we started toward the Honda.

"We've got to get to work," Chad answered. He sounded a little uncomfortable admitting that in front of everyone.

"Oh?" she asked. "Where are you working?"

"Two Penny Farm," he answered as if he hoped that would end the discussion. Cheryl, however, didn't intend to forget about it so easily.

"I suppose you're still paying off your car?" She smiled, and although her voice was honey sweet, I could detect a sarcastic undertone.

I saw Chad turn pale.

"Yeah," he said and jerked open the car door. "Some of us have to work for what we want."

"Too bad," Cheryl said. She gave a triumphant laugh and swung her blond head back to the others as if she was dismissing us.

Chad's jaw was rigid as he climbed into the Honda and reached across the front seat to unlock my door. I wanted to tell him that I understood what he was feeling, and that I, too, had been snubbed by Cheryl. But as we drove out of the parking lot I sat very still, scarcely breathing, because it was obvious he didn't want to talk about what had just happened.

"That was some car," I said, trying to make conversation after a few moments of silence had elapsed. By that time we were on the main road. Chad still sat stiffly, his fingers curled tightly around the steering wheel.

"It makes this car look like a piece of junk, doesn't it?" Chad asked suddenly. His tone was mocking.

"I don't know about that," I answered. "Your car may not be fancy, but it's clean and it runs really well."

"But that's all you can say about it," Chad said flatly.

"No, it isn't," I said firmly. "It also gets you where you want to go, and as far as I'm concerned, it's a lot nicer than riding to school on the bus."

Chad took his eyes off the road for a second to look at me. "If you're serious about that, thanks. Some girls believe that every guy they date has to have a lot of money and a fancy car," he muttered.

I didn't know what to say, so I said nothing. It was obvious that he was talking about Cheryl, and I was surprised at the hard edge in his voice. It was so unexpected, and I felt a strange, nagging worry begin to form in my mind.

I knew that Cheryl had embarrassed Chad when she'd mentioned that he had to work to pay off his car loan. But I wondered if it really bothered him that he didn't have a lot of money? Was Chad jealous of Dan's Porsche? Did he think that if he had a fancy car he would get Cheryl back? Most important, did he *want* Cheryl back?

I didn't want to think that he still cared for her. Even though I didn't believe in miracles, one small part of me continued to hope that Chad would come to like me as more than a friend.

As long as Chad didn't have a steady girl-friend, there was a chance that something special could develop between us. The time we spent together was wonderful. We had a lot of fun talking and seemed to know how to make each other laugh. At times we were also able to communicate without even speaking, something I wanted to believe only happened between people who cared for each other. But I couldn't be certain, and I sure couldn't summon up the courage to tell Chad how *I* felt.

Many times I thought I would burst because I wanted him to know how I felt. But I only got as far as opening my mouth before I discovered that I didn't have the nerve. Deep down inside, I knew it was because of my looks. My boyish figure made me feel much less attractive than other girls I knew, especially someone like Cheryl Williams. And that thought brought me back to wondering whether or not Chad wanted her back.

Suddenly I wanted to know, but didn't have the courage to ask him directly. I was afraid that Chad would think I was prying— and he'd have been right. So I asked what I hoped was a safe question, but one that might help me learn more about how Chad felt.

"Why did you and Cheryl break up?" I asked, my voice small and tight. I hoped I didn't sound overly curious.

Chad didn't seem to notice. He also didn't answer me immediately. I saw an odd expression flicker in his blue green eyes.

"Cheryl can be difficult to get along with when she doesn't get her own way," he finally answered in a flat tone. "I guess you could call her spoiled, although she'd never admit it. Anyway, we broke up because the day after I bought the Honda, she refused to let me drive her to school. She had expected me to buy a *new* car and insisted she wouldn't be caught dead riding in this heap."

Chad's mouth twisted slightly when he said

the word "heap," and I imagined the hurt he must have felt. I also wondered *why* he would have such a strong reaction to her—unless he still cared about her.

A wave of despair washed over me. It was impossible to concentrate on anything for the rest of the day. All I could think about was Cheryl. And when I tried to do my homework later that evening, I jealously thought about her looks, her self-confidence, and her ability to attract boys.

At one point I felt so torn up that I had to close my books and turn on the radio. Listening to music always helped me relax. After a while I decided that even if my relationship with Chad never developed any further than the friendship we now shared, he'd still be working at the farm. I would still see him every day. I could gaze at him when he wasn't looking and work with him whenever I wasn't busy doing something else.

It wouldn't be perfect, but it was still comforting. I finished my homework and then drifted off into a dreamless sleep. No matter what our relationship was, I would continue to look forward to the time Chad and I spent together. Having him as a friend was better than not having him at all.

Chapter Eight

It rained all day Saturday. But Sunday morning the sun was shining brightly. April was already promising fresh signs of spring.

Clusters of daffodils and other colorful spring flowers were popping up in the grass, which was slowly changing from its winter brown to a vibrant green. Even the buds on the trees surrounding the paddock areas were beginning to swell. And it was unseasonably warm, which meant that the stables would be busy.

Everyone had decided to come to the farm and ride. Some owners appeared in well-tailored riding habits, expecting their horses to be ready and waiting. Other people came to take their favorite hack horse out for an hour or two, to go riding through the state park that bordered the farm.

Chad and I did what we could to help the

grooms, especially when my father went out riding with his friend, Mr. Phillips. Every Sunday, weather permitting, he would ride with his friend for an hour or so. He did this because even though Mr. Phillips was an experienced rider, he didn't like to ride alone.

"Whew!" Chad said, collapsing on a bale of hay that was stowed beside one of the barn doors. We had just delivered two horses to their owners and were taking a minute to rest. "Is it always such a madhouse on weekends?" he asked in a tired voice.

"It happens every year," I told him. "As soon as the weather gets nice, everyone wants to get outside."

"Spare me," he groaned as another shadow filled the doorway. "Here come two more."

The grooms all seemed to be busy in other parts of the stable, so Chad and I hurried over to the riders who handed us their horses, gave us each a crisp nod, and went strutting off to their cars.

I saw Chad shrug at their hasty departure and realized that he didn't recognize the mare he was holding. "Follow me," I said as I led the chestnut into the barn.

Fortunately, neither horse was hot and sweaty, so it wasn't necessary to walk either of them. All we had to do was take them into the stable and settle them in their stalls.

The chestnut walked easily beside me, clinking his silvery bits. When I started to cross-tie him in the aisle, he nuzzled me affectionately.

"Your horse belongs three stalls down," I told Chad, pointing straight ahead. "Her name is Peggy, which is short for Pegasus. There's a nameplate on the door."

Then I undid the girth in order to lift off the saddle and continued untacking the chestnut. I had just replaced the bridle with the halter when Sandy showed up and offered to take over. I knew that the chestnut wasn't one of her horses and started to protest. She explained my father had returned from his ride and needed to see me in his office.

I couldn't imagine why. The two o'clock lesson I was supposed to help him with wouldn't be there for an hour, and I was caught up on all my other work. When I walked into the office and saw him talking to a little boy who looked about five, I was even more confused.

"David here wants to learn how to ride," my father explained, ruffling the little boy's dark curls. "He says he's ridden merry-go-round horses and gone for pony rides at the beach, so he's ready to learn how to ride a *real* horse. I suggested he take a private lesson with you."

It was an unusual request. My father rarely gave lessons to children under ten unless they owned their own pony or junior horse. But when I looked down at David, who stood huddled against his father's side, I understood why he was making the exception. Peeking out from under his left pant leg was a metal brace.

David smiled up at me when my father introduced us. He had one of the most open faces of any child I'd ever seen. "Hello, David," I said.

"Hi," he replied. "Can you teach me how to make the horse jump?"

"Sure, but not for a little while. Why don't I introduce you to Scout, first?" I asked. David nodded and took my hand when I held it out to him. We started the lesson by walking around the outdoor ring together. David was riding Scout, a gentle Appaloosa, while I walked beside him. I showed him how to hold the reins properly and use them to guide the horse. We also worked on how to squeeze his legs against the saddle when he wanted to make Scout move forward. I wasn't sure how much control he had in his left leg so I put off showing him how to post until his next lesson.

David learned enough to keep him busy. He could hardly believe that he was really controlling Scout. He pulled the horse to a stop and then signaled him to move forward at least ten times. But Scout took it all in stride. He didn't balk when David asked him to turn left and right over and over again. Then all too soon the half hour was up.

"Why don't you walk him up to where that boy with the blue jacket is standing?" I told David, pointing to Chad, who was just outside the door that led into the stables. I knew Scout would head directly for the barn, and I thought it would make David feel good to ride the short distance by himself.

Chad watched them approach. When Scout got near the doorway, he signaled David to stop.

"That was pretty good," Chad said. He smiled as he lifted the little boy down from the saddle. "Now, how would you like to feed Scout a lump of sugar?"

"Gosh!" David said, his face lighting up. "Could I really?"

"Sure. Just ask your instructor here," Chad said. He pointed at me. "She's got all sorts of goodies hidden in her vest pocket."

I saw David glance at me, then back at Chad. "How'd you know what she has in her pocket? Is she your girlfriend or something?"

I felt my face turn crimson at the boy's abrupt question. In order to avoid Chad's gaze I started running up the stirrups on Scout's saddle. I was mad at myself for reacting so self-consciously and wished I could have just laughed. If the question had been directed at anyone else, I would have. But I'd lost my sense of humor where Chad was involved. All I could do was stand there, holding my breath and waiting for him to answer.

"That depends. What's the 'or something'?" Chad asked quickly. I had to admit it was a pretty clever way of getting out of answering. And it saved me the embarrassment of hearing him say, "We're just friends," even though it was true.

A few minutes later I brought David back to the office where his father was waiting and said goodbye to them both. By then it was close to two o'clock, which gave me very little time to grab a sandwich and get Dancer ready before the junior riders started showing up.

The lesson was held in the large indoor ring. And because it was a beginning-intermediate class, everyone knew how to trot and canter. My job was to ride in front of the class and lead them through their paces. It wasn't the most exciting job in the world, but it gave me a chance to exercise Dancer, something I rarely had time for on a busy weekend.

As the class followed me around the ring, my father stood in the center calling out commands in a low voice. He'd ask us to trot, then look at each rider to see whether he or she was posting on the proper diagonal. Everyone usually had it right until my father instructed us to start cutting across the ring in a figure eight. The moment the riders had to sit a beat to change their diagonals without stopping for more than a moment, many of them ran into trouble.

Near the end of the lesson I noticed that Chad was watching us from the far corner of the spectator stands. He was sitting in the second row with his feet propped up in front of him. I tried not to look at him each time I passed by, but I couldn't help it. My eyes were drawn to him like a magnet. He seemed to be watching me, too, and one time he even gave me a thumbs-up sign.

I felt lighthearted for the rest of the lesson. When it was over, I helped Chad walk some of the horses. I found myself staring down at the scuffed boots he wore beneath his faded jeans, even though I really wanted to look into his eyes. I wasn't sure if he was still thinking of David's question; I knew I was. In fact, I couldn't stop thinking about it or about Chad's response. He hadn't answered David straight out, and I wasn't sure why—unless he was trying to tell me something.

Then I forced myself to shrug that thought off. *You're making a mountain out of a molehill,* I scolded myself. Chad wasn't the type to play games, and he wasn't shy. If he had something to tell me, he'd say it right out.

Monday morning two weeks later there was a break from our morning routine. After Chad had parked the Honda, I thanked him for the ride as always, then started to walk away.

"Wait a second, I'll walk you," he said, glancing over the hood of the car.

My heart flipped over. Chad had never offered to walk me *anywhere* before. Every other morning he always rushed off to join his friends, who always gathered around a blue Buick.

Then it occurred to me that maybe his friends weren't there. I looked where they usually gathered, and to my amazement, they were there, just as always. Few things in the world could have thrilled me more than having Chad walk me into school, but I was puzzled. Why the sudden change?

I kept my eyes straight ahead as we approached the front steps, hoping I didn't look as shaky as I felt. Chad had shortened his stride to match mine, but I was still afraid I would trip over my own feet—especially when some of the other kids turned to stare at us. It was all I could do not to blush. I had never been the center of such attention before, and while I found it exhilarating, it also made me feel a little awkward.

Diane was leaning against the side of the building, and I saw her eyes grow wide as we approached. I called out a friendly hello as we passed, and like a true friend, she didn't come rushing over. I knew she was dying to ask all kinds of questions, but she just looked on silently as Chad shifted his books to one arm in order to open the door for me.

"Where's your locker?" he asked once we were inside.

"That way," I said and pointed to the left. I knew Chad's locker was on the other side of the building and figured that he would probably head that way. Instead, he turned in the direction I had just pointed.

"It's down at the very end of the hall," I warned him. It was only fair.

"No problem." Chad shrugged and started down the long corridor. It was empty except for a few students who were standing by their lockers. When we got to my locker, I dropped my books on the floor, and the thud echoed up and down the corridor.

"You sure keep it neat," Chad exclaimed when I opened the door to hang up my coat. He stood facing me, leaning slightly against the locker next to mine.

I smiled at him and shrugged.

"You can help me clean mine anytime," he said teasingly.

Just tell me when, I wanted to respond. "You sure you mean that?" I asked instead. "I always thought boys' lockers were *supposed* to be messy." *How dumb can you be,* I thought.

Fortunately, Chad laughed. Just then the warning bell rang.

"See you later," he said, taking off toward his own locker. Although there were five minutes until the final bell I understood why he was in such a hurry. Throngs of students were pouring into school, and within minutes the corridor was filled with their loud voices and the clanging of lockers.

"Don't you ever do that to me again," Diane said as she came up behind me.

I was just picking up my English book, and I spun around completely confused. "Do what?" I asked.

"Leave me hanging in suspense like that," she said. "I didn't dare come near you until the bell rang, but it's been killing me. I was dying to know what you were doing with Chad this morning."

"I don't know. Honestly, that's the truth," I said. "When we got out of the car, Chad told me to wait, and then he walked with me." I grinned. Diane took a deep breath. Then she said, "Well, if you want my opinion—and even if you don't I'm going to give it to you—I'm willing to bet this is the first step. Chad is working up the courage to ask you for a date."

Chapter Nine

For the next few days I held on to the hope that Diane was right, that Chad wanted to ask me out. He walked me to my locker every morning, and during lunch he'd occasionally stop over to talk for a few minutes. But he never mentioned anything about a date. By Thursday I was losing all hope. I had thought I could accept just being Chad's friend, but the truth was that I couldn't. I wanted more than just friendship. I wanted to be Chad's girlfriend.

But he still hadn't said anything by the time we got into the car Friday afternoon, and I was convinced I would be spending another weekend at home watching reruns on television. Paul, the boy I'd sometimes dated, had stopped calling when he saw Chad and me driving to school together. It wasn't any great loss. He'd been a bore. The only thing I did regret was that now I had no one.

I sighed and tried to let the spring breeze that was coming through the open window ease my disappointment. We were driving through the center of town then, which meant we were about halfway to the farm. As we passed the twin movie theater, I noticed they were changing the marquee. "It's about time they got new movies," I commented. "The other ones had been there for ages." I was just making conversation and was caught totally off guard when Chad turned to me and smiled.

"Would you like to go to one tonight?" he asked. There was a sudden roaring in my ears.

Is he really asking me for a date? I'd been waiting for this moment for two years.

"OK," I said. I forced myself to shrug because I wanted to appear casual. Inside, however, my heart was doing flip-flops. "Which movie do you want to see?" There was a choice between a romantic comedy and a western spoof. Both were supposed to be good, and I hadn't seen either.

"You pick it," Chad said quickly. That was something new for me. The times Paul and I had gone out, he'd always decided beforehand where we would go or what movie we'd see. This was a welcome change.

The way Chad had asked me out was also different from what I was used to. He was a lot more casual about it. The thought crossed my mind that maybe he didn't think of it as a real *date*, but I quickly dismissed the thought. I didn't want to spend my time wondering what Chad thought. I wanted to enjoy myself, because real date or not, I knew this would be a special evening for me.

Chad picked me up at seven-thirty. I'd chosen the romantic comedy because of the time it started, and we sat in the middle section about halfway back.

During the movie Chad didn't put his arm around me or touch me except when our fingers bumped briefly when we both reached for the popcorn at the same time. But I was still aware of him. Each time he shifted his position, each time he moved his hand toward the popcorn, all I could think of was that his body was just inches away.

At the end of the movie the lights didn't come on right away so Chad took my hand and led me up the aisle. I expected him to let go once we were outside the theater, but he didn't, and I was too happy to say anything.

My hand felt good in his—as if it belonged there. We walked along the darkened sidewalk, neither of us talking. It wasn't until we had gone about a block that I realized we weren't heading toward the car.

"Where are we going?" I asked.

Chad stopped and turned to look at me. "I'm sorry, Julie. I just assumed you'd want to stop somewhere. Do you want a soda or something?"

There was that "or something" again, and before I realized what I was doing I found myself answering Chad the same way he had answered David. "That depends. What's an 'or something'?"

Chad laughed. "I guess I asked for that."

"I guess you did." I giggled. "And a soda would be great."

"Are you sure?"

"Absolutely," I said. He led me into Amy's, the local hangout.

It was already crowded when we got there. Automatically, I found myself searching for Cheryl. I didn't really want to see her. I mean, I wanted her to see me holding hands with Chad, but I was also afraid that somehow Cheryl would spoil the evening for us.

As it turned out she wasn't there. But I did

spot a lot of other kids that I knew. They sat mostly in groups of four or six around the Formica-topped tables and in the booths that lined one wall.

Chad and I both nodded to people we knew before joining his friend Ben and a girl named Carol at one of the tables. They were waiting for two other friends to join them, but they assured us there would be room for all six of us. At first I was nervous, but Ben and Carol went out of their way to make me feel welcome. They included me in all their conversations, even when they complained about a teacher that I didn't know who taught junior English.

It was easy to like Ben and Carol. I usually feel awkward around people I don't know, but with them I wasn't at all uncomfortable. When the waitress came around, I ordered a chocolate soda and Chad asked for a slice of pizza. It seemed strange to hear him order that in Amy's which had once been strictly an ice cream parlor. It still served mostly ice cream, but now the owner had added things like pizza, hot dogs, and hamburgers to the menu. There was even a new jukebox at the far end of the soda fountain that constantly blasted out the latest rock songs.

We must have sat there talking for over an hour. When I looked up at the clock, I was amazed that it was almost midnight. I didn't really have a curfew, but since I worked on weekends, I always tried to make it home by twelve.

My parents knew I was with Chad, but I was still afraid they would worry if I was late getting home.

"I don't mean to be a stick in the mud," I said in what I hoped was a light tone. "But I've got to work tomorrow."

"Are you telling us you need your beauty sleep?" Ben asked me.

Carol gave him a playful slap on the arm as Chad slid his chair back and got to his feet.

"Now I understand why you always look so terrific," Chad said as I stood up. "There's a lot to be said for getting to bed by midnight."

I laughed along with everyone else, and we said good night. When Chad and I walked to the car I silently made a wish on the brightest star. I wished that I would have many more dates with Chad because I had just had one of the most wonderful evenings of my life. Everything about it was etched in my mind: how he had looked, standing at my front door earlier in the evening; the way he sat in the movies with his long legs spread out under the seat in front of him; and his words just before we left Amy's.

Chad had said I always looked terrific. I could hardly believe it. Maybe Diane had been right after all; maybe there *was* hope. It hadn't seemed possible before, but now I was ready to believe in miracles.

Chad turned the car into the wide lane leading to the farm. We had made it home with five minutes to spare. "Thank you, Chad. I had a wonderful time. And we even got home early," I said as he walked me up the steps to my front door.

"You should have told me your parents expected you home by midnight," he apologized.

"I didn't think I'd have to," I admitted. "I had no idea we'd be out so late."

"See what happens when you're having a good time?" he said. Then he suddenly became serious. "You really did have fun, didn't you, Julie? Not just the movie, but afterward—sitting in Amy's with Ben and Carol?"

Chad's voice was so full of concern, so anxious. I couldn't believe that he could possibly wonder if I'd enjoyed our date.

"Honestly, Chad. The movie and Amy's—and everything—were just terrific."

"I'm glad," Chad said in a soft voice. Then he kissed me gently on the cheek and left.

"Is Chad with you?" my mother called from the den where she and my father were watching television.

"He already left," I answered. "Did you need to tell him something?"

"No, it's OK. His mother just called around eight to say she and his sister were going out and might not be home until late. But she said she'd leave him a note on the refrigerator."

The mention of a note on the refrigerator brought a smile to my face. I thought we were the only family who left messages there.

"She sounded very nice over the phone. We had a long chat," my mother continued while I shrugged off my coat. "I told her how pleased we were with the job Chad was doing at the farm, and she seemed very glad to hear that."

There are times when I can tell exactly what my mother is thinking just by looking at her face. The way she smiled that night told me that she was pleased with a lot more than Chad's work. She was happy to see that Chad and I were hitting it off so well. And both my parents seemed to have stopped worrying that I wasn't spending enough time with kids my own age. In fact, I was certain that Chad and I were getting along even better than they had hoped we would.

That night I snuggled into my covers and hugged my pillow, wishing it were Chad. I had to agree with my mother—things were working out well. I had had a perfect evening, and I felt confident that the next day would be just as perfect.

Chapter Ten

I should have known that just when things were going great something would happen to ruin them. In this case, the something was Cheryl Williams. She showed up at the stables on Saturday morning, the first time she'd been there since the fall. The sight of her coming down the aisle in a snug blue ski sweater and tight fitting breeches paralyzed me. I felt the blood drain out of my face—I couldn't move.

"Julie!" she cried when she saw me. The tone of her voice made it sound as if we were best friends. And her smile was so radiant that it was almost blinding. "I need some help with Jupiter. Can you tell me where Chad is?" she asked.

My head felt heavy, and there was a dull ache behind my eyes. I didn't answer Cheryl right away, and I could tell she was getting annoyed. She kept tapping her riding crop against one of her boots.

"Well?" she asked impatiently.

I couldn't understand why Cheryl said she needed Chad's help when she knew it was the grooms' job to get horses saddled and ready for their owners. I also couldn't believe she had the nerve to ask him for anything after the way she'd treated him the other day. But then I remembered that Cheryl turned the charm on and off, depending on what she wanted.

I wished that I could lie and tell her Chad wasn't in yet, but I knew I couldn't. Just then Chad walked into the barn leading a black mare, and Cheryl spun around to face him.

"There you are!" she said, her voice dripping honey. "Since all the grooms are busy, Mr. Peterson told me to ask you to help me saddle Jupiter."

Chad's face registered total surprise, and he stopped dead in his tracks. He seemed as astonished to see Cheryl as I'd been. My father's request also caught him off guard. He flashed me an odd look before turning back to her, and for a moment I thought he was going to offer an excuse. Only it never came.

"OK," Chad said. "I'll be back to help you

as soon as I deliver this mare to her groom."
Cheryl smiled broadly.

I glanced down at the floor, so she wouldn't see the expression of hurt and anger on my face. I'd hoped Chad would refuse to help Cheryl even if it meant going against my father's request. But, of course, he wouldn't have been Chad if he'd behaved like that.

Cheryl still wore a satisfied smile when she turned back to gaze at me. "I understand you and Chad were at Amy's last night," she said smoothly. She carefully examined her nails, which were polished the same glistening shade of pink as her lipstick. "I don't know how you guys can tolerate that place. It's become so noisy since they added the jukebox."

The way she said "you guys" made it sound as if we were social misfits. "To be perfectly honest," I answered in an indifferent tone, "we didn't notice the noise. We were having too good a time."

Cheryl was about to say something when Chad came back and announced that he was ready to help her. She turned her back on me and stepped up to Chad saying something to him that made him laugh. That almost drove me crazy. I wondered if it had anything to do with our date. Would she tell him what I'd just said about it? What would Chad do?

Would he confirm what I had told her, that we had had a good time? Or would he pass the evening off with a shrug?

I didn't wait to find out. I could hardly suppress the tears in my eyes. Hurrying into the office, I curled up in a tiny corner of the couch.

I didn't want to lose Chad just when he was beginning to like me. But I had a horrible feeling that that was exactly what was about to happen. At the same time, though, I knew I wouldn't blame him if he chose someone like Cheryl over me. I mean, she was gorgeous. What boy wouldn't want to go out with her?

I stayed in the office for the next ten minutes, tears running down my cheeks. I found myself wishing that Chad had never come to work at Two Penny Farm. Everything would have been so much easier. I'd still be able to dream that someday Chad would notice me. Instead I was miserable, all hunched up on the couch, afraid that Chad was about to slip away.

It hurt to think I could lose him so easily. But knowing Cheryl, I figured she'd try to win him back just to spite me. And she probably didn't like not having a regular boyfriend. Even though she was beautiful and dated a

97

lot, maybe she hadn't found anyone she liked as much as Chad. Chad, I was almost sure, would be thrilled at the prospect of getting Cheryl back.

I punched the cushions on the couch at the thought that Chad would rush back to Cheryl. If she could have seen me just then, I knew Cheryl would have been pleased; I could even imagine the look in her cool blue eyes. But I had to do something about my anger. After the way she had treated Chad, it made me furious that he might still want her back.

But there was nothing I could do. I blew my nose and wiped my eyes. Then I went to the window to watch the riders in the outdoor ring with their horses. I wasn't aware of the amount of time that passed. When Chad came looking for me, I felt his presence in the room even before I turned around.

"Are you OK, Julie?" he asked when I turned to face him. He was standing by the door. "You look sort of funny."

I wanted to yell, "How would you look if your heart had just been broken?" Instead I smiled. "I never felt better," I managed to answer. My voice didn't sound convincing to me, but Chad seemed relieved to hear that nothing was wrong.

He did, however, glance my way a lot during the morning, as if he were checking up on me. But when Cheryl returned on Jupiter, his eyes switched from me to her. He guardedly watched her as she spoke to some other riders she knew and as she flirted openly with a few of the male riders. I wondered if Chad was jealous. I kept expecting him to say something to her, but he made no move to get her attention. In fact, the minute he saw her turn Jupiter toward the barn he disappeared.

I couldn't believe he would purposely avoid Cheryl, so I figured he must have gone to wait for her at Jupiter's stall. Then just a few minutes later I spotted Jupiter standing alone in the aisle, still fully saddled and bridled, his neck dark with sweat. Cheryl had left him there without even bothering to loosen his girth.

I couldn't believe anyone could be so thoughtless and cruel. How could she leave a horse standing like that?

Three more horses came in just then, so I knew that no one would be free to take care of Jupiter for another few minutes. I untacked him, threw a light blanket over his back, and took him outside to walk until he cooled off. Ten minutes later, there was still no sign of Cheryl and my temper was growing short. I had visions of her sitting with Chad in the tack room, sharing his lunch. That reminded me it was well past one o'clock. If someone didn't come soon, I would probably starve to death, and it would serve both Cheryl and Chad right.

Finally Jupiter's groom came out. When he saw me walking the horse, he apologized, saying he had thought Miss Williams would take care of him. *Miss Williams*, I thought, *takes care of no one and nothing but her precious little self.*

I was a little relieved to learn that Chad and Cheryl *hadn't* been in the tack room together while I was stuck with Jupiter. But her presence at the stable still upset me. She virtually ignored me and followed Chad everywhere. I'll never know how I managed to get through the remainder of the day without crying or exploding. I went to bed thinking that I'd never had a lousier day.

Cheryl showed up on Sunday, too. She arrived just before I was scheduled to give David his lesson. I wondered if David could sense how angry and frustrated I was. He hardly talked until we were almost halfway through his lesson, which was when Chad came out of the barn, with Cheryl on his heels. David and I saw them at the same time.

"Hey, Chad," David called out gleefully. "Want to watch me post?"

"You bet," Chad said and he walked up to the fence. Cheryl was close behind him.

David showed how he had learned to lift himself up from the saddle while I kept Scout at a walk. I was so proud of him. It was amazing how well he posted, despite his brace.

"Why, isn't that terrific?" Cheryl said to Chad. Her voice was loud enough for both David and me to hear. "Julie's such a good instructor, she can even teach a handicapped child how to ride."

I gasped at her thoughtlessness and immediately turned to David. He had slumped down in his saddle, a look of painful embarrassment on his face.

Chad also saw David's reaction to Cheryl's words. He seemed stunned. *Say something*, I urged silently. But all he did was grab Cheryl by the elbow and yank her away.

"I don't like that girl," David spoke in a low voice. "Even if she is Chad's girlfriend."

"I don't like her, either," I said squeezing his good leg. I didn't correct him about Cheryl's being Chad's girlfriend. For all I knew, it was the truth. But I didn't have time to dwell on that. I had a little boy to take care of, and I knew I had to get him posting again, before he lost any more self-confidence.

"Come on, David. I'd like to see you post again," I said.

He shook his head. "I want to stop now," he told me. But I wasn't going to let him get off the horse without doing it at least once.

"I'll make you a deal," I told him, remembering how my father had sometimes bribed me when I was younger. "I'll let you feed Scout one lump of sugar for every four times you post."

It worked. Before the half hour was up, I owed David four lumps of sugar. I promised him we would try posting at a slow trot the next week. That made him almost bubble over with excitement. When I delivered David back to his father, he once again wore a big smile.

I didn't have time to speak to Cheryl after David left because I was pressed for time the rest of the afternoon. But as soon as I finished with the beginner-intermediates' lesson, I intended to approach her. I didn't want her to think she could say whatever she wanted to David and get away with it—at least not in front of me.

When I went to look for Cheryl, however,

she was nowhere to be found. Neither was Chad. I searched up and down every aisle in the stables, but there was no sign of either of them. Then I spotted Chad standing beside Cheryl just outside the barn, talking to Cheryl's parents. His hands were jammed into the front pockets of his jeans and he kept shifting awkwardly from one foot to the other. I wasn't sure why he was so uncomfortable. Then Cheryl slipped her hand through his arm, and in a high voice she said, "Chad has *promised* to take extra good care of Jupiter for me. So we don't have to worry about a thing."

Is that so, I fumed. I raced back into the stables and ran headlong into my father. My eyes were misted over and the look on my face should have told him something was wrong. But he was so busy that he didn't seem to notice. And, actually, I was relieved that I didn't have to explain anything.

"I have a special job for you," he said. He patted the glowing coat of a horse in one of the stalls. "I need someone to exercise Star. He hasn't been ridden for four days, and I can't let it go until tomorrow."

I scowled at my dad because he knew I didn't like Star. The dark bay gelding was a nasty horse and always flattened his ears back when someone came near his stall. Once, when I attempted to fill his water bucket from outside his stall, he even lunged at the partition.

"Can you have his groom tack him up for me?" I asked, unaware that Chad had returned to the barn.

My father spotted Chad behind me and asked if he'd mind helping with Star. Chad said, "No problem," then took off down the aisle. A few moments later he led the bay gelding out the back door all tacked up and ready to go.

I didn't know what to say to him because my anger at Cheryl still gnawed at me, and the fear that I had lost him overwhelmed me. I nodded a curt thanks and put my foot into the stirrup ready to swing up.

"Are you giving me the silent treatment?" Chad asked. "You've hardly spoken to me all weekend."

I took my foot out of the stirrup and twisted around to face him. I hadn't intended to say anything to Chad because I was afraid I'd sound like a jealous girlfriend. After all, I didn't have a claim on him. But now that he had brought it up, I couldn't control my temper any longer.

"You noticed?" I said. I smiled sweetly, but

there was a cold note in my voice. "I was sure that since you were so absorbed in your *girlfriend* you wouldn't even realize. She's really something, you know that. And her comment about David's leg was really terrific."

"Wait a minute!" he protested. "I can't control what Cheryl says."

"You're right," I said. "So in the future please make sure to *keep her away from David*. That little boy is going to have enough problems learning how to ride without Cheryl's comments to hurt him."

Chad looked as if he wanted to say more, but I didn't give him a chance to reply. Snatching the reins out of his hands, I put my foot into the stirrup and swung up into the saddle. Star immediately started fussing. He shook his head, sidestepped, and pawed the ground restlessly. I adjusted my stirrups, ignoring Star's complaints. When I gathered the reins and turned him toward the bridle path, he wrestled with the bit, trying to lower his head and buck.

I knew the welfare of every horse was an enormous responsibility that my father took very seriously. That was why he didn't approve of my taking a horse out on the trail alone. But I needed to get away from Chad and the farm in order to think. I figured the only thing that might happen to Star was that he'd work up a good sweat, because I intended to ride him hard. I never thought he'd be so skittish, but just as I had pushed him into a brisk canter, a squirrel darted across the path. Star veered out of control, and my foot came out of the stirrup. That alone wouldn't have been a problem, but the nervous horse also lost his footing and his hindquarters buckled under him. The motion jarred me out of my seat.

And when he stood up with a fierce motion, I sailed over his head and landed on my side on the hard ground. It knocked the wind from my lungs, and for a moment everything was pitch black. I made a huge effort to open my eyes and saw some light. Through a dizzy blur I saw a bright flash and reached up to cover my head as Star's hoof swished by me. The bay gelding had completely regained his footing, but he was more spooked than ever.

I was still a little dizzy, so it took me a few seconds to sit up. When I did I realized that Star was no longer beside me. Free of his rider, he had probably taken off for the stables. That left me with the unpleasant task of walking back and time to ponder what my father would say when he found out what I'd done.

At least I wasn't seriously hurt, I figured. Standing up, I dusted myself off and started walking. I hadn't gone more than a quarter of a mile, however, when Chad rode up astride one of the hack horses.

"Are you hurt?" he asked. He looked both concerned and amused.

"I'm fine," I snapped, which was almost true. My body was fine, but my heart wasn't.

I didn't want Chad's concern or his help, so I stormed down the side of the bridle path, brushing away tree branches that got in my way. If I couldn't brush them aside I snapped them off, twisting the green ones and flinging them to the ground.

I had just broken the branch of a white birch tree when Chad lightly touched me on the shoulder. He'd dismounted and was walking beside me, leading his horse.

"Julie," he said. He still had his hand on my shoulder. His grip tightened, and he turned me around to face him. "I'm really sorry about what Cheryl said. But I don't think she said it to hurt David."

"No? Then who was she out to hurt—me?"

"Exactly." A chuckle escaped Chad's lips. "You must realize that she's jealous of you," he added.

"Come off it!" I pulled away from his grasp

and lifted my eyes to stare at him. "Why should Cheryl be jealous of me. *She's* the one who has everything."

"That's where you're wrong," Chad said. He put his arm around me, and my heart started beating faster.

"Cheryl may act as if she has a lot going for her, but you've got something she can never have," he continued with a tender smile. "You're happy being yourself, and she isn't. I admire that about you."

Then he took a step closer to me. I knew he was going to kiss me. I could almost feel it, and as his mouth came closer and his features blurred, a current of emotions flooded through me.

When his lips finally did meet and cling to mine, I thought that no kiss would ever again feel so warm and so right. A dizzying response washed over me. The sun was suddenly very bright, so I closed my eyes tightly and brought my arms around his neck, trying to block out everything but the incredible joy of Chad's nearness.

When at last he drew away from me, I stared at him in wide-eyed wonder. "What was that for?" I asked.

"Simple," he said huskily. "I wanted to kiss my girlfriend." His arms went around me to draw me closer, for an all-enveloping embrace. "You are my girlfriend, aren't you?" he asked.

"I guess I am," I said in a quiet voice. His kiss had been so wonderful, but hearing Chad say I was his girlfriend was the best of all reasons to cling to him.

Chapter Eleven

I noticed nothing around me as Chad and I rode back to the farm together. Chad was in the saddle, and I sat behind him with my arms wrapped around his waist, my head against his shoulder. It felt good to be so close to him. The solidness of his back sent little shivers through me. I felt so secure and safe that it was hard to believe that I'd doubted Chad and run away in anger.

Chad's promise to take care of Jupiter still annoyed me, but it no longer seemed important to ask him about it—not after our kiss and his words.

Before he had ridden out to find me, Chad had gotten Sandy to agree to walk Star out and not tell my father he had come back riderless. He also said that the horse had returned to the farm without a scratch, his leg wasn't even injured from his stumble.

Both pieces of news reassured me. Eventually I would have to tell my father what had really happened, but at least he wouldn't be waiting to yell at me the minute we got back.

"Think we'll make it?" Chad asked, breaking into my thoughts. He was looking at the sky. I followed his gaze, and it was then that I first noticed the dark gray clouds that had moved in above us.

I tilted my head back and allowed the wind that had come up to brush against my face and whip out tendrils of my hair. "Who cares?" I shouted defiantly as a single raindrop touched my face. I was too busy nestling close to Chad to be concerned about a little rain.

Who said miracles can't happen, I almost said out loud. A joyful sense of well-being was bubbling up inside me, and riding through a storm with Chad seemed like the most romantic thing that could ever happen to anyone. Another raindrop landed on my forehead. As we came out into the open field that bordered the farm that rain began to pelt us, and I could tell that Chad was eager to get inside the barn before the skies opened up.

"You can let go now," Chad said when we'd reached the barn. I made no move to release my hold. "Come on, Julie," he said, chuckling. "You're going to get us both soaked."

"Who's afraid of a little rain?" I muttered, but I reluctantly slid off.

I wanted to stay close to Chad, but it was pouring, and even if I didn't mind getting wet, I knew it wasn't fair to the horse. Chad knew this, too, because he quickly dismounted and led the animal into the shelter of the barn.

Horses poked their heads over stall doors when they heard us coming down the aisle. Some whinnied softly, and I responded absently, stroking their velvety noses with my fingertips or running my hand along their necks. I could hear my heart pounding in my chest and wondered if everyone else at Two Penny Farm could hear it, too. Then I realized that I didn't care. It no longer mattered if everyone knew I was crazy about Chad, I realized happily. Because he was crazy about me.

The smile on my face stayed for the rest of the afternoon, as Chad and I helped the grooms dry the tack that had gotten wet when other horses were caught in the downpour. We wiped down saddles, took bridles apart, and removed the mud from the stirrups. Then, once everything was cleaned and dried, we put it all back together again.

"Want a lift to the house?" Chad asked at the end of the day.

It was still raining hard so I accepted the offer, glad for the chance to spend a few extra minutes with him.

"I wish I didn't have to rush home," he said when he pulled up to the door by the kitchen. "But I've got a big biology test tomorrow, and last night I didn't get much studying done."

He let the sentence hang there, and I wondered if he was going to tell me he had had a date with another girl. I sat there staring at the windshield wipers as they swished back and forth, hoping he would add something else to what he had just said.

"See, my dad came to visit and wound up taking my sister and me to dinner last night," he said almost apologetically. I let my breath out slowly. My suspicions were pointless; doubting Chad was one habit I'd have to work on breaking.

"No problem. I'll see you tomorrow." I started to put my hand on the door handle.

The moment Chad saw me do that he killed the ignition and reached over to pull me against him. "Do you know what happens to girls who forget to kiss their boyfriends good-bye?" His eyes gleamed wickedly. "They get attacked by the kissing monster." Then he

113

began raining little kisses all over my face and neck.

I laughed and struggled playfully to avoid his kisses until his lips brushed against mine and stayed there. Then the laughter died in my throat, and my hands fell to my sides.

His lips felt so warm and sweet I didn't want the kiss to ever end. But a moment later, Chad pulled back a little and looked into my eyes.

"I'd—uh—better get going," he said, and I nodded as though I were hypnotized.

"See you tomorrow," he added.

"Right," I answered softly. I opened the car door and dashed toward the house. A few drops of rain hit me, but I didn't care. My feelings for Chad ran so deep, and as I watched him drive off, I wondered if I was falling in love.

The next morning as we walked into school, Chad held my hand. It wasn't long before we were the main topic of conversation. I pretended not to hear the whispered comments, but the open stares were more difficult to ignore.

At lunchtime Chad met me by my locker. We had arranged to eat together. I was a little nervous because I'd never sat with a boy before, and I wasn't sure what kind of a reaction I would get. Then I saw Ben and Carol and relaxed when we went to sit with them. But Cheryl did look a little shocked when she passed by.

"Well, well," she said and then laughed in a mean way. "Look who's sitting in *my* old seat."

Every muscle in my body stiffened. I began unfolding a napkin in my lap, very carefully.

"Just ignore her," Carol whispered across the table. I nodded. Then Chad reached over to put his arm around me. That made me feel better. It was one thing to have everyone know that Chad and I were a couple, but quite another to have him show how much he cared for me by sitting with his arm around me.

Before long I forgot all about Cheryl. Conversation at the table was fast and funny, and I talked and joked with everyone else. Toward the end of lunch the boys went to get second desserts. That was when Carol brought *her* name up again.

"Cheryl's really not a bad person, Julie. She's just a little spoiled," Carol told me. "She's so used to getting everything she wants that it's hard for her to accept losing.'

"Losing?" My eyes widened. "When has Cheryl ever lost anything?"

"I was referring to Chad," Carol said.

"You mean *he* broke up with Cheryl?" I asked, startled.

Carol reached across the table and squeezed my hand. "You got it," she said, laughing. "Cheryl knows how to be sweet, and Chad did like her. But once she started acting—well—the way she acts, he got annoyed. Anyway, *he* dumped her, which is why Cheryl likes to give him a hard time now and then."

I don't know why, but I was almost dizzy with relief. I felt a little lightheaded. Learning that Chad had broken up with Cheryl meant *I* could feel more secure about us and our relationship. Contentment flowed through me. By the time lunch was over, word had spread all around school that we were the "new couple."

All through the day, I felt more confident than I ever had before. I walked down the halls and said hello to all the people I usually spoke to, but I felt as though I was seeing them through new eyes. Happiness spilled out of me. I had time to chat with anyone who stopped me; I listened gladly to Diane's weekend plans; I went out of my way to speak to a transfer student—I'd meant to do it for a month and that day, I did.

I was still the same Julie Peterson I'd always been. My hair and eyes were the same

color they'd always been. But because someone I liked—maybe even loved—cared for me,
I no longer felt like an ordinary sophomore. I
felt like someone special. And I was. I knew I
was very special—to Chad.

Chapter Twelve

I'm not sure exactly why, but having a boy-friend helped me accept myself the way I was. I didn't worry so much about my boyish fig-ure and the fact that I wasn't stunningly beau-tiful. I realized that I had other things going for me. After all, I was cute, with nice eyes and pretty auburn hair, and most importantly, I didn't pretend to be anything I wasn't. That was one of the things Chad had said he liked best about me. Knowing that made me feel comfortable.

Through Chad I met a lot of juniors, and I was spending more and more time with kids who were a year or two older than I was. So I hesitated when Chad and I were invited to a party Diane was having. I was afraid he might feel uncomfortable being the only junior there. But when I mentioned it to him and explained that I would understand if he didn't want to go with me, he shook his head.

"Not go to a party!" he said, looking at me as if I were crazy. "Who cares if I'm the only junior there?"

And as it turned out, there were several other juniors at the party, including a cute boy whom Diane had had her eye on for weeks. His name was Peter Walker, and he was a cousin of one of our friends. Diane flirted with him between dances with Doug, who had lasted—I thought—longer than most of Diane's boyfriends. Before the party was over Doug was history and Peter had asked Diane out.

"Diane sure falls in and out of love quickly," Chad observed. Diane had dragged me from his arms a moment before to whisper the news, which I'd relayed to Chad. Before she'd interrupted us, we'd been dancing to a slow song in a corner of the family room. I treasured the feel of his arms around my waist and his body pressed against mine.

"She's got lousy timing though," I said. The song was over, and a loud rock song blasted from the stereo.

Chad laughed. "Come on. Let's go get something to drink," he said, reaching for my hand. He slipped his fingers in between mine.

There was a large glass bowl filled with strawberries and fruit punch on the table against the wall, but I wanted a soda. I went into the kitchen to ask Mrs. Cummings for one. When I returned to the family room, Chad was stretched out in an overstuffed chair by the bay window. He had one leg draped over the arm of the chair and the other one stuck straight out in front of him.

"Any room for me?" I asked teasingly. Before I knew it I was pulled onto his lap and encircled by a pair of arms that felt like steel bands.

"What kind of a question is that?" he whispered into my ear.

I rested my head against his neck and for the next few minutes we just sat there together, not talking but just enjoying being together. We rarely saw our friends, except during school. We worked all week at the farm, and we spent most Friday and Saturday nights at my house watching TV or playing Trivial Pursuit because of Chad's tight budget. Sometimes I thought that was more fun than going to a movie or to Amy's, especially when my parents were out for the evening. On those nights Chad and I would stretch out on the floor to watch TV with our heads on one big pillow and our arms entwined.

But I'd never shown affection for a boy in public before. I was embarrassed when one of Chad's classmates made a big deal out of our sitting together in the chair.

"Will you look at the lovebirds," he said, pointing in our direction. He gazed around the room to make sure everyone had heard him.

"Knock it off, bozo," Chad said. He tossed his empty paper cup at the guy's head.

Unfortunately, I was blushing, which gave everyone else a reason to continue the teasing and make a lot of jokes. It was all meant in good fun, but I didn't particularly enjoy being the center of so much attention. I sat up straight in Chad's lap.

"Want to dance?" he asked, and I nodded. Dancing helped us blend in with all the other couples and diverted attention from us until the party broke up just before midnight.

"I hope you don't think those guys intentionally picked on you," Chad said as soon as we got in the car, "They'll go after any couple who look happy."

I didn't want to ask how he knew that because I was afraid of what he would say. "I just wish I hadn't blushed," I said, knowing that had been the cause of the prolonged teasing.

"Don't worry about it," Chad said. He smiled and took a hand off the steering wheel to squeeze my arm. "You look cute when you blush."

I knew he was just trying to make me feel better, and he was reassuring, but he couldn't completely erase the embarrassment I had felt earlier.

I pressed myself back against the seat and tried to enjoy the ride. It wasn't long before Chad turned into the lane leading to our farm and parked in front of the house. My parents weren't home when we went inside, but my mother had left a note on the refrigerator saying they would be back by midnight and to offer Chad some brownies that were wrapped in foil on the counter.

"I knew I was glad the party ended early," he said as he came up behind me. I'd just finished unwrapping the brownies, and he stared at them hungrily. "I just didn't know why."

I felt a lot more comfortable being alone, so I let myself lean back against him. "Where should we eat these?" I asked after we'd placed a few on a larger plate.

"What do you say we go into the den and find ourselves a large chair to sit in together?" Chad asked.

My parents found us in that large chair when they came home a while later. We hadn't heard them come in because the television set was on. They smiled as if it were the most natural thing in the world to find me sitting on Chad's lap in the den. And while I felt a little flustered for a moment, I made no move to get up and neither did Chad. Instead we stayed there telling them about the party. When we got to the part about being caught sitting in the chair together, they smiled.

I felt terrific because I knew they understood. They, too, had been teenagers and knew there were times when you wanted to be close to each other.

"I see you found my note," my mother said when she spotted the empty plate on the rug.

"We sure did, Mrs. Peterson," Chad answered. "And the brownies were great."

"I hope you left us some," my father said, joking. I was about to say yes when Chad slapped his hand up against his forehead and frowned.

"Gosh, Mr. Peterson. I don't think—" he said. "I mean, Julie didn't say anything, so I just kept eating—"

For a moment there was silence in the room. I watched my parents exchange startled looks, but the moment they noticed Chad grinning broadly, they realized they had been had.

My father shook his head, smiling. "I had that coming," he admitted. "But I'm still going to check and see if there are any brownies left. Come, dear," he said, leading my mother toward the kitchen. They told us good night, and in a few minutes I heard them go upstairs.

"Your parents sure are great," Chad said, pulling me closer against him.

"You're not so bad yourself," I responded. I pressed my forehead against his cheek.

"Is that right?" he said.

"Yep." I nodded.

Few words were spoken after that. I leaned against Chad's chest, and we sat watching television and enjoying each other's closeness until the movie was over and he got up to leave.

"See you tomorrow," I said, walking him to the door. It was almost two o'clock, but that didn't make it any easier to say good night.

"Can't wait," he replied. He gave me a quick kiss before backing out the door.

At that moment I was happier than I'd ever been in my life. I dreamed of Chad that night and woke up Sunday morning with a smile on my face. It didn't matter that the sky was overcast and a fine drizzle was falling against my windowsill. I was in love.

After a shower, I went downstairs to find my parents sitting at the kitchen table reading the Sunday *New York Times*. It was a time-honored ritual in our house. Every Sunday my father would go to the stables at the regular time, then at nine-thirty he would return to the house to eat breakfast with my mother. I used to join them before I'd started dating Chad. But since I stayed up later on weekends, my parents allowed me to sleep in on Sunday mornings.

"What time did Chad leave last night?" my mother asked from behind the newspaper.

"Two," I answered.

"Are you sure you were watching television all that time?" my father asked. I had just sat down at the table with my glass of orange juice.

"Dad!" I gasped. My father folded his newspaper and sat back in his chair sipping coffee. I was going to ask him what he thought we'd been doing, but something about the twinkle in his eyes stopped me.

"Chad's a nice boy," he said after a few moments. "In fact, I've been watching him help you with Dancer these past few weeks. He knows his stuff. That's why I'm going to ask him to work with a few of the younger junior riders during their practice session today."

My jaw dropped, and I sat there staring at my father. It was unheard of for him to allow anyone other than a trained instructor to coach riders.

"Does Chad know this?" I asked, ignoring my muffin that had popped up in the toaster.

"Not yet, but I intend to tell him as soon as he gets here," my father said. "I left word in the barn to have him stop by the house."

"You did!" I exclaimed. My hands flew to my head.

I had washed my hair and instead of blowing it dry right away I'd decided to leave it wet until after breakfast. I didn't care if my parents saw it clinging to my head in long wet strips. But I didn't want Chad to see me looking like that.

"Why didn't you say something!" I asked. I shoved my chair away from the table and bolted up the stairs as my father's hearty laugh echoed in the background.

Twenty minutes later I returned to the kitchen, where my mother told me that I had just missed Chad. He and my father had already left for the stables.

"Wait a minute, Julie," she said as I started to put on my boots. "I know you're anxious to talk to Chad, but you've got to have some breakfast before you go anywhere."

"Oh, Mom," I groaned as she pointed to my place at the table.

A moment later she put a plate before me. I forced myself to choke down a few bites of scrambled egg and half a muffin.

"OK?" I asked. I finished gulping down the orange juice that I'd left sitting on the table earlier. She nodded, and I dashed from the house. The rain was hardly more than a mist.

Chad was standing in the office with my father when I burst through the door, and when he saw me he smiled. A few wet strands of hair hung down on his forehead and his jacket was all wet, but to me he'd never looked more handsome. I wanted to throw myself into his arms, but of course, I didn't.

"Congratulations," I said softly.

"Are you going to kiss him?" a voice asked from behind me. I whirled around to see David. The little boy had been sitting on the couch next to his father when I'd come in, and now he stood beside me looking up at us.

Chad wasn't quite so taken aback. "Do you think she should?" He flashed David a grin.

"I don't know," he said and shrugged. Then he seemed to give it more thought. "Won't that make her your girlfriend?"

Everyone in the room laughed then, and it was David's turn to blush. He started to run to his father, but Chad caught him around the waist and hauled him back against his legs.

"Want me to let you in on a big secret?" he whispered out loud, and David suddenly forgot about his embarrassment. He nodded excitedly and turned to look up at Chad. "She already *is* my girlfriend."

I saw David's face go from surprise to confusion, to surprise, all in the matter of seconds.

"If Julie's your girlfriend, what about the other girl I saw you with? The one who laughed at my brace?" David asked.

I felt my body go rigid and had to look down so Chad wouldn't see the sudden hurt in my eyes. I thought I'd successfully put Cheryl from my mind. But hearing David's question brought all my doubts rushing back.

How is Chad going to answer this? I wondered as I stared at the toes of my boots. Then I heard him speak and my breath caught in my throat.

"That girl owns one of the horses at the

farm, so I *have* to be nice to her," Chad said softly. "But she's *not* my girlfriend."

I had the feeling that his words were spoken as much for me as for David. I relaxed, and when I lifted my gaze to meet Chad's, I was once again all smiles.

Chapter Thirteen

The rest of the day flew by. Chad was a hit with the junior riders and some of the girls started flirting with him. After they finished a round, they would trot their horses over to where he stood and listen dreamily while he listed any mistakes they might have made.

"Good round, but your horse chipped the first wall," Chad told one girl with dark brown pigtails. She sat in the saddle blushing while he explained how she should correct her mistake the next time around.

Chad rarely missed an error, which helped the riders learn what they were doing wrong as well as what the judges would spot in a show. And after his words that morning, I wasn't jealous of the flirting that went on during the lessons. In fact, I found it amusing because it reminded me of when I'd had a crush on Dave, one of the instructors my father had hired to work with a group of us before horse show season a few years ago. Chad was just as lovable as Dave had been, but more importantly, Chad was all mine.

It had broken my heart when I'd learned Dave was engaged to be married, just as I knew it would break these girls' hearts to learn Chad and I were going together. So I was careful not to let it slip.

At school, however, everyone knew. It was now Chad and Julie this, or Julie and Chad that. Kids no longer asked, "What are you doing tonight, Julie?" It was always, "What are you and Chad doing tonight?"

And they no longer stared when they saw us sitting at lunch together or walking down the hall hand in hand when we had classes near each other's. Diane and Peter were the new topic of conversation with my friends, not Chad and I.

They had been seeing a lot of each other since Diane's party, and I was glad that my best friend was also dating a junior. Even though Chad and Peter didn't hang around together, they had many of the same classes and seemed to get along well. We even double-dated one Saturday night after my first horse show of the season.

I had placed third in a field of twelve in my

jumping class, which wasn't a bad beginning. In fact, I was pretty pleased with my ribbon, and I was proud of Dancer, too. It hadn't been a rinky-dink show, either. Along with my ribbon, they also awarded me points that would go toward my season total. A high point total would allow me to compete in more prestigious shows in the future.

I had wanted to do well in the show, not only because it was my first, but because Chad had been there to watch me. He'd managed to get out of staying with the junior riders to spend all day with me. That was unusual because at the other shows we had attended since mid-April when the season started—shows I hadn't entered—we had rarely seen each other. I had to help out wherever my father needed me, and the only time Chad and I had together was at the van between classes.

But that day Chad helped me wash and braid Dancer's mane when we first reached the grounds. Then he looked on while I warmed him up in an open field.

When my number was finally called, I moved Dancer to the entrance gate, and Chad gave me a quick nod. "Good luck, Julie," he called as we trotted onto the field. Then he settled back against the railing to watch.

I could see Chad from the corner of my eye as I headed Dancer toward the green brush jump. The wind had picked up and blown a lock of hair over his forehead, but he didn't seem to notice. His eyes were fixed on me, and his arms never moved from their folded position on the top of the railing.

I talked to Dancer continuously under my breath as I always did over a course, and when we reached the green brush jump, he soared over it like a spring breeze. I shot Chad another quick look while I pulled Dancer back to a brisk hunter pace, and this time he gave me a thumbs-up sign. The rest of it was a blur. Dancer swept over the wide gate edged with flowers and the in-and-out jump without any problem, and when the final results of the class were given we rode out third to accept the yellow ribbon. I was thrilled.

"I understand we're celebrating something," Peter said when we slid into the booth opposite him and Diane at Amy's that night. They had gotten there first and had waved us over.

"I'm not," Chad said, feigning surprise.

"Me, neither," Diane said gruffly. She was finding it hard to suppress her smile. "That leaves Julie."

Three sets of eyes turned on me then, and all together they said, "Congratulations!"

I blushed and leaned back against Chad's shoulder until the waitress arrived to take our orders. "What are you having?" I asked Chad when he turned to look at me.

"The usual," he said. That meant pizza with extra cheese and a soda.

Diane and Peter also ordered pizza so I did the same, and we wound up with a large pie cut into eight slices. When it arrived, Diane scooped up a slice and set it on my plate. Then she did the same for herself and the guys.

"When do you guys have another horse show?" Peter asked when he had finished all but the crust of his first slice.

Chad and I looked at each other and shrugged. "I don't know, why?" I asked him.

"Diane and I thought we'd get a few couples together for a beach party."

Chad's eyes lit up. "It can't be next weekend though," Diane said between bites. "My parents want me to go with them to visit my grandmother."

"How about the following weekend, then? That Saturday?" Chad asked, reaching for his glass of Pepsi and taking a sip. "Even if there is a show, we should be back in time."

I sat back in my seat and said nothing. I couldn't believe they were really serious. It was the first weekend in May, but the weather could still be very cold and windy on the beach at night. Yet nobody seemed to have given that any thought.

"Isn't it still too early in the year for a beach party?" I asked. Diane rolled her eyes heavenward.

"Spare me, Julie Peterson," she said. "Haven't you ever heard of blankets and body heat?"

I didn't know what to say or do then. My cheeks burned, and I hoped Chad didn't think I was being deliberately innocent. The truth was that I'd never been to a beach party before and didn't realize it was just an excuse to wrap up in blankets.

Fortunately, Carol and Ben walked in then and when they spotted us in the booth, they came right over. "Room for two more?" Ben asked. We immediately scrunched together so they could each have a seat at either end of the booth.

"See what I mean about body heat?" Diane asked. She fit herself into the crook of Peter's arm the minute he put it around her shoulder.

Peter and Chad hooted with laughter, and I joined them in spite of myself. Ben and Carol looked puzzled, but they didn't say anything. They merely looked at each other across the table and shrugged.

"We've decided to have a beach party," Chad said, to let them in on the joke.

"No kidding!" Carol looked around the table in surprise. "When?"

Chad grinned and gestured with one hand to Peter. "Ask him. It was all his idea."

"It sounds great!" Ben piped up.

"I'll second that," Diane said. Everyone's enthusiasm was getting to me.

As I sat there listening, they made plans to hold the beach party in two weeks. Peter informed us that everyone would be responsible for bringing his own blanket, but added that he would bring the firewood for the bonfire if someone else brought the soda and hot dogs.

"What about marshmallows?" I suggested. I couldn't imagine a camp fire without marshmallows.

"Good idea. If you can also bring the soda, Carol and I will take care of the hot dogs," Ben volunteered.

We decided we'd invite only two more couples to join us so the party wouldn't get out of hand. Then we talked about *where* on the beach we could hold the party. Carol suggested someplace near the parking lot so we wouldn't have far to walk. But that was immediately vetoed because it wouldn't give us any privacy. A few more suggestions were offered and discarded. Finally Peter described a cul-de-sac in the dunes. "I assure you, it will not only keep out much of the wind, but it will be *very* private," he said.

"All right," Chad said. "It's all settled then."

"Great," Diane said, clapping her hands. "We'll talk to one another and decide where to meet."

I muttered something about hoping the weather cooperated.

"The weather?" Chad said in my ear. "I will keep you warm through rain and snow and sleet and ice—or however that goes."

"You'd better," I told him in a voice only he could hear. "Or else."

"Or else what?" Chad asked.

"Or else we'll *both* be cold," I said as I reached for another slice of pizza.

Chapter Fourteen

Those two weeks before the beach party passed in a blur of happiness. On the next Saturday there was another horse show, and for the first time ever I rode someone else's horse. I had been schooling Baxter under my father's watchful eye for months and had learned to anticipate his dives and little habits. He still wasn't perfect, but his owners were impressed with the way he was performing. They wanted to enter him in the show, provided I agreed to ride him.

"Should I?" I asked my father before answering. I wasn't sure Baxter was ready, and I didn't want to make a poor showing.

"It's up to you," my father said, looking at me thoughtfully. "But I think you've got Baxter moving well enough to earn some points."

Chad thought it was too good an opportunity to pass up. "I'd go for it if I were you," he told me.

So with two experts behind me, I did. When I placed high enough to win a ribbon for Baxter's owners, they were thrilled. I was pleased with the results, too, and even a little proud of having placed so high my first time out on a new horse. But all my energy was focused on Chad as I rode home next to him in the van. Just being with him made me so ridiculously happy I couldn't stop smiling.

As the day of the beach party drew closer my happiness swelled. All our plans were finalized at lunch on Friday, and I had a hard time concentrating on schoolwork that afternoon. My thoughts kept wandering; I kept thinking how lucky I was to have the most wonderful guy in the world as a boyfriend. I started drawing hearts with Chad's initials in them across the top of my notebook.

I didn't realize Mr. Simpson was behind me until he commented on my scribbles and told me to see him after class. When the bell rang I was given a lecture on the hazards of letting my social life interfere with my schoolwork, so I was twenty minutes late leaving school.

When I burst through the front doors and

saw the student parking lot empty except for Chad's car, I broke into a run. I didn't stop to ask myself why he wasn't standing outside the car, waiting for me as he usually did. Until I spotted two heads in the front seat instead of one, it hadn't occurred to me that Chad might not be alone.

I stopped dead in my tracks as the sunlight glistened on a mass of long, blond hair. There was only one person who had a mane like that—Cheryl Williams.

My heart was racing. She was looking at Chad with a dreamy expression on her face. For a moment I just stood there, unable to move. Chad had reassured me countless times that he didn't care about Cheryl anymore, but seeing him with her in the car made fresh doubts form in my mind. I couldn't ignore the fact that she was stunningly beautiful. I also knew that she didn't see anything wrong with making a play for someone else's boyfriend.

I walked over to the passenger side of the car, and the minute Cheryl saw me, she opened her door. "Hi, Julie," she said giving me a smug look. "What took you so long? We've been waiting for you forever."

I mentioned something about having to talk

with Mr. Simpson. *What is she doing in Chad's car?* I asked myself.

"Nothing serious, I hope," she said, turning sideways in her seat as if she was preparing to get out and move to the back. Only, instead of getting out so I could sit next to Chad, she pulled her seat forward.

"Hop in," she said and grinned at me wickedly.

I stared at her for a minute, and then leaned down to look at Chad. I was sure he wouldn't let her get away with that, but I was wrong. Perhaps he didn't understand the pleading in my eyes. Maybe he didn't want to start trouble. In any case, instead of insisting that Cheryl move to the backseat so I could sit next to him, he merely looked at me and shrugged.

A sharp pain jabbed at my heart; at that very moment, I also caught the look of triumph in Cheryl's eyes. She looked like the cat-who-swallowed-the-canary, and it hurt to think Chad wouldn't stand up to her for me. Didn't he realize that *I* was his girlfriend and by all rights should be the one sitting next to him in the front seat?

Then a terrible fear hit me. Maybe what I had once dreaded was finally happening. Maybe Chad wasn't saying anything because he was having second thoughts about our going together now that he realized Cheryl was still interested in him. I hesitated for a moment before climbing into the car.

"I'm so glad Chad offered me a ride to the farm this afternoon," Cheryl said, bubbling victoriously as I slumped down into my seat. "It saved me the trouble of calling a cab and gave us time to talk alone. Did you know we used to go out?"

I saw Chad glance at me in the rearview mirror, waiting for a response, but I didn't answer her. I couldn't. I was finding it difficult just to breathe, how could I talk?

That didn't seem to bother Cheryl, though. As Chad started out of the parking lot, she continued to talk about all the wonderful times they had shared. She didn't even bother to look at me. It wasn't until Chad had stopped for a traffic light at the edge of town that she gave me a quick glance over her shoulder.

"Don't you just love this little car?" she asked. "Except for the bucket seats, of course."

I couldn't believe it. When Chad had first bought the car, she had refused to even sit in it, yet here she was carrying on about how wonderful it was.

"What's wrong with bucket seats?" I asked. I was aware I sounded snippy but I didn't care. It was just the way I felt at the moment.

"You've got to be kidding," Cheryl said, turning a warm smile toward Chad. "Haven't you noticed that they keep you from sitting next to the driver?"

I could have strangled her then. She must have known how upset I was, but she continued to turn on the charm. I found myself imagining secret meanings in her laugh and hidden messages in the glances she sent across the front seat. I thought I heard Chad mumble something occasionally, but I couldn't be sure. All I knew was that he had stopped trying to make eye contact with me in the rearview mirror, which seemed to confirm my worst fears.

I felt myself shrivel up inside, and by the time Chad pulled into the wide lane leading to the farm my lips were trembling. I knew I was about to burst into tears. The minute he stopped in front of my house, I bolted from the car.

"See you in a few minutes," I heard Chad call after me. But I didn't bother to turn around until I was inside the kitchen with the door closed. Then I stood with my forehead pressed against the cool glass panes of the window watching Chad and Cheryl drive off together.

I didn't think I could hurt any more, but I was wrong. When they pulled up by the barn, they didn't get out of the car right away. The aching inside me grew worse. *Is this how it feels to have a broken heart?* I wondered a little wildly. I saw their heads bent together, and I was convinced it was over between Chad and me. The tears I'd been holding back spilled down onto my cheeks.

"Julie, what is it?" my mother asked as she walked into the mud room. I must have scared her, standing by the door with my books clutched tightly against my chest and my body trembling with painful sobs. "What happened?"

I wiped my tears. "It's—nothing—really," I murmured, not sure I could talk about what had just happened with Chad.

"Yes, it is," she said. She came up behind me and placed her hands on both my arms when she saw I couldn't control my sobbing.

That was my undoing. I spun around and buried my face in her shoulder, letting the tears spill freely. "It hurts so much," I cried while my mother stroked my back.

"I can see that," she whispered against my forehead. "Do you want to tell me why?"

I took a deep breath before lifting my eyes to look at her. "Chad's in love with Cheryl," I whispered brokenly.

She looked at me, surprised by my words.

"When did he tell you this?" she asked.

"He—he didn't," I said, sobbing. "But it was so obvious even a blind man would notice."

I tried to explain how Chad had offered Cheryl a ride in his car and how she sat with him in the front while I was forced to sit in the backseat alone.

"I see," my mother said, slipping her arm around my shoulders and leading me up the stairs to my room. "But are you sure that means he loves Cheryl?"

"What else could it mean?" I asked her.

"Maybe nothing," my mother replied. She bent down to brush her lips against my forehead. "Don't pass final judgment on this until you see what happens when you get to the barn."

"I can't!" I lurched away from her and sank down onto my bed. "Don't make me go to work this afternoon, please!" I begged. "I just can't face Chad now, not with Cheryl there. Please, Mom. I'll see him tomorrow, but right now I just need to be alone."

Through the mist of tears I saw my mother frown. "All right," she said after a few minutes thought. "If you really feel that strongly about not seeing Chad, I'll let you skip work this afternoon. Tomorrow things are bound to look better."

They didn't.

When I woke up Saturday morning after a fitful sleep my eyelids were so heavy from all the crying I'd done it was a struggle just to open them. As far as I knew, Chad hadn't missed me at the stables. He didn't call after dinner, something he did every night since we had started dating. I sat by the phone all evening waiting for it to ring, and every time it did I held my breath, praying it would be Chad. But all the calls were for my parents, except for one—Betty Comden needed the English homework assignment from me.

By eleven o'clock I gave up waiting and dragged myself up to my room. I ached for sleep because it would stop me from thinking about Chad and how much it hurt to lose him, but it didn't come. Long after my parents went upstairs to bed I still lay wide awake with the blankets tucked up under my chin.

Too good to be true, too good to be true, echoed in my head until two o'clock in the morning. Sleep finally put me out of my misery.

Chapter Fifteen

At breakfast I told my parents I didn't think I would be able to go to work that day.

"Are you sick?" my mother asked, giving me a quizzical look across the table. I nodded. I was dying of a broken heart which was worse than any illness I could imagine. "You don't feel feverish," she said, putting her hand on my forehead. "You're probably just tired."

"Does that mean I can't stay home?" I asked.

I saw her look at my father; he shook his head.

"I'm afraid your father needs you in the barn today," she said.

"Dad," I said and turned pleading eyes on him, but before I could get another word out he cut me off.

"You know how busy it is at the farm this time of year. I can't afford to let you take off just because you and Chad had a misunderstanding." I wanted to shout. That was the understatement of the year. The boy I loved more than anyone in the world had just dumped me for another girl. Surely that was more than a *misunderstanding*.

I fixed my eyes on my mother, hoping for some sympathy from her. But there was none. "Your father is right, Julie," she told me. "You can't hide from Chad forever."

"Neither of you is being fair!" I blurted out. "You don't understand."

"On the contrary. We understand a lot more than you're giving us credit for," my father said, folding his newspaper and laying it on the table. "That's why I expect to see you at the barn in an hour." When he stood up to carry his dishes to the kitchen sink I knew the subject was closed.

My mother and I remained at the breakfast table after my dad returned to the barn. She refilled her coffee cup and tried to get me to eat some toast, but there was no way I could choke down any food.

"Oh, Mom," I whispered. "What am I supposed to say to Chad when I see him?"

"Just act normal," she said, laying her hand over mine on the table. "Then see what happens."

"I don't know if I can," I mumbled in a shaky voice. "I really don't know."

Upstairs, I struggled into my breeches and a long-sleeved shirt. It was too warm for my down vest, so I pulled on a cotton sweater instead, not bothering to check my reflection in the mirror. I was sure the rough night still showed on my face, and I didn't want to see the dark circles under my eyes.

When I stepped out the back door I saw Chad right away. He had just come out of the barn, leading a bay mare by the halter. He spotted me immediately.

Be casual, I told myself as he released the horse in the paddock and started toward me. *Don't let him see how much you hurt.*

"Hi, Julie," he said. He smiled, but there was something strained in his voice and in the way he walked. "Glad to see you're feeling better."

That wasn't the opening I'd expected, and I stopped in my tracks. I was sure that Chad had been coming over to tell me he no longer wanted to go out with me, and I'd already braced myself for rejection.

"Really?" I said dryly. "I'm surprised you care."

He gave me a puzzled look. "What do you mean by that?"

"Oh, I don't know," I said. "After yesterday in the car—you and Cheryl—" I broke off the sentence and started walking again. It was no longer possible for me to act casual.

"Look, about yesterday—" Chad began, falling into step beside me.

We weren't actually touching, but he was so close to me that I could feel the warmth of his body. I knew if I turned my head I would see the fine stubble of beard he had on his chin.

I took a deep breath. "Go on," I urged, trying to hide the ache. "I'm listening."

He glanced at me then and looked away. But not before I saw the crimson flooding his cheeks.

"Can we talk over there?" he asked. He jerked his head toward a large tree. "It's more private."

Here it comes, I thought, and a heavy thudding started in my head making my skull feel as though it was about to split wide open. *Don't let me cry, please don't let me cry.*

"Why don't you just say it here and get it over with," I said, trying to keep my voice steady.

Chad's body became rigid. "Say what?" he growled.

"Whatever it is you have planned. You just told me you wanted to talk, remember?" I said stiffly.

"Sure I did, but if this is your attitude, forget it!" he snapped, and stalked off.

Too stunned to move or speak, I watched as he stormed over to the paddock fence and thrust his elbows onto the top railing. I'd never seen Chad so angry before, and it made me uneasy.

I swallowed hard and slumped against the side of the barn, trying to sort out the jumble of emotions churning inside me. Even though I was hurt and angry at Chad, something prevented me from walking away. At that moment, all I knew was that deep down I still loved Chad and I didn't want him to be angry with me.

"Chad—" I called in a hoarse voice. He turned to look at me, wariness in his eyes. "I'm sorry. You wanted to talk?" I said.

"Are you sure you're ready to listen?" he asked after twenty or thirty seconds had elapsed, and I nodded. Since I had already accepted the fact that I'd lost Chad, I didn't think that anything he could say would make me feel any worse than I already did. Still, walking over to where he stood by the railing was one of the most difficult things I'd ever had to do. My knees began to wobble, and the blood roared in my ears.

Neither of us said anything for a few minutes. We didn't look at each other. I stood with one shoulder against the top railing, my hands shoved into my pockets. I stared at the ground, while Chad gazed at the cloudless sky and the tall trees that surrounded the paddock.

"Look, Julie," he said after a long silence. "I want you to know I'm—I'm *really* sorry for everything that happened yesterday. I didn't mean for you to be hurt. You've got to believe that. Things just happened so fast," he said.

I felt hot and cold. I wasn't sure what he meant by "things" and opened my mouth to ask. But he wouldn't let me speak. "Don't say anything, Julie. Not yet. There's something we have to get straight first." Chad's voice became stronger. "I realize now that I was crazy to think Cheryl could act like a decent human being in the car. She's forgotten how. But just because I offered her a lift to the farm doesn't mean I still care for her, because I don't. It's over between us. Finished. I swear."

"If that's true, why did you offer her a lift?"

"Because your father asked me to," he said quietly. "One of the riders I instruct outgrew her pony, and her parents made an offer to buy Jupiter. Since Cheryl is listed as his owner, she had to sign the papers."

For a second I was too tongue-tied to speak. I didn't even move. Now I understood why Chad had agreed to take care of Jupiter, and why Cheryl had needed a ride to the farm the day before.

"Oh, Chad, if only you'd told me this yesterday," I whispered.

"I tried to," he said, turning to face me. "When I realized how things must have looked—me with Cheryl and all—I came up to your house to apologize. But your mother said that you weren't feeling very well—that you wanted to be alone. She said that maybe I should wait until today to talk to you."

"She did? I mean, you came—" Suddenly I remembered what I'd said to my mother. That was why she had told Chad to wait to talk to me until that day. *But why hadn't Mom said something this morning about Chad coming over yesterday?* As if in answer to my silent question, Chad continued.

"I made your mother promise not to tell you that I'd been there. After everything that had happened, I was afraid you'd never want to see me again. Honest." He drew his fingers across his heart, and I had to believe him.

I was learning to trust, and when he reached out to take my hand and give it a gentle squeeze, all the hurt disappeared. I leaned my head against his shoulder.

"That's more like it," he said softly. "I love you, Julie."

My heart felt so full, I was afraid it might burst. Although I wasn't sure that I'd ever feel really comfortable around Cheryl, I was sure that I no longer needed to be afraid of losing Chad to her. I trusted Chad, and if he said that he loved me—Julie Peterson—then I had to believe him.

"I'm sorry for acting so horrible. I should have trusted you from the very beginning," I murmured as we started back toward the barn. "Forgive me?"

"I will if you promise to roast me some marshmallows at the beach party tonight," he answered tenderly.

"I promise," I said, linking my arm through his and looking up into his beautiful green eyes. "I'll roast you more marshmallows than you could possibly eat." Pausing, I looked down at my feet. Then gazing back at Chad, I went on. "And, Chad—I love you, too."

Arm in arm, we headed into the barn. It was a sunny spring morning, and there wasn't a cloud in the sky. And with Chad beside me, I knew that every day would be just as perfect.

THE PROBLEM WITH LOVE

Rosemary Vernon

This one is for you, Eileen

Chapter One

"Here we go!"

Needles of icy spray stung Cathy Meyers' face as the rubber raft plummeted down the American River rapids. The boy sitting next to her, Derek Sorenson, instinctively clamped a hand around Cathy's sun-browned arm while she held onto the aluminum frame for dear life.

It was spring, and the first run of the season for the five life-jacketed teenagers. The river was high because of the melted snow runoff from the Sierra Nevadas, and it was full of debris it had gathered along its route.

Cathy ran her fingers through her tangled, shoulder-length brown hair, dark blue eyes wide with anticipation. She loved the exhilarating rough-and-tumble ride down the river, which carved a roaring path past her hometown. It was a ride that made her scream and laugh, a ride that was always full of surprises.

1

The five always rode together, with Marty Mason as self-appointed leader of the group, which consisted of himself, Cathy, his sister Jan, Tracy Wilder, and Derek Sorenson. Marty and Jan's family owned the raft, and Marty was one of the best "river rats" there was. He always took great precautions, scouting the river before a run, and he knew how to read the language of the water better than he read his homework assignments. He was one of those single-minded boys who could discuss nothing but white-water sports.

Cathy loved rafting, but she wasn't dedicated to it the way Marty was. In fact, she found it hard to be serious about anything for long. If Cathy was dedicated to anything, it was the idea of trying *everything*—and having fun, ambitions her parents did not value very highly.

Her room at home was littered with roller skates, old ballet shoes, half-finished crafts projects, and dusty paperbacks she'd bought and never read. She had also gone through a period when she had developed a great interest in photography, so her walls were covered with nature photographs she had taken. Some of them had even appeared in the school newspaper. But when she had been asked to join the staff, she had refused. Taking pictures as a job would take all the fun out of it, she decided. Besides, the staff met third period every day, and she didn't want to load up her class schedule. Anyway, by the time they got around to asking her, she had lost interest in photography and found another hobby that took up most of her time and attention—boys.

"We wish you'd be more serious, Cathy," her father often complained. "All you think about these days are boys and parties."

Her standard reply had always been: "Well, you can't complain about my grades, can you? I always manage to get by pretty well, even without studying. There are a lot more interesting things to do than study."

Then came algebra. . . .

Cathy was *not* getting by in algebra. In fact, she was in big trouble. So much trouble that she had done something really dumb. She had told her parents that she had left her report card at school and hadn't had a chance to look at it herself. It was a desperate move to postpone the big scene with her parents until Monday because she had a big weekend planned: the raft trip, a party that night, and skating Sunday. She knew her parents wouldn't have let her out of the house if they had seen her algebra grade.

3

Still, when she hadn't brought home her report card, the "look" had passed between them—the knowing look that Cathy had learned to read as "we don't believe you."

Ever since Cathy's father had started teaching at her high school, Sierra Heights last fall, substituting for Ms. Curtis in English, Cathy had felt smothered. She had always been fairly popular and had many friends, but with her dad teaching at Sierra, some things had changed.

For instance, now she was categorized as "Mr. Meyers' daughter," Herbie Franklin, who had never had two words to say to her before, now wanted her to smuggle him the answers to her father's English exam. Of course, she had told him to get lost. Eric Merritt wanted to take her out—she found out later that he was hoping to insure himself an A on his report card.

One of her friends had even stopped coming around, finding it difficult to maintain a friendship with Cathy when her father was her English teacher. "I don't know how to act now," Katy Willis complained. "It's so weird being at your house, talking about boys or clothes, with your dad teaching English. I feel like I ought to be discussing prepositional

4

phrases or something. Why don't you come to my house instead?"

"Why should it matter? You never even noticed my father before he was your teacher!" protested Cathy. She was hurt.

Tracy and Jan had tried to console her. "Look, Katy's not your only friend. You've got us. We don't care if your father's a teacher at Sierra."

It was okay for them to say, but when Jan and Tracy ate dinner at Cathy's, they discussed English assignments with her father. School seemed to be invading her whole life.

"Why does it bother you?" Mrs. Meyers questioned. "I think it's wonderful the girls are so interested."

"It bothers me because they're my friends and Daddy is monopolizing the conversation!" Cathy exploded. "We hear enough about schoolwork at school."

"But school is important."

"I'm glad you teach elementary, Mom. I couldn't stand having both of you in the same school with me all day long."

Her mother looked hurt, and Cathy wished she could say things in a nicer way. But it seemed that since school had started in September, she hadn't had a nice thing to say to either of her parents. Of course, she loved them, but having parents who were teachers could really be a drag sometimes, especially when you were in high school.

Always outspoken, Cathy now took the defensive position in every argument. It didn't matter what they talked about. If her parents said the sky was blue, Cathy would insist it was gray. She found herself taking a stand against them even when she knew she was wrong.

To Cathy, her parents seemed dull and set in their ways. All their responses were so well worn that Cathy thought they sounded like a couple of tape recorders. All *they* talked about, it seemed, were grades and education and careers. Cathy couldn't believe that they had ever really *lived* at all. She knew they were happy the way they were, but she couldn't understand how they could be. . . .

"Hey, Cath, are you still with us?" Jan asked, startling Cathy and bringing her back to the present. "How 'bout rowing for a while?"

Cathy accepted reluctantly. She didn't like rowing much, though she'd never say so to her friends. Her oar strokes were shallow and noisy, and she hated the burn in her shoulders after a little steady rowing.

"When you splash like that, you're not getting anywhere," criticized Marty. Marty was a thin, red-haired, freckle-faced boy, and his sister resembled him in hair color and pale skin, minus the freckles.

Tracy smiled. "Cathy's got her own crazy way of doing things. You ought to know that by now, Marty."

"Loony, but an individualist," summarized Marty. "Now just row over to that bank, Cathy, and we'll get out."

"Don't trust my driving, huh?" Cathy joked, maneuvering the raft through the slower water to the bank, where everyone climbed out.

Derek offered her his hand. "How are you getting to the party tonight?"

"Any way I can. Bus, skates, train . . ."

"Okay, smarty. Have it your way." He pretended to sock her in the arm. "I thought you might like to ride with Jan and me."

"Sure. That's the best offer I've had yet." Cathy grinned. She and Derek went out occasionally, but just as friends.

The five teenagers hoisted the raft onto the top of Marty's Dodge van and lashed it onto the rack, then climbed inside.

"Turn on the heater, man, I'm freezing," Derek demanded, through chattering teeth.

7

"I second the motion," said Tracy.

"I can't wait to take a shower," Cathy muttered, shivering in her soaked cutoffs and bikini top. "Hey, Marty, are you coming to the party? Or are you gonna spend tonight patching the raft?"

The others chuckled. Marty shrugged. "Aw, I might come. It depends."

Marty was the only one of the group who was not social. The other four loved parties.

Cathy leaned between the front seats to talk. "Well, if it wasn't for you, Marty, keeping the raft shipshape, the rest of us wouldn't get to float."

"No kidding, Cathy?" he said, obviously amused. "Without my undying dedication, you would all be up the creek, huh?"

Laughter filled the van as it swung into the Meyers' driveway.

"See you tonight." Cathy jumped out of the van, wearing a thick purple velour towel around her slim waist.

"We'll pick you up," yelled Jan, before Derek slammed the sliding door shut between them.

Cathy ran inside and yelled, "I'm home." After stopping in her bedroom to grab jeans and a plaid shirt, she padded down the tiled hallway to the bathroom, where she turned on the shower full blast. She peeled off her clothes, showered, shampooed her hair, and quickly dressed. Her mother knocked at the door.

"When you get out, your father and I want to talk to you."

Cathy held her breath. Uh-oh. "Okay, Mom." By her mother's tone of voice, she knew she was in trouble. Reluctantly she crept down the hall, on the lookout for her parents.

"Boy are you in the doghouse!" Cathy's thirteen-year-old brother Matt said, as he peered out of his bedroom. In the last year, since he'd entered junior high, Matt had grown from a little stick figure into a broad-shouldered, wisecracking creature one inch taller than Cathy. Cathy teased him about being like their puppy Horace, who had changed from a ball of fur with big feet to a huge red setter with all the right proportions.

"What's up, Matt?" Cathy whispered conspiratorially. The two weren't really close, except when joining forces against their parents.

"Your report card!" he said, rolling his eyes.

"They know?"

"Only about your algebra grade. Marcus spilled the beans."

9

Mr. Marcus was Cathy's algebra teacher. She clutched at her throat. "Oh, no. Pray for me."

She found her parents in the den. They turned when she entered: her father, a broad, barrel-chested man still in his golf shoes and Arnold Palmer T-shirt (he usually changed as soon as he got home), her mother looking her usual, slightly disheveled self in a pair of jeans and a paint-speckled blouse. Sybil Meyers was not very concerned about her appearance, maintaining that many other things were more important than how a person looked.

"Well, sit down, Cathleen."

Whenever they called her Cathleen, she knew she was in for it. She lowered herself into a deep leather arm chair.

"We want to talk about your report card," her father said. "Mr. Marcus informed me that you received a D in algebra."

Cathy swallowed hard, her voice sticking in her throat. "Yes."

"I hope this isn't an indication of your other grades, young lady."

"It isn't." She hadn't received a bad grade in anything else, although her father would probably criticize her for dropping from a B to a B minus in American history.

"I hope for your sake, that this time you're telling the truth. You must realize that lying certainly hasn't helped so far."

"Cathy," her mother explained patiently, "we've been very understanding until now, and we haven't interfered with your social life at all. But you're a very bright girl. There's no reason why you should be so close to failing a subject. If you can't buckle down by yourself, we're going to have to help you. For starters, we've hired you a tutor."

Cathy's mouth dropped open. "A tutor?" Gripping the arms of the chair, she asked, "Who?"

"John Crowley, a boy in one of my classes," said Mr. Meyers. "Do you know him?"

"No. Well, maybe. I might've seen him around. Isn't he kind of a creep?" It wasn't the right thing to say to her parents, she knew, but she also knew the sort of person they would choose. It was true she couldn't quite place John Crowley, but she had a vague idea of who he might be—tall, dark-haired, with glasses—one out of a small group of studious, silent types who would view her from the pedestal of the Honor Roll as if she were a real dummy for needing a tutor.

"He isn't a creep, Cathy. He's a very responsible young man, and I think he can help

11

you." Stephen Meyers' explanation was firm.

"I don't want his help, Dad. I don't care what you think of him. I don't want a tutor." Cathy crossed her arms angrily, trying to think of some way out of this whole mess. How embarrassing—having a nerd tutor her in algebra! "Look, I'll study harder, I promise, and I'll get Derek or Jan to help me."

"Cathy, you've made promises before. Besides, you know you wouldn't get much studying done if one of your friends tried to help you. What you need is someone totally uninvolved."

Fidgeting, Cathy jumped to her feet. "Can I go now? I've got to get ready."

Her mother's eyebrows shot up. "Oh? And where are you going?"

"I'm going to Lisa Shuler's party, Mom. I told you that a week ago, remember?"

"Call Lisa and tell her you're not going. And don't make any more plans for the weekend, Cathy," her father said firmly. "Officially, as of now, you're grounded."

"Daddy!"

"We're serious, Cathy."

Her mother looked at her husband, then back at Cathy. "I'm sorry, Cathy, you have to learn. A few weeks' work with John will help

12

you, I'm sure. You've got to concentrate on your studies more."

"Thanks for ruining my whole life!" Cathy turned and ran out of the den. She was ready to explode. Be tutored by John Crowley? What did her parents think they'd accomplish by sticking her with him?

And tonight, of all nights, she was grounded. They had no right to do this, she fumed, thinking of all the good things she wouldn't be allowed to do now—Lisa's party, skating tomorrow, and whatever else the gang came up with.

Suddenly the four walls of Cathy's bedroom seemed to press in on her like a cell.

Chapter Two

"I forgot to ask if you're allowed visitors." Jan stood on Cathy's doorstep, dressed in cream slacks and a bright orange blouse, a begonia pinned in her curly ginger-colored hair.

Tracy walked up the stone path behind her friend.

"Yes, I'm allowed visitors. Come on in." Cathy motioned to them. Horace, the Meyers' red setter, followed the girls in the hope of getting some attention.

Jan seated herself carefully on Cathy's striped bedspread, while Tracy preferred to stand, not wanting to crease her white cotton embroidered dress.

Surveying them both in their party clothes, Cathy said, "I sure wish I was going with you. But I guess I'm stuck here until my algebra gets better—or they invent a new kind of computer for me to swallow."

"Ugh—algebra. It sounds like some kind of

disease, doesn't it?" Tracy wrapped her tongue around the word and tried it out several different ways, until the word sounded funny and foreign to their ears, and they burst into giggles. "Well, anyway, it's a good thing your problem isn't English. You'd really be in the doghouse with your dad."

"Yeah, luckily I've always done well in English without really trying. Dad's only cause for complaint there is that I don't spend my free time curling up with Shakespeare or inventing new uses for the comma."

Jan laughed. "Cathy, you really are too much. So what are they going to do to you?"

Cathy leaned her head back against her rattan headboard. "You mean besides keeping me in solitary confinement? Wait until you hear. You won't believe it. You'd think I was going to be a brain surgeon the way they worry about my math grades. I mean, who needs algebra, right? It's really embarrassing. I can't—"

"Cathy!" Jan interrupted. "Will you just tell us already?"

"They hired someone named John Crowley to tutor me."

"A tutor? What for? That's crazy."

Cathy shrugged. "I don't know why. They just went ahead and hired someone."

"Who's John Crowley, anyway? Does he go to Sierra?"

"Is he cute?" Tracy asked. "I've never heard of him."

Cathy sighed. "I have him pictured as one of those studious types with thick glasses and an armload of books. I'm not sure. He's in one of my dad's classes, though."

"Wouldn't you know it."

"We'll have to check him out." Jan's eyes lit up mischievously.

Cathy knew what that meant. Jan would want to check John's entire class schedule, what he ate for lunch, who he ate with, his daily habits in general. Personally, Cathy thought Jan read too many detective stories and that she applied detective tactics to finding out facts about interesting boys. Then, when she talked to them, she could weave the information into her conversation.

Cathy's strategy was different, however. When she wanted to get a boy to notice her, which she never found difficult, she simply flirted with him. She seemed to have a knack for figuring boys out, for tuning in to their personalities. In this case, though, she wasn't going to bother. She wasn't interested in getting John Crowley to notice her. They would get to know each other soon enough, and, anyway, she was already certain he wasn't her type.

Her type was a popular, outgoing boy, who liked to go to parties and football games, and, above all, liked to dance. Cathy dated regularly but so far, had never fallen for any-one. She thought it was sort of scary to get that involved with a boy. She had seen what happened to her friends when they fell in love—they couldn't concentrate on anything else, and they were crushed if things didn't work out. She was certain she wasn't ready to go through that yet, if ever. She never wanted to lose control over a relationship the way she had seen other girls do, or be inseparable from a boy. At least this way, Cathy knew she wouldn't be the one to get hurt.

Tracy's deep voice cut into her thoughts. "I'm glad my folks aren't teachers. I'm sorry, Cath."

"Don't apologize. I understand. Believe me, I often wish they weren't teachers, either."

"If only you could think of a way to get them off your case." Jan sighed.

"You mean like a brain transplant?" asked Cathy.

"Oh, come on, Cathy," said Tracy. "We know you're no dummy. Just look at all the things you know how to do." She looked around

Cathy's room. "You can skate, you're a good photographer, you can dance—lots of things." She glanced at her watch. "Uh-oh, it's getting late. Sorry, Cath, we've got to go. Anybody you want us to kiss for you?"

Cathy stuck out her tongue. "Get out of here, will you? Kiss them all for me." She laughed, making a grand gesture with her arms.

"Oh, by the way," said Jan, "when is J.C.'s first tutoring session?"

It took Cathy a moment to figure out who Jan was talking about. She was always calling people by their initials. "Oh, you mean John Crowley. I don't know when he's coming."

"Good luck, anyway," Jan said, walking out of the bedroom.

"Thanks, I'll need it," Cathy said, following her friends down the hallway. At that moment Matt roared into the driveway on his go-cart.

"See you!" Cathy shouted above the din. "And have a good time for me."

Chapter Three

At school on Monday Cathy looked around for John Crowley but didn't see him. She wasn't really sure she knew what he looked like, but she thought it would be nice to find out so that she didn't have such an unformed image of him in her mind.

During lunch, conversation consisted entirely of what had happened at Lisa Shuler's party.

"I couldn't believe it," Jan was saying. "Rob McKay and Tracy danced together *all night*. And God only knows what happened when he took her home."

Tracy jabbed Jan in the ribs with her elbow. Tracy was the only one of the three whose embarrassment didn't show itself like a red banner. "Cut it out, Jan," she warned. "Nothing happened after we left. We just"— her eyes grew misty—"kissed."

"Oooh. When are you going to see him again?"

Picking a piece of lint off her slacks, Tracy pretended to be casual. "Oh, probably in biology this afternoon."

They all started laughing.

"And what about you, Jan?" Tracy taunted. "You sure spent enough time talking to Eddie Harrington, in the dark corner next to the stereo."

"We were talking about records, Tracy." Jan made a big deal of pushing a comb through her curly, obstinate hair.

"Wendy and Phil got into a huge argument, as usual. Lisa had to ask them to leave."

"Why'd she do that? They always put on a good show." Cathy grinned, imagining the couple at each other's throats. If ever there were two natural-born actors, they were Wendy and Phil. They couldn't go out for a hot dog without creating a big scene, but to everyone watching, it was kind of entertaining.

Cathy admired people who could scream their heads off in public and get everything off their chests, then feel great afterward. Her parents were the sort who didn't argue much at all, believing that most disputes could be solved by discussion. But Cathy thought they dismissed too many things just for the sake of keeping peace. They enjoyed silence and protected it at any cost, even if they had to ignore problems to do so. If either she or Matt blew up at home, they were always met with their parents' combined wall of frigid disapproval.

"I found out that J.C. is in the one and only fourth year Spanish class," said Jan, her mouth full.

"What? What's that got to do with anything?"

"Well, you know he's a real brain if he's in fourth year Spanish, Cath. There are only about eight kids in the class. You have to pass first, second, and third year to get into it. They're reading stuff like *Don Quixote*."

"I just wonder what I can do to spice up the tutoring. I mean, algebra is so deadly dull. Even writing the numbers in different-colored ink isn't going to do much for it."

"Who knows? John might be a nice guy, even if he's out of it," suggested Tracy.

"I don't know. Maybe I can tell jokes or something."

The thought of spending an hour bent over an algebra text with a boring boy at her side was enough to make Cathy start squirming.

After school Cathy went home and fixed herself some chocolate milk and cookies. It

21

was ten to four, and her mother would be home soon, and shortly after that, John would arrive. She laid her report card on the kitchen table. It was dogeared, because she'd been nervously twisting the corners between her thumb and forefinger all day.

At that moment her mother's station wagon drove into the garage. Cathy went to her room to brush her hair. The doorbell rang, and she hurried to answer it, thinking that her mom had forgotten her key.

"Uh, hello. I'm John Crowley. Is this the Meyers residence?"

The tall, lanky boy on the doorstep shifted the stack of books from one arm to the other before stepping inside. Cathy was startled. He was handsome! He had dark hair, cut shorter than most of the boys she knew, a long, slender nose, and a strong, angular jaw. He did wear glasses, as she had guessed, but they seemed to set off his dark brown, almond-shaped eyes.

Cathy's first thought was: why haven't I noticed this guy before?

Slightly thrown off guard because her idea of what he would look like had been so wrong, she needed a moment to gather her composure enough to speak—which was unusual for her.

"Oh, hi. I'm Cathy, the resident math genius. Come on in."

The click of her mother's low-heeled, sensible shoes sounded across the linoleum. "Oh, hello, John. I see you've already met our Cathy."

"Our Cathy." Cathy's ears burned at the pet phrase. Her mother's fingers touched her elbow, and her smile, expressly meant for John, was that of a person who has just met a comrade after days of battling with some enemy. John was on the side of the teachers, while Cathy was definitely in the league of incorrigible students.

"I was about to make some lemonade. Would you like some, John?" Sybil Meyers asked.

"Uh, yes. That would be nice, thank you," John replied formally.

Cathy drew in her breath. Lemonade, how cute. John seemed so stilted yet so gorgeous. She sneaked another look into those big brown eyes and wondered what he'd look like without his glasses.

"I think the study would be the best place for you two to work, don't you, Cathy?" Sybil said as the frozen lemonade plopped into a plastic pitcher. "There's a nice desk in there and lots of light."

"Or outside," suggested Cathy. "Do you ever do your homework outside, John? I always find that fresh air really gears up my brain. How about you?"

He replied very seriously, "No, I don't. I usually study in my room."

"How original," Cathy muttered under her breath.

Cathy's mother placed two tall glasses on a tray. "Here you go. And here are some cookies Matt made last night."

"Sugar cookies—my favorite," John commented, following Cathy and the tray into the den.

Sugar cookies and lemonade. This boy is just *too, too* far out for me, Cathy thought. Well, she considered, he surprised me once, maybe can surprise me again. And *he is definitely good looking.*

She placed the tray on her father's desk. "This is the place," she announced.

"Your mother was right. This is a good place to work, don't you think?"

Mom is just going to love this guy, I can tell, thought Cathy, as she watched him sit down stiffly in one of the leather chairs.

"Terrific!" Cathy agreed, with mock enthusiasm, but John didn't seem to notice he was

24

being teased. "Well, what do we do first? she asked him.

"Well, why don't you tell me what you're having trouble with, and maybe we can work on it."

Right down to business. At least he could have asked her what her favorite subject was. She wondered if he was aware that he was staring at her peach-painted toenails.

John cleared his throat nervously. "Maybe you could show me your homework and your algebra book?"

"Oh, sure. Just a sec." Cathy skipped off to her room and brought the textbook to him. "Here. Pages two twenty-one through two twenty-four. That's what we're working on now."

Casually perched on the wide arm of his chair, Cathy leaned slightly over him as he read. She was sure her closeness bugged him, so it didn't surprise her when he suggested, a little stiffly, "Shouldn't you find your own chair?"

"Oh, yeah. Sure." Quickly she spun around and flopped into the chair directly across from him, where she could watch him better.

"Where did you start having trouble with algebra, Cathy?" John inquired evenly.

"In Mr. Marcus's class, the very first day." It was the sort of Goldie Hawn answer she was famous for. She studied John's impressive profile to see how he would react. He didn't. What did it take to loosen somebody like him up? she wondered. "I've never been very good at math, but algebra is just impossible for me."

"Do you understand sets and subsets?" he asked, flipping through the book.

She shrugged. "It kind of goes in one ear and out the other. They're so uninteresting they don't stick."

"Uninteresting? I think math is really challenging."

She stared at him as if he had a screw loose, and she wondered whether he was putting her on. There was the slightest twinkle in his eye—or was it just the reflection off his glasses?

John went on. "But I think I understand your problem. A lot of girls are afraid of math. I think it's the way they're brought up. They think they're not supposed to be interested in stuff like that. And it's too bad, because there's no reason why girls can't do as well as boys in algebra, or anything else, for that matter. I—"

"Wait a minute!" Cathy interrupted. "Me?

26

Afraid? Are you kidding? Listen carefully, John," she said slowly, as if explaining something to a child, "the reason I hate math is because *math is boring!* Besides, I happen to have better things to do with my time than play around with sets and subsets. And another thing, I am not 'a lot of girls.' I'm me. Okay?"

But John kept right on talking, as if he hadn't heard a word she'd said. "Anyway, math just might come in handy someday when you're looking for a job. A lot of people are finding they need to go back to school and take calculus and trig in order to get promotions."

"Well, I don't think that applies to me." Cathy let out a sigh and tossed her hair over her shoulders.

"Why not? What are your plans for the future?"

"Plans? What plans? I'm only sixteen, you know. I don't have to have my future all mapped out already." The question made her a little uneasy, though, so she fired it back at John. "All right, Mr. Mathematics, what do *you* want to do?"

"I want to be a doctor," he told her simply.

I should have known, she thought. Why does he always have to have an an answer for everything? "Well, I've still got a lot of time to decide what I'm going to do. And meanwhile, I just want to have fun."

"Well, you seem like a smart girl. You can be or do anything you want, you know, if you take things seriously."

Cathy glared at him, remembering her parents' concern and the way they kept telling her she had to be more serious about studying if she wanted to go to college. She was sure she had plenty of time to decide about college and plenty of time to get her grades up if she had to. But John's certainty seemed to underline what her parents had told her and to increase her own insecurity. "Gee, John," she said teasingly, "that's the most romantic thing any boy has ever said to me. I hope you don't say that to all the girls."

He changed the subject abruptly. "So, let me see you work some of these problems," he said, handing her the algebra book. "Then I can get an idea of what you can do."

Cathy scanned the page, her brain closing up shop at the sight of the equations she'd never really looked at. "I can't do any of these without help," she admitted.

John bent over the algebra book and launched into a long, detailed explanation of sets of integers, but Cathy lost his drift entirely. Instead, she stared at his square-nailed fingers and at the golden hairs on the back of his hands that glistened under the lamplight as he moved. She also liked how his hair curved neatly against his neck and had a slight wave to it.

"Do you understand?"

When John looked expectantly at her, all she could do was shake her head. "John, don't you ever smile?"

"Of course I do." He managed a quick, self-conscious smile, just to prove to her he had the ability. "When there's something to smile about. You brought your homework, too, right?"

"Yes. Here." She yanked a mimeographed sheet from the book.

"Okay." Again, John explained each problem patiently, looking to Cathy for the answers.

If he had asked her for a description of his hands or the way he held a pencil, she could have given it readily. As it was, all she could do was smile and make wisecracks. "Do you get paid by the hour or by the problem?" she asked.

"Cathy, will you cut out the jokes and pay attention?" His patience was starting to wither. "Now did you see how I got that?"

"I saw it all right, but I sure didn't understand it."

He explained once more how he had arrived at the answer.

At last John and Cathy were finished, the homework done, ready to turn in to Mr. Marcus the next day. While Cathy slipped her homework paper back in her book, her fingers accidentally—or slightly on purpose—touched John's, and he drew back quickly, as if he'd touched fire.

Cathy stole a glance at him and noted that his color had risen to the roots of his dark hair. Ah-hah! she thought. He's not just a human computer after all.

"I guess I'll see you tomorrow," John said as they walked to the front door.

"Okay." Cathy leaned against the doorjamb and watched him walk down the path to his bike.

On impulse, she yelled out, "John!"

He turned in surprise, nearly losing his footing.

"Smile!" She smiled Cheshire cat-style—something she'd practiced in the mirror so often she knew how to do it without looking.

John stared at her with an expression that was half laugh and half grimace, but then, he managed a brief smile as he hopped on his bike and waved goodbye.

Well, what had happened? Cathy had planned to be bored, not interested. Math still wasn't interesting, but John was. She had expected him to be ordinary looking, but he was sensational looking, even if he didn't have any idea he was.

And, he certainly wasn't like any of the other boys Cathy knew—which left her pleasantly confused.

Chapter Four

"What's he like?"

Cathy shrugged as she twisted Jan's hair onto an electric roller. "He's good looking, believe it or not. I sure was surprised when I saw him on the doorstep. Only trouble is, he's fascinated by math."

"That's not all bad." Tracy sat on the edge of the bathtub, watching. "Maybe he'll be a famous scientist someday. Is he interested in sports or anything like that?"

"I don't know. He doesn't say much about himself. We just talked about algebra. He did say he wants to be a doctor."

"We just asked what he did for fun," Jan said, "not what his life's ambitions are."

"How am I supposed to know?" Cathy giggled. "He's strictly business, Jan."

"Who does he hang around with?" Tracy wanted to know.

"I don't know. Hold still, Jan." Cathy

pushed in a thick bobby pin to secure one of the curlers. "Boy, your hair has a mind of its own."

"That's what it keeps telling me," wailed Jan, and they all laughed.

"Can't you just imagine Derek or Tom Williams tutoring you? Or Tim Bryant?" Jan rolled her eyes. "You'd never get any work done, Cathy. No wonder your parents chose J.C. I know those guys are really smart, but their brains never get in the way of having a good time."

"Yeah. *They're* all good students, and *they* still manage to play sports and go to parties," Cathy said thoughtfully. "I guess they don't make a steady diet of studying. I mean, John just seems so—serious. The guy hardly ever smiles."

"That's really something," Tracy marveled. She took an apothecary jar full of polished stones from the shelf and picked through them. "You get smiles out of a boy pretty easily, Cathy. Ms. Personality Plus, that's you. You know so much about boys you could write one of those advice columns in the newspaper. I'm sure your advice would be better than theirs. Hey, maybe you'll be a world-famous psychologist some day."

"I'd rather be a world-famous actress. That would be a lot more fun," Cathy said dramatically.

"How about the first woman president?" Jan suggested. "I can just see you out on the campaign trail."

"Listen to you guys," Cathy complained. "Even you're bugging me about my future now. Why can't anyone just let me enjoy being sixteen for awhile? Anyway, getting back to John, he did smile a little, but I just don't think there's any chemistry between us." Then she remembered that second when their fingers had touched. But she didn't mention it to her friends. She squirted some setting lotion on Jan's hair and mopped up the drips that ran down her neck. "I wonder if he's got a girlfriend."

"He's a senior, isn't he?"

"Yeah, I think so."

"Marcia Hutton. She's been nominated valedictorian," supplied Tracy. "She sounds like his type."

Cathy visualized Marcia's pert, owlish face next to John's and tried to imagine the two holding hands or dancing, but the image seemed cartoonish. "No. They'd both be too embarrassed to fall for each other."

"Marcia's nice, but she's in love with Shakespeare," Tracy said. Marcia was the only girl in Sierra Heights who could give a believable portrayal of Ophelia. She really got into her part.

Jan squealed. "Can't you just imagine kissing a guy who talked in prose like that?"

"Sort of like Cyrano de Bergerac," dreamed Tracy.

"What difference does it make how the guy talks when you're kissing him, Jan?" Cathy demanded.

Tracy started laughing so hard that she slid from the edge of the tub to the fluffy pink bath rug. "You are crazy!" she sputtered.

"I recall having very little to say to Jack Engel when we were going out," Cathy said, unplugging the rollers. "He kissed so well, words would've been a waste of time."

"He still does kiss well, I hear," maintained Jan. "His lips will soon be world famous. By the way, Tim Bryant asked me about you, Cath. Look what you're missing, holed up here at home."

"Tim Bryant had arrived at Sierra in the fall as a new student and had received a lot of attention from the female population there already. "What did Tim say?" Cathy asked.

She had known for several weeks that he'd been eyeing her.

"He asked me if you were dating anyone, and I said no. I told him you were grounded, and he just said, 'Oh.' He sounded disappointed."

"How can you tell he was disappointed from just an 'oh'?" Cathy was skeptical. "Are you sure you're not reading more into the conversation than really exists?"

Jan shook her head. "I know a disappointed boy when I see one."

"He's awfully cute, Cathy," Tracy cooed.

"How long are you grounded for, Cath?" asked Jan.

"Until I get a good grade on my next algebra test. I have to show signs of improvement."

"Let's see how no parties, no dances, no boys affects you," Jan directed a painted fingernail at her. With hairpins protruding at odd angles from her rollers, Jan looked like a Martian. "You'll be itching to get loose in another week."

"Yeah, you're probably right." Cathy rose and slipped on her thongs. She thought of John's dark brown eyes, so full of concentration while he patiently explained problems to her. She pictured him masterfully juggling

36

numbers and tossing them to her, except that she kept fumbling with them and dropping them all over the floor.

Could she ever learn anything from him? She could never learn to concentrate the way he did, but she at least had to get through this semester. With boys, social stuff, and most of her schoolwork, Cathy was pretty sure of herself. But now, with algebra—and John Crowley—a flutter of doubt crept in where only self-confidence had been. Quickly Cathy brushed those disquieting thoughts aside. One hour five days a week with John was bound to make a difference.

She turned to Jan. "Come on. Let's go outside and watch your hair curl."

"John's coming after dinner tonight," Cathy announced at dinner, having just talked to him briefly on the phone.

It was a disappointing conversation. He was Mr. Business and had only said what he needed to say, nothing more. Cathy didn't really know why she felt he should have said more, especially since he'd be at her home right after dinner but still, the conversation seemed too abrupt.

37

"John is such a nice boy, isn't he?" Sybil Meyers said as she spooned peas onto her husband's plate. "Don't you like him, Cathy?"

She glared at the bold brown line around the edge of her stoneware plate. "I guess so. I hardly know him. One tutoring session does not a friendship make, Mother."

"His father suffered a back injury recently, you know. He's recuperating from surgery now. I suppose John's trying to earn some extra money for the family."

"No, I didn't know," Cathy said. "John didn't mention his family."

"Did you do better on your homework, Cathy?" her father asked.

Cathy rolled her eyes and motioned that her mouth was full.

"Wait," Matt interjected on her behalf. "Can't you see the poor girl's masticating her food?"

"Is that one of your vocabulary words for this week?" Stephen Meyers inquired with amusement.

"It's a bonus word, Dad. I've got to think up sentences for all of them," Matt explained.

Cathy cleared her throat noisily to get their attention. "If anyone's still interested, I didn't get my homework back yet, but John did help me with it, and, yes, I think I did better."

"Bravo." Her father smiled. "Mr. Marcus ought to be happy about that."

John was wearing a light blue pinstriped shirt with dark blue cords, which looked nice on him, Cathy thought. Except that John never looked casual. Other boys could somehow make the same combination look casual, but not John.

Cathy sat across from him on a cushioned rattan chair.

"I never see you around school, John. Do you spend a lot of time at the library counting the books?" Cathy propped her chin in her palm and waited expectantly for his answer. She had put on green eyeshadow and new mascara, hoping he would notice that something was different about her.

"Sometimes."

She winked. "You sound so mysterious. Do you play sports or anything?"

"No, I don't." Looking uncomfortable, he crossed and recrossed his ankles, then opened a book in his lap. "I do play chess."

"I'm glad to hear you play something." She couldn't resist a smile.

His blush rose from his collar. "Let's do some algebra, Cathy."

"Okay, okay," Cathy agreed. "I just didn't want to jump right into it, you know? My heart can't take so much excitement all at once. You're my only contact with the outside world, and I've got to make the most of it, you know. I'm grounded until I get a decent grade on the next algebra test. Did my folks tell you?"

He shook his head.

"We have them every two weeks, so I'm hoping to up my score on the next one."

"I think it might help if you changed your attitude a little."

"It sounds like *you've* been taking lessons from my parents. You have this funny way of sounding *exactly* like them. Look, I can have fun and still get by. I've done it all through school . . . Besides, you're going to help me."

"I can't pass algebra for you, Cathy. You've got to do some of the work yourself. Don't think I'm going to save you."

"Thanks a lot. It's nice to know my tutor has so much confidence in me."

John sighed. "Why don't we just cut out the personal stuff and get down to work, okay?"

"It's okay with me. Go ahead, Professor Crowley, sir."

". . . Apply the distributive law and re-write each collection of symbols without parentheses as illustrated in the examples."

He handed her a freshly sharpened pencil.

Cathy accepted the pencil daintily. "Why, thank you." After dinner, she had changed into a sleeveless white T-shirt that showed off the beginning of a tan. Now, she was getting cold and excused herself to get a sweater.

When Cathy returned, John looked annoyed, but he didn't say anything. She concentrated for a few minutes on one problem, then said softly, "I need your help, John. I can't do this."

Seeming reluctant, he moved closer to her to help. "Look, all you have to do is add five plus two, then multiply by three."

Slowly, Cathy worked several problems. And John stayed next to her the whole time.

"There!" She finally sat back and handed him her work.

He studied the sheet carefully. "This one is good, Cathy, but the others are wrong."

Cathy frowned at him. "What do you mean, wrong? I did what you said!"

"Well, let's go back over them." Patiently, he showed her what she had done wrong. Then together they arrived at the correct answer.

"How exciting," said Cathy under her breath, not without sarcasm.

"You're doing great," John said, consulting

41

his watch, which let her know there wasn't much time left.

She was amazed at how good those few words of praise from him made her feel. "You really think so?"

"Sure."

Cathy stared at him, noting how his eyebrows were hidden by the tortoise-shell rim of his glasses.

"You know, John," she said teasingly, "most girls would probably want you to take off your glasses, but I think you look terrific with them on."

"Oh, I guess you don't want to see me turn into Superman, then, huh?" John said with a straight face.

She laughed. "You're funny, John. Did you know that?"

He stacked up his books, ready to leave. "No one has ever called me funny before, Cathy. I'm not a funny person."

"Maybe you are, and just don't know it. I think you have a hidden fantastic sense of humor," Cathy ventured, "Who are your friends? Maybe their funniness has rubbed off on you," she joked, but it was also a sly way of getting information.

"Do you know Paul Eisley and Jud Donnalan?" he asked, placing his pencil in his shirt pocket.

"No."

"Those are my friends," he told her, the corners of his mouth tilting slightly upward with only the hint of a smile. "And now, I've got to go. See you tomorrow."

"'Bye."

After he was gone, Cathy lingered in the study, thinking: Wow, he's even got a sense of humor buried deep down under all those equations. John Crowley is certainly full of surprises.

Chapter Five

When Cathy arrived at school the next morning, there was a noisy commotion in the hallway, and she couldn't get to her locker.

"What's up?" she asked Lisa Shuler, who was craning her neck to see over a sea of heads.

"Somebody put a bra over the George Washington bust in the display cabinet," Lisa informed her.

"You're kidding. Do they know who?" Cathy, being short, had to stand on tiptoes to catch a glimpse of Ms. Fisher, guidance counselor, extracting the bra from the cabinet, getting the strap hooked on Washington's nose en route.

"Of course not. It was probably some freshman, though. Who else would do such an immature thing?"

Cathy laughed. Lisa behaved as though immaturity was a sin, she thought, stopping at her locker, then hurrying to her algebra class.

Mr. Marcus, Cathy's algebra teacher, was a good friend of her father's, and close to the same age. He looked older to Cathy, though, with stripes of gray hair on either side of his head. Ever since he told her father about her grade in his class, she had considered him to be against her. She behaved all right in class—well, maybe she talked a little more than she should. But even when she was quiet, Mr. Marcus always managed to look at her with a slight air of disapproval, which really bothered her.

Now she passed her homework paper forward, feeling relief that she'd done the work and knowing that it was probably correct, too. What would she do without John? Actually, he'd done most of the work. She smiled to herself, thinking about how cute he looked when he was concentrating.

On the inside cover of her notebook, Cathy absentmindedly wrote the names Paul Eisley and Jud Donnalan, then doodled around the two names. Those were John's friends. What were they like? Were they as serious as he was? Even she had to admit, her experience with this type of boy was limited—she who could attract nearly any boy she wanted.

Cathy clapped a cold palm to her cheek, as if trying to bring herself to her senses. What was she thinking? Why should she be concerned with attracting John, anyway? He was—well, he was a challenge, that's what he was, and sort of a mystery, too. Besides, he really was good looking. But she certainly didn't want to get serious about him. It was just fun imagining the possibilities. If she ever got to know John and he liked her back, the excitement would fizzle out of their relationship like carbonation out of an open soft drink, just the way it had with all the other boys.

When the bell rang, Cathy jumped out of her seat and made a dash for the door. Often her dad would come to Mr. Marcus' room after first period to talk, and she didn't want to run into him today.

"Hey, Cath." Derek Sorenson clapped her on the back, tipping her slightly forward.

"Derek, you have the heaviest hands of anybody I know!" Cathy exclaimed, recovering herself.

"Oh, sorry, I forgot. I don't know my own strength." He looked bashful. "I wanted to know if you wanna go rafting this weekend? Marty's taking us out again this Saturday."

Her parents' restriction tightened invisibly around her. "Oh, you know I'd love to, Derek, but I'm grounded. Didn't you know? I'm pretty sure I can't go."

He shook his head in dismay. "Too bad. Love to have you aboard, you know. Can't you talk 'em out of it?" His face was hopeful.

"No. It's because of my math grade. I have to bring up my algebra before they'll let me off," she explained.

"Well, I'll be thinking of you as we race over that white water." He grinned.

"I'll be thinking of you, too." Ahead, Cathy spotted John standing in a triangle of sunlight at the end of the hall. It was the first time she'd seen him at school. "See you, Derek," she said absently, hurrying toward John.

He was talking to two boys she didn't know.

"John!" she called, waving to him.

His head jerked up. The sound of her voice had obviously startled him. "Oh—uh—Cathy, hello. How are you?" You couldn't exactly say John sounded pleasantly surprised, but that didn't stop Cathy.

"Oh, you know me, John, laughing on the outside, crying on the inside, as usual. Hey, do you realize this is the first time we've ever met in public?"

"Yeah, well, I guess it is." He looked like a trapped animal desperate for escape. Cathy noticed the other two boys eyeing her with curiosity and interest. But John made no move to introduce them. In fact, he seemed to be trying hard to pretend that the whole episode wasn't happening. But Cathy plunged ahead. "So, these must be the friends you were telling me about." She turned to a freckle-faced boy of about her own height. "Hi, I'm Cathy Meyers."

"Oh, yeah, Mr. Meyers' daughter, aren't you?"

She sighed and flipped her hair over her shoulder. "Why is it I'm only recognized as 'Mr. Meyers' daughter'? What if he was Cathy Meyers' father? How would that be?"

The boy blushed, making his freckles all the more prominent. "Sorry. I didn't mean to offend you."

"Oh, no big deal," Cathy said.

"I'm Jud Donnalan, by the way," the boy said.

Cathy grinned. "Nice to meet you, and nice of John to forget to introduce us." She shot a half-smile John's way.

The other boy chuckled and looked at John.

John cleared his throat. "Well, Cathy—" he

48

began, but she cut him off, turning her attention to the other boy.

"And you must be Paul." Cathy smiled. Paul, a milky-skinned, towheaded boy, nodded and said hi.

"Well, listen, would you like to go out for a Coke after school, instead of meeting at my house, the way we usually do?" she suggested, looking directly into his dark eyes. Jud and Paul were getting more and more curious, but Cathy didn't notice them. A thrill passed through her as, for once, John looked right back into her eyes and gave her his full attention. But it only lasted a second, and then he was backing away again.

"Look, Cathy, my next class is in there, and I'm going to be late, and so are you." He nodded toward one of the art rooms.

She was vaguely aware of Paul and Jud shuffling into class. By John's body language, she could tell that he more than half wanted to be in his classroom. In fact, about three-quarters of him wanted to be sitting in front of that teacher, and only one-quarter wanted to talk to her.

"Well, do you want to?" Cathy persisted, clutching her binder demurely against her chest, following him to the door. He was looking intently at her again. Then the bell rang above them, making John jump. But Cathy stood her ground.

"Look, I can't ... I'm sorry. I'll see you later ... 'Bye. I'm late." He was gone.

Unbelievable, Cathy thought, as she trudged down the stairs. Any other boy would have been happy with her invitation—but not John.

That evening, when he came to tutor her, Cathy said casually, "I guess you had something to do after school today?"

"My father asked me to come straight home from school," he replied, not looking up from the algebra homework he was correcting.

"Oh, are you in trouble?" In Cathy's book, having your dad summon you straight home from school meant trouble.

"No, nothing like that. He just needed me to drive him somewhere."

From the closed look on John's face, Cathy knew it was the end of that conversation.

What bugged her was why he didn't take a rain check on her offer. Why did he say absolutely nothing about it? Was he just too shy or embarrassed?

It might be the end of the conversation, Cathy decided, but it was only the beginning of the J.C. Mystery.

Chapter Six

"You got a B on an algebra test. Cathy, you've really made some progress!" Stephen Meyers praised his daughter. He lay the test paper on the coffee table. "John must be just the right tutor for you."

She shrugged. It annoyed her how her parents wanted to take credit for everything. They chose John, therefore they were the ones responsible for her good grade. "He helps," she replied. "He's madly in love with numbers, and he's trying to make me see how wonderful they are, too. Have I got news for him."

"John's a nice boy, don't you think?" Sybil smoothed the Indian print skirt she wore, which looked to Cathy like a garage sale find. Knowing her mother, it probably was.

"Sure, he's nice. Kind of boring, though."

"That's unfair, Cathy. And you know what John must be going through with his family right now." Sybil Meyers frowned disapprovingly.

"I don't know anything about him, Mom. He never talks about himself to me."

It was completely true. In the two weeks she'd been working with John, as much as she had tried to unearth something about his personal life, they had never talked about him, only about algebra. Cathy suspected that he was inclined to confide more in her parents than in her, which for some reason made her slightly jealous. They were just parents, for crying out loud, not friends.

She had tried to draw him out, flirting with him a little, and more than once she had detected a flicker of interest on that intelligent, watchful face. But then, he always seemed to back away. She couldn't figure him out. Oh, well, at least she hadn't lost her touch with other boys.

"Since I'm doing so well with my algebra, can I go out tomorrow night, maybe?" Cathy asked casually. Tim Bryant had asked her to go with him to a dance at the school. She had waited to get her parents' permission until she had got her algebra test score. Now she held her breath, praying they'd say yes.

"Oh, dear. I don't know." Sybil Meyers looked to her husband for a reply.

Cathy's father sucked thoughtfully on his pipe. "I suppose so. You do deserve a night out, and we did promise we'd lift the restriction if your grade improved. But—" he adopted a sudden, stern tone— "this doesn't mean we're back to the old fun and games, young lady. No more all play and no work. You're still going to have to work hard on that math, so there will be no going out on school nights."

"Sure, I know. Thanks, Dad." She went to her room to phone Tim.

He was extremely popular, and Jan and Tracy were both drooling when she told them he had asked her out.

"You're looking good, Cathy," Tim complimented her as he held open the door of his orange Karmann Ghia. Tim Bryant was tall with dark, curly hair, and a perfect muscular build.

"Why, thank you, so are you." She smiled and fluttered her eyelashes.

Cathy did look good, with her bangs combed to one side and her hair gently curled at the ends. She had on a red blouse with billowy sleeves and a Hawaiian print skirt—since the theme of the dance was Hawaiian.

Suddenly she started wondering how John would like her outfit. Then she remembered who she was with and nestled closer to Tim.

"Hey, that's nice," he commented.

Cathy looked at him. "You're getting a great tan," she said. "Are you out in a sun a lot?"

"Yeah, pretty much." He shrugged. "I'm pretty athletic."

"You're a center on the basketball team, right?" she cooed.

"Well, yeah. I spend a lot of time inside a gym, too, you know." He turned and winked at her, and she flashed a smile at him.

"That Hawaiian shirt really shows off your tan," Cathy added.

"Oh—thanks," he replied, obviously flattered.

Cathy was glad to see she hadn't lost her touch.

"What were you grounded for, Cathy?" Tim asked as they parked in back of the auditorium where the dance was being held.

"My report card. Algebra, mainly. But I've got a tutor who's helping me." The air was

54

growing chilly, so she slipped on her sweater.

"Why didn't you ask me? I'd tutor you." He grinned at her and slid an arm around her shoulders.

"My parents chose my tutor. He's good. Do you know John Crowley?"

Tim frowned in concentration. "Oh, yeah. I know him. *He's* tutoring you? He's in my trig class."

"Oh, really?"

"Did you know John won a CSF scholarship?" Tim held her hand as they strolled into the auditorium.

"No, I didn't know," Cathy replied, feeling a twinge of jealousy. Why did everyone in the world seem to know more about John than she did? "John never tells me anything."

"I just happened to know because Pete Price got one, too, and he's a close friend of mine." He squeezed her shoulders. "But wouldn't you rather have me? I bet John's kind of dull, isn't he?"

Cathy didn't answer as they passed under the straw arch that was supposed to look like a grass shack but looked more like a lopsided arrangement of hay bales. Fortunately, there wasn't time to dwell on Tim's question, for they were greeted by Tracy and her new interest, Rob McKay. Jan was with Eddie Harrington, and they waved from across the dance floor, then came over.

"Hi, you two." Jan winked at Cathy. "So you got out of the house, huh, Cathy? This is going to be a great dance."

"I hope so. I have to make the most of tonight, since I'm not allowed to go out during the week."

They talked for a few more minutes. Then Tim suggested that he and Cathy head for the refreshment table. Jan took Eddie's hand, and they went off to dance again.

After Tim had sampled everything at the refreshment table, he and Cathy danced. Cathy loved to dance, and she was good at it, having taken lessons for a year and a half. The rhythm got under her skin and moved her almost of its own will, and she flowed with it as if she were going for a ride. When she danced, she came to life, momentarily forgetting everything else, except the music and her partner.

Tim's hazel eyes shone with admiration as he spun her around and around. Cathy's heart rose into her throat as she looked at him. He was so good looking—every girl's dream of an ideal date. And he was a good dancer, too, though she knew he was not her equal.

She wondered if John danced. . . .

Cathy and Tim danced almost every dance and Cathy was sorry when the evening was over. Tim suggested driving along by the river. It was a balmy, romantic night. The headlights blazed a bright path through the darkness. They could see tiny waves glittering by moonlight, and on the horizon, pines merging with a starless, deep purple sky, creating a feeling of immensity that took Cathy's breath away.

At Cathy's house, they sat in the car, talking quietly. Tim draped an arm around Cathy's shoulders, stroking the silky sleeve of her blouse. Then he turned to kiss Cathy good night and drew her eagerly into his arms. Her pulse leaped when his lips touched hers.

The thought stole, unbidden, from the back of her mind: *how would John kiss me?*

And then, Tim's arms tightened around her, and she felt the hard ridges of his ribcage beneath his shirt, pressed close to her body. John's kisses would be altogether different, Cathy told herself. She imagined herself in his arms instead, running her fingers lightly along the spare contours of his face, memorizing them. . . .

A cricket's monotonous song, woven into the steady gurgle of the distant river, suddenly sounded loud to Cathy, reminding her of the time. Gracefully, she extracted herself from Tim's embrace.

"I'd better go in now," she whispered sweetly.

He grinned and kissed her one last time. "Okay, I wish you didn't have to. But see you Monday, okay?"

"Okay."

Cathy watched Tim's car roar off down the road before she slid the key into the lock and went inside.

Chapter Seven

"Do you like to dance, John?" Cathy leaned back in one of the leather chairs and watched John organize his lesson for the day.

"No, and I don't like loud music, fast cars, or football, either. I'm a total loser as a teenager, Cathy. I've got more important things—"

She was so furious she stopped him in mid-sentence. "Why do you always have to put other people down for having fun? Just because you don't know how to have a good time yourself."

"And why do you always try to embarrass me by asking silly questions when I'm trying to teach you something?"

"Well, maybe there are a few things I could teach *you* if you weren't afraid to learn—like how to dance, for instance."

"Look, Cathy. I'm here to do a job. I'm getting paid to teach you something. Maybe you don't care whether you learn anything, but I hate to take your parents' money for nothing.

Some of us do have to take life a little more seriously than you do, Cathy. Believe me."

She was ready to make another smart remark. But then she took a good look at him. He looked terrible, really exhausted and rundown. Why hadn't she noticed it before? "Listen, why don't we take a quick break, go out for ice cream, and then start all over, okay?" She smiled to show him there were no hard feelings.

John smiled back. "Okay. My treat."

At last, Cathy thought gleefully, he's coming under my spell.

Matt met them in the hallway and was immediately indignant. "Hey, where are you guys going? Knocking off early, I see? Aren't you supposed to study until five?"

"We're taking a break," explained John.

Matt grinned. "I bet I know whose idea this was. My dear sister's, that's whose." He made a face at Cathy.

Cathy returned an equally ugly face. "Just tell Mom we'll be back in a little while."

Away from her house, perhaps John would loosen up a little more, Cathy thought, walking beside him. She hoped so.

"There's an ice cream shop nearby —Sally's," she offered.

"Fine," John said.

"Would you call this a date?" Cathy asked teasingly.

"I call it a mid-afternoon break." He looked down at her, his long strides giving her the feeling that she was running to keep up with him.

"Do you have brothers and sisters?" she asked.

"Two sisters and a brother," he answered.

"I don't know about yours, but my brother drives me crazy."

"Mine's about the same age."

"Oh, yeah?"

"Yeah."

Cathy tried as hard as she could, but she could extract very little information from John. He answered her questions in as few words as possible.

Once inside the pink-and-white-striped ice cream shop, Cathy took an interminably long time to decide that, out of forty flavors, she wanted a vanilla ice cream soda. John rolled his eyes in exasperation.

"All that time to choose something so simple?"

"I could've chosen plain and simple vanilla ice cream," she reminded him, scooping out some of the ice cream with a long spoon.

John folded his hands in front of him on

the clear plastic tabletop. "I want to talk to you."

She grinned. "Go ahead. You want to know all about me, right?"

"No."

The word came out so abruptly, Cathy was taken aback, practically choking on her ice cream.

"I want to talk to you about your most un-favorite subject. You're bright, Cathy, and there's no reason in the world why you can't learn algebra if you want to. But it will take you twice as long if you keep goofing around like this." His dark eyes were so earnest.

"Like what? I thought we needed a break. You agreed." She tried to stop her voice from thinning into a whimper. She hated whimpering girls, and she suspected boys did, too.

"That's not the point, Cathy. You make it hard for me to teach you. You have to get that grade up, and just because you did so well on the last test doesn't mean you can relax now."

My fears exactly, John, she thought, but instead she put on a smile and said, "I'll do just fine, John. With you by my side, how can I go wrong?" Her fingernails grazed his palms, and she wiggled her fingers. "Tick-lish?"

He pulled his hands into his lap.

62

"I bet you are ticklish, aren't you?" she persisted, watching him while she took a sip of her soda. He didn't respond. "You're a very mysterious person, John. I mean, I know next to nothing about you!"

"Mystery is only a fringe benefit," he said darkly. "Algebra is what I'm paid to teach you."

She giggled. "You sound exactly like my father, you know that?"

"Cathy, you're making this difficult for both of us."

"You're beginning to repeat yourself."

"I mean it."

Her anger simmered very close to the surface. "I thought we were going to relax for a minute. But I don't think you're capable of it."

"And I don't think you're capable of being with a boy for five minutes without acting like a ridiculous flirt."

Cathy felt the anger spreading, pushing them apart. "John. . ." her voice was a stunned whisper that he cut off.

"Why am I spending my time trying to teach you what you don't want to learn? I may need the money, but I don't think it's worth it." His once softly expressive eyes now blazed at Cathy, making her wish she were invisible.

Her mouth dropped open, but no words would form. It was obvious that there was nothing she could do or say to alter what was happening. John stormed out of the shop, louvered doors banging behind him, his slender back rigid with anger.

Chapter Eight

Cathy had no more desire for her soda after John walked out, so she left it and shuffled dazedly back home. How could things have gone so wrong? She had really tried to help John relax. Why had he gotten so angry?

When she got home, she looked hopefully for John's old black bike, which he usually propped up against the brick planter at the side of the house. It wasn't there.

Stepping into the cool hallway, Cathy wondered what she should tell her mother and hastily sifted through the possibilities: a) John suddenly had got sick and had gone home; b) John had to get home early today and do something for his mother; or c) the truth—she and John had had a slight (?) disagreement.

"John left." Matt thrust his tousled head out of his room to report. "Just took off like a bullet on that old bike of his."

Cathy scowled. "Did he say anything?" The less said, the better.

"Nope. Not to me. He told Mom he had to get home early today, and not to pay him as much because he didn't put in very much time." Matt studied her closely, as if looking for something that would let him know what had really happened. "What's the matter? Did you have a fight or something?"

A wave of relief swept over Cathy—*Thank you, John, for not spilling the beans.* He had paved the way for her with Mom.

She was suddenly aware of Matt's piercing gaze. "Oh, uh, a fight? No, I don't fight with *John,*" she told him, as if the idea were unheard of.

"I heard you asking him if he danced. Geez, Cathy," Matt wagged his head in disgust.

"Eavesdropper. What do you know at thirteen?" she countered.

He grinned out of one side of his mouth, an oil smudge on his right cheek making him look comical. "You'd be surprised!" He laughed, then sauntered back into his room, which was a veritable pig's sty, in Cathy's opinion. You couldn't enter without breaking an ankle on an electronic game or a mechanical part. The closet doors were emblazoned

66

with decals and flourescent posters of cars and motorbikes; the dresser was covered with models in various stages of construction. For his birthday Cathy had bought him a notice that read: *Enter At Your Own Risk*, which was hung on the door.

Cathy went into her room and gazed out at the garden through her bedroom window. A bluejay hopped on a camellia bush and flitted from branch to branch. The whirlybird sprinkler flung drops against her windows, and she felt a stab of annoyance at her mother for placing the sprinkler too close to her room. Now her mother would make her clean the windows again soon.

Sometimes she could look outside and forget any troubles she might have—which had never been very many. She'd managed to breeze through adolescence without the problems many of her friends had. Good old Cathy, she was never down for long.

But today Cathy could not quiet her troubled and confused thoughts. The events of just forty-five minutes before played over and over again in her mind, and a sick, twisting ache of regret rose from her stomach. In the past she could usually tell in advance how people—especially boys—would react to her teasing. But with John, even when she was trying to be nice, her plans always backfired, and he ended up getting angry.

Restless and unable to study, Cathy tiptoed so nobody would hear her down the hall to the den, where she retrieved her algebra homework. John had left it neatly folded on top of her binder.

A lump rose in her throat as she gazed longingly at the leather chair where John had sat. She thought of his hands pale against the dark leather, his elbows jutting out, his expression serious as he talked about algebra.

Knowing that lump was holding back tears, Cathy quickly scooped up her things and went back to her room. Eager to get her mind off her misery, she dialed Jan's number.

Jan sounded strange, as if she were talking into a handkerchief.

"Are you disguising your voice?" Cathy teased her.

"No, eating a bologna sandwich. I've got to keep my strength up. Mom's threatening to make another casserole tonight, and I just can't swallow another bit of casserole!" she said emphatically. "So, how was old J.C. today?"

"That's what I want to talk to you about. Can you come over?"

"Sure, I'll be right there."

" . . . So he got up and stomped out of the ice cream parlor and just left me sitting there. I couldn't believe it."

"I guess you got him pretty upset," Jan commented. "What did you say, anyway?"

"Nothing; I was really trying to be nice and put him at ease. I just can't figure him out. I mean, you can't carry on a normal, everyday conversation with him like you can with other boys."

Jan glanced sideways at her friend. "Cathy, you never have been known to carry on a normal, everyday conversation with boys. Every word drips with honey—even to guys you don't like."

Cathy frowned. "You make me sound terrible."

"What's so terrible about it? I think you're just naturally flirtatious. Nothing wrong with it, really. Boys love it. You can see the marvelous results."

"Not anymore," Cathy said sadly.

"John's cute, but he's really not your type,

Cath. Take my word for it. Unless old J.C. has already broken your heart," she teased.

The corners of Cathy's mouth twisted against her will, as they did when she knew she was about to cry. "Don't be ridiculous." She tried to laugh, but the laugh emerged false and brittle.

Jan changed the subject. "Hey, are you going out with Tim this weekend?" she asked.

"He hasn't asked me."

"Derek says he's going to," Jan informed her.

Cathy smiled, recalling how Tim had pushed so urgently past other students in order to sit next to her during the assembly today at school; how their shoulders had touched, how he had drummed his fingers against the seat of the folding chair, while she'd wondered if he really wanted to hold her hand. But, for once, she'd had enough of thinking about boys.

"Am I ever hungry," she said.

"Ugh. I'm not in the mood for Monday casserole, I'll tell you that," grumbled Jan.

Cathy laughed. Jan's mother went on wild food binges whenever she bought new appliances or cookbooks. When she'd first purchased a new blender, everything was served pureed. They ate soup and stew for the month after she bought a slow cooker. Now her sister had bought her a casserole cookbook, so Mrs. Mason was still trying out new recipes on the family.

"No such luck," Jan complained grimly. "I hate my food all mushed together. It's like eating baby food. I mean, if I was one hundred years old and had very few teeth, perhaps I'd appreciate what she's doing for me."

"Maybe you can eat at my house," suggested Cathy. "I think it's a pretty safe bet my mom won't be fixing a casserole tonight. I saw some pork chops thawing." There was no telling what her mother would do with those chops, however. She experimented with so many different varieties of food you never knew what you'd be getting: Indian, African, Chinese, Mexican, Polynesian—the list was endless.

"Thanks for the invitation," Jan breathed. "I think you might've just saved my life."

The idea occurred to Cathy that having Jan for dinner would discourage her mother from asking about John.

John's words played back: *Cathy, you're making this difficult for both of us.* Jan had said she couldn't carry on a normal, everyday conversation with a boy without flirting. Was that really true?

It just couldn't be, she decided. Perhaps Jan was more correct in saying that John wasn't her type. *That* she could buy much more easily.

Chapter Nine

On Friday, Cathy took an algebra test, which she knew she did badly on. All week she'd been on edge, unable to concen-trate, antici-pating this failure and yet feeling helpless to do anything about it.

John had been no help, either, though he might have thought he was helping. "Are you sure you're ready for this test, Cathy? You've got to do well on this one, you know."

"I'm ready, I'm ready," she assured him, knowing she wasn't. Her mind was a million miles away, and she had grasped at any dis-traction from math: dawdling over clothes, shoes, and record albums.

And all week she thought about John. He didn't want her to be a flirt. But he *did* like her, she knew that. How could he like her and hate her at the same time?

After the math test, Tim Bryant asked Cathy if she wanted to double date with Rob and Tracy, and she readily accepted. Like a convict preparing to meet the executioner, she wanted to cram in as much fun as possible before the ax fell.

Then at lunch Tracy asked her if she wanted to spend the night afterward. "I bought two new albums," she said.

"Oh, sure. Why not?" Cathy grinned, knowing it would be the last time she'd be allowed to for a while.

Of course, the subject of algebra reared its ugly head before dinner, as she guessed it might.

"How did the test go today, Cathy?" her father inquired from the top of a stepladder. He was replacing a curtain rod.

Her mother was putting up applesauce, and the aroma of simmering apples filled the air. Home seemed extra "homey" tonight, and Cathy suddenly wished she didn't have this burning secret to keep from her parents. It made her feel apart from them, and a little ashamed.

Making an unnecessary amount of noise with the silverware, she finally sang out as casually as she could, "Oh, fine. I think I did well."

"Ed did say you were improving," Stephen Meyers said, descending the ladder.

Who else gets daily progress reports on their children, direct from the teacher? Cathy thought bitterly. Still, Mr. Marcus wouldn't see how badly she'd done on this test until he corrected papers this weekend. Just wait until Monday. . . .

She asked if she could spend the night at Tracy's.

"I suppose so, but you'll have to stay in Sunday to finish all your homework," her father warned.

"Can you do the French bread, Cathy?" Sybil Meyers asked. She was ladling steaming applesauce into mason jars. "I've still got a few more jars to fill here. I guess I'll freeze some apple pies, too."

"Now apple pie sounds fabulous." Cathy's father's eyes lit up, and she was glad to see the conversation moving away from algebra. "That's the most ordinary American thing you've thought of in a long time, Sybil."

Sybil Meyers smiled through steam. "Why, thank you, Stephen," she said, winking.

At first, Cathy was embarrassed to see her mother flirting with her father. Then she decided they should try it more often. She ran upstairs to get ready to go out.

* * *

The foursome chose to see a horror movie, which had Cathy and Tracy clinging to their dates' arms.

After the movie Rob grumbled good-naturedly, "Tracy grabbed me so hard I thought she'd rip my arm right off."

"Look at it this way, McKay. When do you ever get girls to cuddle so close?" said Tim.

"That's right." Cathy laughed. "I was ready to climb into your lap a couple of times."

"Why didn't you? You know I wouldn't have minded," Tim said, reaching for her hand. His touch warmed her, and she glanced up to find him gazing fondly down at her. Then, embarrassed, he looked away.

It wasn't hard to figure out that he liked her a lot. Cathy knew that look—she'd seen it on other boys' faces after she'd dated them a couple of times. Their features softened, and their eyes took on an I'd-do-anything-for-you expression. Girls often asked her, "How'd you do it?" as if she had some secret magic charm. Up until now she hadn't been able to answer that question, for it was something she didn't give much thought to. But then Jan's words spiraled through Cathy's mind. *Every word drips with honey—even to guys you don't like.* She put that unpleasant

76

thought out of her mind, however, as they drove to the Viewpoint.

The Viewpoint was a flat, remote turnout that overlooked the entire town, its sparse lights twinkling below like jewels pressed into black velvet.

The Viewpoint was where girls were asked to go steady, where couples broke up and got back together again, where secrets were shared and promises made and broken. Needless to say, it was a romantic place, enclosed by the comforting presence of dense pines and watched over by a star-encrusted sky.

Tim and Cathy sat in the back seat of Rob's car, kissing, while Rob and Tracy strolled along one of the many trails leading away from the Viewpoint.

Tonight, Tim's kisses became more fervent, traveling over her neck and face, sending chills up Cathy's spine, before she pushed him away. "Why don't we go for a walk?" she suggested, freeing an arm from his embrace to motion toward the trails.

"Oh, Cathy," Tim murmured, stroking her hair, which had picked up the static electricity from his shirt. "I really care about you."

Eyes shining, he leaned over to kiss her again, but Cathy inched across the seat to the door. Suddenly his affection seemed to be hemming her in. The tiny compact car with its fogged-in windows and Tim's breath against her cheek was stifling.

"Come on, Tim. It's a beautiful night. Let's walk," she urged.

"Okay," he agreed, but his voice was edged with disappointment.

Cathy smoothed her hair, feeling slightly nervous. She knew she didn't want to get any further involved with Tim. She knew she didn't want him to kiss her again. And she knew she had to find a way to let him know how she felt . . . and soon.

But she wouldn't do it tonight, Cathy decided, as she and Tim strolled along the wide, tree-canopied footpath together. The night was too beautiful, softly cushioning them in its balmy warmth—too beautiful to spoil with any sadness.

Later, after the boys had let Tracy and Cathy off at Tracy's house, the girls put on a stack of albums while Cathy set Tracy's glossy black hair.

Tracy made hot chocolate and toast, then the two lay in twin beds and talked.

"What do you think of Rob?" Tracy asked over and over again.

"He's cute. You know that. What do you want my opinion for?" Cathy finally answered, getting exasperated. "He seems to be crazy about you. So why worry?" She couldn't understand all this concern.

"Oh, he is not."

"Yes, he is, too. I know when a guy is crazy about a girl," Cathy assured her knowledgeably.

"Then you know Tim's crazy about you, too."

Cathy sighed deeply. "I know. I'm not excited about it, Tracy. You think you've got problems. Tim's a nice boy, there's nothing wrong with him that I can see. It's just . . . I don't want to get involved."

"But *why?* You're a cute couple." Tracy propped herself on one elbow to stare at her friend in amazement. "How can you be so unexcited? Haven't you ever felt really special about someone, Cathy?"

"No. I never wanted to, either."

"Do you like playing hard-to-get, is that it?" Tracy pursued. "I noticed you sort of doing that to Tim."

A thin thread of fear wove through Cathy's thoughts as Tracy tried to pinpoint her behavior with Tim. She laughed. "Hard to get?

79

No, I just had to cool him off, Tracy," she explained quickly. "Actually, I don't *play* hard-to-get, I *am* hard to get."

Tracy laughed. "I guess that's what keeps boys crazy about you. Does John have a crush on you, too?"

"I don't think so. He's in love with subsets and integers. He's really much too serious for me," she said.

"Cathy?"

"What?"

"I know you like him," Tracy said softly, her smile shining through the darkness.

"Ha ha," scoffed Cathy. But she did dream of John Crowley that night, his fingers tracing the outline of her lips before he kissed her.

Chapter Ten

Cathy filled her weekend with as much fun as she could, and even went rafting Saturday, but spent Sunday as her father had requested, studying. Attacking her algebra homework, she realized how far behind she'd fallen.

At noon, out of desperation, she phoned John. Wouldn't he be pleased she was asking for help?

Nobody was home at his house. Cathy toyed with the notion of phoning Tim, who would come charging over in a flash, but she thought better of it. There was no reason to encourage him when she didn't want him encouraged.

Alone, she sweated out one page of homework, while Monday morning grew menacingly closer with each passing minute.

On Monday Mr. Marcus handed back the test papers. He called out each student's name, and each had to walk up to the front of the class to receive his or her paper. Cathy squirmed in her seat, legs and fingers crossed, waiting. Why she crossed legs and fingers she didn't know—perhaps in the hope that by some miracle there was an A on her paper. The expressions worn by students returning to their seats were evidence of what kinds of grades they had received, and Cathy hoped her face wouldn't betray her in the same way.

"Cathy Meyers."

The clipped, curt way Mr. Marcus read out her name chilled her to the bone. Under the mossy cliff of his eyebrows, his blue eyes pierced her own.

"I expected better from you, Cathy," he remarked in a low voice, so that the knowledge did not have to be shared with the rest of the class.

"I'm sorry," she whispered, dropping her eyes to her paper. Her stomach twisted at the sight of the many check marks, vicious red slashes across the mimeographed sheet, and the fiercely bright D at the top of the paper.

A D minus! Just this side of an F, which, with a little less effort, it could have been.

Cathy felt sick. Angrily she shoved the test

paper into her binder, wishing she could simply crumple it into a tight ball and throw it in the trash. But, of course, she couldn't do that. The algebra test was the first thing her parents would ask about when she arrived home. There was absolutely no way out.

Quick, bitter strides ate up the distance between class and her locker. To Cathy's surprise John was standing in front of her locker. She forgot to wonder how he knew where her locker was.

"What are you doing here?" she demanded.

His brown eyes flicked over her quickly. "I just wondered how you did on your test."

"John, I'm trying to forget what I got on my test, if you don't mind."

He shifted his gaze to his wrist, but seeing he'd forgotten to wear his watch, he looked away. "I was just worried," he explained. "That bad, huh?"

Cathy jerked her head up to face him. Tears ached at the back of her throat. "Yeah. A D minus is pretty bad, isn't it?"

"Cathy," he said with alarm.

"You didn't have to ask, John," she returned coldly, whirling around to face her locker so that he didn't see the one slow tear sliding down her cheek.

John sighed. "I'm sorry, but I was afraid this would happen."

"Cathy, how could you?" was Sybil Meyers' exasperated response as she smoothed the test paper in front of her on the coffee table in the den.

"John worked so hard with you. I'm just terribly disappointed with this grade." Stephen Meyers wore his disappointment in the forward slump of his broad shoulders. He gave a tired sigh. "This is just inexcusable. What are we going to do with you?"

"I don't know. Send me to reform school?" Cathy retorted smartly, dropping into a chair, draping her long legs over one arm.

"Don't be flip, young lady. Your last grade was so promising, and now this. You realize you'll have to work doubly hard to bring your grade average up by the end of the term. This is your last chance."

She knew everything he was saying was correct, but the knowledge only seemed to fuel her contrariness.

"Who cares whether I learn algebra or not? Is it going to scar me for life?" Cathy challenged, out of the corner of her eye catching her mother's flinch. Instantly she knew she'd gone too far, but it was too late, so she bumbled on stupidly. "I'll probably be a dancer or something," she decided in a split second.

"That would be very nice," her dad told her coolly. "But you'll need some sort of education in order to get yourself a job while you're learning dance." He cleared his throat and, with his forefinger, traced the carving on a wooden pencil pot. "If you don't raise this grade by the end of this school year, you'll have to repeat the class in your senior year, which I don't believe you want to do, do you, Cathy?"

She shrugged.

"Mr. Marcus informs me that you have one more important test this semester, and if you do well on it, you'll pass with a C. As I've told you, your high school grades really do matter when you enter college. They are sent to every college you apply to, and who's going to accept you with D's and F's?"

"Lots of people don't go to college," Cathy argued back. "Thomas Edison, William Saroyan, Shakespeare—lots of people."

"That's very true," her father agreed in his calm, classroom voice. "But those people lived in different times. I don't think they had the social life you do. And I don't believe they had the same attitude you have, either."

It was just as well the doorbell interrupted them at that moment because Cathy did not want to be lectured to anymore.

Sybil rose. "That must be John. I'll answer it."

"Saved by the bell," breathed Cathy.

"You might as well just sit here and wait for him, Cathy. He's almost as concerned about your work as we are." Stephen Meyers turned on his heel and marched out, leaving Cathy sitting in the chair, seething.

John entered, carrying his usual burden of books, but this time he dropped a paperback into her lap. "This one's for you," he said. "I thought it might help you." He sat down in another chair.

She read the title: *Overcoming Math Anxiety* by Sheila Tobias. Leave it to John to think that people can solve their problems by reading a book, she thought. "Thanks," she said. "I'll look at it later." Cathy pushed the book aside and smiled up at John. "Besides, I've decided to study dance instead of math. What do you think?"

"Cathy, you're incredible! You've just blown the most important test of the semester, and you're acting like you don't even care!"

"What do you want me to do, cry on your shoulder? Come on. Let's dance. You can't say you don't like it until you try." Cathy stood up and grabbed both his hands and tried to urge him out of his chair, but he refused to budge. He shrank from her, but Cathy wouldn't let go, and to the surprise of both of them, she dropped into his lap.

"Stop it, Cathy," John said roughly, but Cathy paid no attention.

"Your hair is in your eyes," she purred, stroking stray wisps back and hooking her arms around his neck.

Abruptly he shoved her away, got up, and retucked his shirt. "When are you ever going to grow up?" he shouted. "For some stupid reason I keep expecting you to change, but you won't even try. So why do I keep on trying to help you?"

"I don't know. Why do you? It sure was easier getting D's in algebra before you came along. Now I have to work so hard for them—and put up with so much abuse."

"You know what, Cathy? You're absolutely right. I can't help you. When I take a job, I take it seriously, and I'm just not making any progress with you. It's a waste of my time and your parents' money. Don't you agree?" There was a hard edge to his voice that Cathy had never heard before. "I've had it, Cathy. I'm telling your parents I quit."

Cathy swallowed hard. John looked frighteningly fierce as he gathered up his things. "I need you, John, don't you see? Please don't quit."

"No. I've made up my mind. You'll manage, one way or another. Goodbye, Cathy."

Helplessly, Cathy watched him leave. Then the realization hit her, spreading like a huge, regretful ache inside her. This time he would never come back. She had really blown it. Suddenly she wished she could call back the words she had said, she wished she had been different with John. There was something about her he couldn't stand, and maybe, maybe she couldn't blame him. Or maybe, as she had suspected all along, he just wasn't her type.

Chapter Eleven

"Okay, Cathy. Tell me what happened?" Sybil Meyers' hands twisted in her apron.

Cathy blew her bangs out of her eyes and sighed innocently. "I don't know, Mom. John just got mad at me for no reason."

Her mother studied her with disbelief. "I don't think that's the whole story. John's put up with a lot from you, young lady. And what gets to me is that you've got everything to lose if you don't buckle down and study."

"Oh, Mom!" Cathy threw up her hands in exasperation. "There are other tutors around, you know. John's not the only one. He and I have a personality clash, that's all. We haven't gotten along since the day we met. I mean, he doesn't have a humorous bone in his body. He's just too serious. All he talks about is math."

"We paid him to talk to you about math, remember? We didn't hire you an entertainer." Her mother pinned her down with a piercing stare.

"Tim Bryant will tutor me. He's already offered."

"I'll bet he has." Sybil frowned, obviously keeping some thoughts to herself. "One thing your father and I decided when we hired a tutor for you was that it was foolish to choose someone you knew socially, because you'd never get any work done.

"But we were wrong about that, too. Obviously it doesn't matter *who* we choose, you will look at him or her as some kind of social conquest." She sighed heavily, wiping a strand of auburn hair from her eyes. "I don't understand you, Cathy. When I was your age, I was never so wrapped up in friends or boyfriends that I neglected my schoolwork. My brothers and I were always taught to see the importance of work before play. I suppose your father and I have been too easy on you."

"Too easy? You're always breathing down my neck. What'll you do with me next? Put me in a straitjacket?"

"Stop it, Cathy." For fear of exchanging further angry words, her mother whirled around and left her.

Cathy was shaken by the whole afternoon. It wasn't her family's way to argue; problems always were solved through sensible conversation. Well, sometimes, like now, she didn't feel sensible; she felt about as unsensible as an eight-year-old—or at least, that's the way everyone was making her feel. Being the only one in a family who voiced opinions loudly, the only one who even *shouted*, was really tough.

"So he quit, huh?" Jan shook her head in amazement at the news. "That's a first for you, Cathy."

"Sounds like things have been popping between you two," commented Tracy wryly.

"I told you we didn't hit it off. He's just way too serious, really drab." Cathy remembered how John's eyes had glittered, sparks flying, as he looked at her. No amount of crooning could cool that fire, she thought now, smiling casually for the benefit of her friends.

But Cathy didn't feel any better for downgrading John. Her unkind remarks didn't diminish John in any way, they only flung her anger out in wider circles. Naturally, her friends were eager to hear what she had to say, and being friends, they took her side. After all, wasn't that what friends were for?

Yet deep down, she felt slimy for talking about him this way, because none of it was really the truth. Sure, he was serious, but

91

that didn't make him ugly. The fact that he didn't succumb to her charms made him all the more attractive. And, he wasn't the least bit drab—in fact, his leanly carved features had become more striking to her the more she saw of them.

"Just a passing interest" was how Cathy described John to Tracy and Jan, and since passing interests were in character for her, they didn't question it, although she did detect a twinkle of doubt in Tracy's eye. Jan simply insisted that Cathy was too pretty and popular to mess around with a boy like John, so it was just as well. There were plenty of boys who were just as smart, but not as single-minded as he, who just loved Cathy.

But in spite of everything and everybody, Cathy secretly looked for John every day at school.

Chapter Twelve

The public library was an ivy-cov-ered stone building that had been standing since before the turn of the century. Because of the rot caused by the ivy, the town council had threatened to tear it down, but no move had been made in that direction because so far, the protests of the Historical Society were continuous, loud, and fierce.

Cathy loved the library, just as it was. There was a pungent, earthy scent pervading the structure, which her dear brother Matt insisted was the smell of the rot. She didn't believe him, though.

But rot or no rot, it was the kind of place Cathy didn't realize she missed until she returned there. She loved the heavy, reverent silence which was broken only by the whisper of turning pages or the operation of the Xerox machine.

Tim reached for Cathy's hand as they climbed the steps to the heavy wooden doors, which he held open for her. She ducked under his arm before the door shut behind them.

"I want to look up something in the *National Geographic*," Cathy said, pointing in the direction of the magazine racks.

"I'm gonna look for some books on Egypt," Tim said.

Cathy looked through several magazines. She enjoyed browsing through publications that she didn't see in the grocery store, like the ones on antiques and *Arizona Highways*, which had beautiful photographs.

She saw Tim between aisles, hunched over an Egypt book, no doubt. Her parents had allowed her to go to the library with him, only on the condition that she study here. Tim quickly assured them that that was all he had in mind. Then Cathy took the opportunity to let him know she was in real need of help on her algebra homework (not mentioning what had happened with John), and Tim was more than happy to oblige her.

"Tim, I hate to bother you, but can you help me find the current issue of the *Geographic?*" she implored.

Tim gazed at her, soft-eyed, nearly dropping the thick picture book he was holding. "Sure," he said. "Be right there." Clumsily, he shoved the book back in the case and followed her over to the magazines.

"Here it is, Cathy, right on the rack."

At that moment Cathy spotted John sitting nearby, leaning over to pick up a fallen book from the carpet. As he straightened, their eyes met and locked. Cathy's breath lodged somewhere between her diaphragm and her throat.

"Oh, hi, John. What a surprise," she whispered.

He smiled uncertainly, and Cathy suddenly remembered Tim at her side.

"Studying?" John asked, cocking his head to one side.

"Uh, yes." Cathy tugged nervously at her hair.

"Hi, John. How're ya doin'?" Tim said.

"Great. How's basketball?"

Cathy was vaguely aware of Tim's response as she watched John watching her. Suddenly she heard Tim saying, "Hope you don't mind if I give your prize pupil a few math lessons myself this afternoon."

"Not at all," John said, looking straight at Cathy. "Didn't she tell you I wasn't tutoring her anymore?"

"Well, no, she didn't." Tim looked flustered and confused, as if he could suddenly feel the electricity between Cathy and John but couldn't quite believe it.

"Let's go, Tim," Cathy said. "We've got lots of work to do, and I'm absolutely *sure* John does too. Right, John?"

"That's right," John said, still staring at Cathy.

"See you later," Cathy said, trying to sound cheerful.

John's big brown eyes looked sad as he watched them walk away. "Goodbye, Cathy," he whispered.

"See ya in trig, John. Take it easy," Tim said, handing Cathy the magazine she had been looking for. He led her to a big round table where he deposited his stack of books. "What's going on between you and John?" he asked Cathy.

"Obviously nothing. He's not even my tutor anymore."

"What happened?"

"We just didn't get along. He's just not my type, you know?"

"What do you mean, not your type? He was only supposed to be helping you with your algebra, right?"

"Right. That was all he was supposed to do," Cathy said, a faraway look in her eyes. "Look, I told you we just didn't get along. I wasn't learning anything. Now, are you going to help me or not?"

"Sure, sure. Take it easy. Where's your homework?"

She pulled out her homework paper. "It's really nice of you to help me with this, Tim. You don't know how much I appreciate it," she said. But her voice did not have the usual effect on him. He did not seem as pleased to be with her as he had a few minutes before.

Cathy felt miserable. She realized she had been mistreating Tim as badly as John. She'd lost the boy she really wanted and was still encouraging someone she didn't really care about. What was wrong with her? That day, her ability to concentrate on algebra was the worst it had ever been.

Chapter Thirteen

"You ought to phone John, Cathy, and tell him that you apologize," her father suggested. "I can see you still need his help."

"Are you kidding? After the way he walked out when I really needed him? I'll never ask John Crowley for help again. I guess I'll just have to pass algebra on my own. But I still don't understand why one of you can't help me. What good is it having teachers for parents if they can't even help you with your homework?"

"My algebra is pretty rusty," admitted Stephen Meyers. "Your mother's better at it than I am."

His wife shot him a questioning look. "Oh?" she remarked, and then: "Well, I suppose we could try." She turned to Cathy. "But I don't think you should give up on John. He's a nice boy, and he needs the money. . . ."

Cathy remembered John saying he needed

money that day they had had the fight in the ice cream parlor, but she couldn't imagine why he needed it. It certainly wasn't for soccer cleats or anything like most of the boys she knew would use it for. He didn't play sports. He had no fancy car or clothes to maintain—was relatively conservative in dress and rode that old bike everywhere; he probably even fixed it himself.

Just another one of her mother's excuses to get her sympathy, she decided. "If he needs the money, then why did he quit?" Cathy asked. "It wasn't my idea."

Her mother's appeal on John's behalf rose and fell, a backdrop for Cathy's thoughts. What was it her mom had said was wrong with John's father? He'd had some kind of surgery and was recuperating, which meant virtually nothing to Cathy. Nobody in her family had ever undergone any serious surgery. One summer Matt had had his tonsils out and was allowed to eat a disgusting amount of ice cream, but other than that, everyone had al-ways been in perfect health.

As she bent over her algebra book, Cathy's mind meandered back to John, the sun picking up deep reddish highlights in his dark hair, and the rough but silky way his skin felt against hers. She imagined that if he ever put his arms around her, his embrace would be gentle, considerate.

Just why did he fascinate her so? Was it because *he* played hard to get (she thought she'd cornered the market with that game), or because his wasn't a game at all, but just plain serious business? He had no time for her games—or for her. Every other boy she'd ever met had all the time in the world for her. They fell over their feet for the opportunity to sit next to her. She knew just what to say and do to attract them.

For a few days, Tim Bryant had phoned her to see how she was doing and to see if she needed any help with her algebra. But she had gently discouraged him, and he seemed to have taken the hint. She was relieved now that it was all over.

During the next week, Cathy came straight home from school each day to work with her mother for an hour on algebra. Sybil Meyers kicked off her clogs and touched the textbook as if it were a Ouija board that could magically give her the answers.

"It's been so long since I've done this," she mused. "I'm so accustomed to second grade math."

"That's about where I am, too, Mom." Cathy

100

proceeded to explain what she barely under-stood herself. "See? Even you have to admit you're not using it in your life. How many times do you run across an algebra problem?"

"Not too often. But having this knowledge does offer you more career choices in life. It's required, and it's supposed to make you into a more well-rounded individual."

"Well rounded—ha! And we're all trying to go on diets."

Her mother laughed. Cathy had always thought of her mother as a happy person. She never complained about anything. But she also kept to herself a lot, so it was some-times hard to tell what she was thinking and feeling. But in those hours they spent to-gether muddling out the algebra, Cathy learned a few things about her mother.

Her mother approached math the way she approached other challenges in her life. She had a real curiosity about it and seemed to want to reach out and take hold of it, turn it around, and see why it worked as it did. The results didn't quite match John's, but Cathy had to admit that her mother's spirit and determination put her own efforts to shame.

Sybil Meyers also had endless patience, but even patience couldn't solve some of Cathy's algebra problems. Finally, completely stumped, Sybil quietly laid down her pencil. "I'm sorry, Cathy. I don't know where to begin with these problems. We've got to call John to help you."

"Never! I don't want you to call him. If you can't help me, I'll just have to do it myself."

"Cathy, what happened between you and John? He's such a nice boy. Why did you have to give him such a hard time?"

"I just tried to help him loosen up a little. He could be a really popular guy if he weren't so serious all the time. But whenever I tried to talk to him, we ended up in an argument. It was weird."

Her mother smiled. "Your father and I used to have arguments like that sometimes. But *I* was the serious one. I really hated it when he tried to make me lighten up."

"You and Dad used to have arguments? I can't believe it."

"Oh, we still do sometimes, but I guess we're so used to each other's ways—and we've learned to compromise. If you care about someone, you make an effort to understand and bend a little bit. You'll find that out some day."

Cathy was amazed to hear her mother telling her so much about herself. "Thanks, Mom," she said and meant it.

"Sorry I couldn't be more help with algebra," her mother said, smiling as she walked away. "Think again about calling John, okay?"

"Okay. I'll think about it." Alone again in her room, Cathy took a fresh sheet of paper out of her desk drawer, determined to figure out the rest of the problems. When she shut the drawer, a pile of books and binders toppled off the desk top onto the floor.

She leaned down to scoop them up and discovered *Overcoming Math Anxiety*—the book John had given her the night he had quit. She'd never even opened it. It had been lying under a mound of papers on her desk. But now she was curious. Maybe some of her attitudes *were* holding her back and messing up her life. Maybe there were some changes she could make if she wanted to.

She sat down and read a chapter, then two. There was a direct link between mathematics and vocational opportunities, Cathy found out. Even high school math programs had a great influence on future careers. Traditionally, math had been considered a male subject, according to the author, and women were generally encouraged into nonmath subjects such as humanities, teaching, nursing, and social work.

Cathy thought of her parents, who had always encouraged her to tackle anything she might find interesting. She could now see that she was cutting off her own choices if she didn't at least give math a chance. Maybe there was something to this "math anxiety" stuff, but the important thing tonight was just to get her homework done.

As she was closing the paperback, something caught her eye. On the second page was an inscription: *For Cathy, the girl who has everything, plus a lot of potential to be anything she really wants to be. Love, John Crowley.*

Gasping, Cathy read it over and over again. John had written this for *her!* He had cared enough to write this, and she had never even opened the book before today!

She set the paperback aside and tried to finish her homework. But John's face blanked out the equations; his brown eyes locked with her own. Tomorrow, she would start working on her math anxiety. Tonight, she day-dreamed she was in John Crowley's arms, and he was telling her things he'd always wanted to tell her. . . .

The next day she looked for John at school but he wasn't there. She was very quiet all day, and Jan and Tracy couldn't figure out what was going on.

"Looks like algebra has finally done her in," Jan said.

"Either algebra or John Crowley," Tracy said, smiling.

John must be sick, Cathy thought. I'll find out where he lives and stop by his house after school. If I call him, he'll just say he doesn't want to see me.

When she got home, she looked up John's number in her mother's directory. The address, 41 Pine Street, stared up at her. Should she, or shouldn't she visit him? Maybe she could ask him out for a Coke. That way, he would have to hear her out, wouldn't he?

There was so much she wanted to get straight with him, even if he wasn't interested in tutoring her.

Quickly she dressed in a pair of nice jeans and a cream-colored blouse. She pulled her bike out from behind the garbage cans and headed for his house.

When she got to John's, his black bike was nowhere in sight. Perhaps he parked it in the back yard. But if he isn't there, she wondered, should I wait?

Simple decisions like this had never been a

problem to Cathy before. She had always played everything by ear, and one way or another, everything always had worked out. But with John, her methods hadn't worked that well. Everything seemed so crucial now. He might not like her being here. He might be turned off—he might reject her. Cathy had never had to deal with that, and she didn't know if she could now.

Mentally reviewing what she might say, Cathy took a deep breath and knocked at the front door.

The house was in an older section of town, where many homes were being renovated, and it was set apart from its neighbors by the pleasing contrast of its white and brick-red paint job. A low brick wall planter housed a profusion of flowers, and a huge maple tree dominated one side of the front lawn. A boy of about Matt's age vaulted onto a bike and hurtled out of the driveway, a newspaper sack slung across one shoulder.

"Oh, hi. Who are you?" From the open doorway a pigtailed girl Cathy guessed to be around ten blinked at her questioningly.

"I'm Cathy Meyers," she answered, smiling. "I'm a friend of John's. Is he home?"

"John?" The girl sounded surprised, and

haltingly added, "He's not here right now. Why don't you come in and wait?"

Cathy hesitated. What would John think of her waiting for him? It wasn't really her style to wait for boys—they usually had to wait for her.

The little girl watched her expectantly for an answer, so she finally agreed to come inside.

"I'm Lucy," the girl introduced herself, guiding Cathy through cool, dark hallways. Judging by the maze of hallways, several rooms had been added onto the original structure over the years. Cathy could tell by her brief introduction that the home was quite comfortable, sort of like her own.

"Do you and John go to the same school?" asked Lucy, surveying Cathy through a pair of brown eyes nearly identical to John's.

"Yes. He used to tutor me," Cathy ventured, not knowing what John had told his family about her. "He wasn't in school today, so I came by to see if he's all right."

"Oh, so you're the one." Lucy seemed to study her with new interest. "I always wondered what you looked like. You're so pretty. Don't worry about John. He's not sick. But he has been getting pretty tired lately, so my father let him sleep late today. He's picking up my mother from work right now."

"We have a visitor, Lucy?" A deep, male voice preceded its owner into the room. A man in a wheelchair rolled into the room. His eyes lit up when he caught sight of Cathy. "Well, well. Hello," he greeted her, extending a large, workworn hand. His handshake was firm. "I'm J.D. Crowley. And who might you be?" J.D. winked at her.

She introduced herself quite formally, telling him that she went to John's school. "I heard you had surgery recently," she continued. "I'm sorry." She didn't know whether or not sorry was the right thing to say.

"Yes, I am too, but it beats the pain of broken parts. Surgery's amazing nowadays. They can fuse your bones together. Did you know that?" He quickly shrugged it off before Cathy could respond. "Of course, you wouldn't be interested in that. An old man's grumblings about his operation."

"Oh, no," she protested, for she didn't think of him as old. She guessed he was about her father's age. "It sounds really interesting. I didn't know that they could do that."

"Would you like something to drink?" he asked. Cathy nodded, and Lucy went off to

108

the kitchen. "Lucy and I are the only ones here right now. Lucy's my nurse, you see." He winked again. "My wife Mary works at the hospital, my daughter Jennifer has a job in a boutique, and Chad has a paper route. John had a tutoring job and will be getting another soon. So you know John?"

"Yes," Cathy said. "I wanted to talk to him about something."

A sudden wince of pain flitted almost imperceptibly across Mr. Crowley's face, but it didn't interfere with his interest in Cathy. "Oh?"

Not wanting to tell John's father that she was the person John had been tutoring, Cathy was relieved that Lucy reentered the room at that moment and said, "Here's some lemonade." She gave tall glasses of pink lemonade to her father and to Cathy. Cathy thought she seemed awfully adult for her young years.

"Thanks, Lucy."

They sat in the dining room, where several woodworking projects were in various stages of completion. There was a round table top with four curvy legs lying next to it. Mr. Crowley noticed Cathy looking at them.

"John found those legs at the flea market,"

he explained. "I'm making a table top for 'em, and Mary will stain it, and it'll be one expensive-looking piece of furniture."

"Take a look at this." He wheeled his chair over to a rocker that was minus its rockers. "We had to carve new rockers for this baby. We'll put some oak stain on her, and she'll look as good as new."

Cathy was accustomed to flea markets and garage sales, since her mother's idea of fun was picking over somebody else's musty cast-offs. But she had never seen secondhand furniture refinished as beautifully as Mr. Crowley's, and she told him so.

"My mom collects a few old things, but she doesn't know how to repair and redo them like you do," she said. As she took a better look around, she saw that there were many more lovely things. "Did you do all these pieces?"

"Most of them," J.D. answered proudly. "That clawfooted table, for instance. Had to scrape about five layers of paint off it before we found the wood. But look how pretty it came up."

"And that cabinet is my pride and joy," he went on, picking out other objects in the room, relating their history. Cathy lost track of time, as though she were being given a museum tour. Old hurricane lamps, a gossip bench, tea cart, rockers, and an heirloom hope chest she just knew her mother would love.

"And look at this." Lucy emerged from the hall toting a doll bed of very old wicker, painted white. Hidden beneath folds of frothy, yellowed lace was a china doll with a mended face.

"How pretty," exclaimed Cathy, and she was genuinely surprised at herself for thinking so. Her mother had brought home a doll much like this one when she had been very little. An old doll with a cracked face and torn, dirty clothes. Cathy had hated it and thought it was horribly ugly. Her mother had wanted to fix it up, but Cathy didn't want it, so it was given to an aunt in Oregon.

It could've been a beautiful doll, Cathy thought now, if only I'd given it a chance. Why don't I ever give things a chance?

The late afternoon sun slanted into the living room, right across Mr. Crowley's face. Lucy had gone to her room, so Cathy jumped up to adjust the shades. "Relax, young lady, I won't melt, you know."

"Please let me make myself useful while I'm here, Mr. Crowley. Can I get anything for you while I'm up?"

"Well, you might grab the bottle of pills in the cabinet above the sink and bring a glass of water with them, if you don't mind."

"Of course I don't mind."

When she returned, Mr. Crowley thanked her and said, "I suppose John's caught in traffic, Cathy. I thought he'd be home by now. You know, my family has really been pitching in since my accident. I'm pretty useless to them right now."

"Useless? How can you say that after showing me all the beautiful things you've restored? What kind of work did you do for a living?" Cathy asked.

"I was a welder," he said, and seeing her confused look, he explained, "A guy who sews metal together."

"Oh." She flushed at her ignorance. "How did you hurt your back?"

"Metal pipe fell on my spine," he said matter-of-factly.

"Oh." That was all Cathy could say. She just couldn't imagine anything so horrible happening to someone she knew.

"It's not a nice thing to remember. But I'm a very lucky man. I know that."

"You're a very *special* man, Mr. Crowley. I can see now where John gets his determination."

"You sound like you know John pretty well. But he doesn't talk about girls much at home . . . and they certainly don't come to visit him very often," he said, chuckling. "He'll be jealous of his old dad for keeping you to myself."

Cathy blushed. "I'm not so sure of that." She changed the subject abruptly. "You know, I think it's really great the way you can fix things up. I keep thinking of that china doll. I never would have suspected how beautiful it could be. And it's all because of your patience and your skill—and your love for things, isn't it? Do you think—do you think maybe I could come by sometime and watch you when you're restoring something? I'd really like to learn how to do it."

"Come by any time you like," Mr. Crowley said, smiling. "I'm sure John will second the invitation."

"Thank you, Mr. Crowley. Now I'm afraid I'll have to be going. My mother will have a fit if I'm late for dinner. Please tell John I'm very sorry I missed him."

"John will be sorry he missed you, I'm sure."

"Goodbye, Mr. Crowley. Goodbye, Lucy," she called. "See you soon." Cathy hopped onto her bike, with a new and valuable knowledge of John Crowley in her heart.

Chapter Fourteen

She had been wrong about John all along, thinking he was boring and too seri-ous. Life *was* serious to him. It wasn't one great long party as it was for her.

Since his father's injury, Cathy guessed that nothing had come too easily to the Crowleys. The entire family, including little Lucy, was pitching in to make everything run just as smoothly as ever. Their quiet humor and sense of togetherness surprised and warmed Cathy.

Suddenly, she felt ashamed of herself for the way she'd acted—toward John and to-ward her parents. She had placed too much emphasis on being popular and having fun. Of course, John had tried to tell her that in his own way, but she hadn't been willing to listen.

She had breezed through life with such ease! The road she had traveled had been completely smooth, but it couldn't be that way for everyone, and it might not continue to be that easy for her, either, she realized. Now that she had met John and his father, she knew that life would never seem quite so simple to her again.

How silly and frivolous I've been! she thought, pedaling vigorously down the hill to her house. Of course, I still think John has something to learn about having fun, and maybe I could teach him if he'd let me. But I certainly haven't gone about it very wisely so far.

How could she change? Cathy had been Cathy for as long as she could remember. There were not too many other personalities she could readily adopt. Maybe she would just have to settle for shaving off the rough edges of her character for now.

Smiling to herself, she coasted into the garage, nearly hitting Matt as he stepped out the kitchen door.

"Where've you been?" he demanded. The frayed T-shirt he wore was smeared with jelly and grease.

Cathy whirled him around, and he fought to extricate himself from her grasp. "I just went over to a friend's."

"Mom's looking for you, you goon," Matt grumbled, climbing onto his decal-plastered go-cart.

"Cathy, where have you been?" Sybil looked up from the pile of workbooks she was correcting.

"I just went over to John's," she blurted out.

Sybil Meyers tried hard to conceal a smile. "Oh? Do you think you might like to make some tea and tell me about it?" She laid down her pen and tucked a wisp of auburn hair back into its bun.

"Yeah, okay, Mom." While she made tea, Cathy told her mother all about John's father, the expertly refinished collectibles that her mother would absolutely love, and Lucy.

"I told you John's family was having a hard time." Her mother sighed. "Your grandfather had back trouble, you know. But I guess you just have to see things for yourself. No one can tell you anything."

Cathy set out cream, sugar, and the teapot. "Do you think he might reconsider tutoring, Mom?" she asked, pouring an amber stream into her mother's cup.

Her mother studied her closely. "It depends on why you want him to reconsider. John's not about to waste his time—but you can try, Cathy," she said encouragingly. "You've just

116

got to show him that you mean it about working."

Just then, the doorbell rang. It was a crazy chime that Sybil had picked up at a flea market and Stephen had repaired.

With a swish of her ruffled skirt, Sybil Meyers answered the door.

"Oh, John, come on in. I have your check."

Cathy's heart leaped into her throat. She hurried into the front hall, putting on her best smile. "Hi, John," she said shyly.

John shoved his fingers in his front pockets. "Hi, Cathy. How are you?"

"Oh, fine." Cathy leaned against the doorjamb, at a loss for words for the first time in her life. Her mother rustled off to get John's check, her voice trailing behind her.

"Won't you sit down with us and have some tea, John? Cathy just made some."

"Oh—uh—no, thank you. I'd better be getting back." He glanced sheepishly at Cathy.

Impulsively she reached out and touched his arm. "John, wait," she whispered. He flinched. "I wanted to tell you I'm sorry for causing you trouble. I didn't realize, I mean—just accept my apology, will you?"

He nodded, his smile tentative. "Okay."

"And, John, I wanted to tell you I finally read that book you brought me. And I've learned a few things since I saw you last—about algebra and about John Crowley."

He blushed deeply and said nothing. But the stiffness seemed to have left his posture, so she felt it safe to continue. "What I really want to ask you is, would you consider tutoring me again?" Cathy watched his face shift as he thought about the question. *Say yes,* she wished, hoping her brain waves would reach out and influence him.

John bit his lower lip, obviously thinking it over very carefully. That was John—careful, cautious. Cathy bet he never jumped into anything.

Do you know what, John? You look just like that Rodin statue of The Thinker. You really do. All serious and thoughtful. She held back her own feelings, waiting for his answer.

"Let me think it over, okay, Cathy?"

Expectation slid from her face, tinkling down somewhere inside her like shattered glass. Think it over! What was there to think over? Her pride rose up in mute surprise. Numbly, she muttered, "Oh, sure. Uh, think it over."

Her mother returned with John's check.

"I'm sorry I can't stay," John addressed her. "I'd better get going."

118

Sybil's smile was expansive. "Thanks so much, John. And don't make a stranger of yourself."

"I won't. And thank you." He indicated the check, then turned to Cathy, who was pretending to be engrossed in a painting on the wall that she'd only stared at thousands of times before. She was thinking: maybe now he'll change his mind and say yes.

"I'll think about it, Cathy, and let you know," was what he said.

She turned and nodded, speechless, angry at herself for bothering to ask him at all.

That night at dinner, Cathy was as quiet as her family had ever seen her. Fortunately, even Matt seemed to respect her feelings for once, and nobody pressed her to take part in the conversation. As they were finishing dessert, the phone rang, and Matt ran to answer it.

"Oh, yeah, she's here. Hi, John. How're ya doing?" Matt made a face at his sister as he handed her the phone.

Cathy felt a knot in her stomach. She hoped her voice wasn't shaking as she said, "Hi, John. How are you?"

"I'm fine. How about you?"

"Fine."

"My dad told me you stopped by."

119

"Yeah. I liked your family."

"That was nice of you—to come by, that is."

Now that all the amenities had been spoken, what else did they talk about? Cathy felt sudden panic. *Here it is, proof absolute that we are too different—John and I have nothing in common except a discussion of the weather and our health.*

After a lengthy, awkward silence, John cleared his throat and said, "Listen, Cathy, I thought over your offer, and decided that I would come back and tutor you. But"—his voice held a note of reservation—"I can't put up with your kidding around. Otherwise, we're just wasting our time."

Cathy smiled into the receiver. *You've got my undivided attention, John—I can't think of anything else!* "You've got it," she announced brightly. "I told you, I'm sorry for how I behaved." She was going to add, "it was inexcusable," but decided against it. There was such a thing as laying it on too thick, which John would be suspicious of. She must be careful not to drive him away again.

"We'll start, let's see—what time is good for you?"

Anytime—tonight, she nearly blurted out but checked herself. She was supposed to be going skating that night, anyway. But she could cancel that. "Tonight?"

"Tonight I've got a meeting of the chess club. How about tomorrow, after school? Say around four?"

So he was the one who was busy, Cathy thought. Were the tables turning?

"Oh, sure," she replied, glad he couldn't see the stunned expression on her face. "That would be fine."

Cathy hung up and did cartwheels down the hall, her joy bubbling up inside her like an oil gusher.

"Yippee!" she squealed as she whirled past Matt, who frowned at her with disdain.

"What a jerk," he commented. "You're really out of it, Cathy. Shall I call the little men in white coats?"

"Call anyone you want, Matt," she cried gaily, backflipping onto her bed.

Chapter Fifteen

John stretched his arm along the backrest behind Cathy as she worked on her homework. She imagined his arm tightening around her shoulders, his lips against hers, the algebra book sliding off her lap and onto the floor with a muffled thump.

But that didn't happen. She had to concentrate. There wasn't much time left until the end of school and report card time, and she had to use what was left to the fullest—no fooling around.

It was funny how, since John had begun tutoring her again, her brain had opened up and she really felt like she was learning something. Maybe it was the book he'd given her that was helping, too, showing her the importance of what she was studying.

"You've been working so hard, Cathy," John said, checking her answers. "I'm really impressed. It shows."

"Really? That book you gave me really helped. I decided I didn't want to be among the majority of girls who have a math avoidance problem," she told him knowledgeably.

John looked amused. "I don't blame you. Why let the boys enjoy all the math subjects?" He glanced back at her paper. "You got all of these right."

"You're not seeing a mirage, are you?" she inquired sweetly. She had been ever so careful not to tease him, biting her lip when the wild comments threatened to burst forth. After all, he was probably pretty wary of her by now.

"No. It's perfect. Congratulations."

John's elbows were propped on the arms of the chair, and he looked relaxed. Cathy wanted to hug him, but instead, she said, "Thank you. But I couldn't have done it without you, John. You know that."

He threw back his head and let out an unrestrained laugh that surprised Cathy.

"What's wrong? What did I say?" she prodded. "I mean, it's nice to see you laugh once in awhile, but not at me!"

"You're so funny, you know that?" He laughed again. "You only needed someone to show you that you could do it. You've been

123

acting like I was going to bite you for a week now, and I can't understand it. When have I ever been a threat to you, Cathy?"

She felt herself blush. "Now you're embarrassing me, John," she replied. "I've only been concentrating on my algebra."

"You haven't been flirting with me or trying any of your usual tricks." John shook his head, pushing up his glasses with one finger. "Gosh, I wonder what happened to the old Cathy. She was a lot of fun."

"What are you getting at?"

"I don't suppose the old Cathy might like to take in a movie tonight, would she? That is, if her parents allow her to go out with her tutor." His ears turned a pale shade of pink. "And we could bring the new Cathy along, too, just to keep the old Cathy under control."

Cathy socked him lightly in the shoulder. "Now you're making fun of me. You make me sound like a split personality. How would you like it if—"

He cut her off. "Come on, it's my turn to make the jokes. Do you want to go to a movie, or not?"

"What do you want to see? A documentary?"

"That doesn't sound bad, but I know something better. Do you like comedies?"

"Of course I do! What do you think I am, anyway? A girl without a sense of humor?" Faintly, she remembered once thinking John had no sense of humor.

"I don't know," he said, his expression deadpan. "You haven't been that much fun lately."

Cathy rose, folded her homework paper, and laid it on the desk. "Well, that's really something, John Crowley, coming from you." She pulled her hair back into a ponytail and wound a rubber band around it.

"Is it a date, or not?"

Cathy noted his confident stance, leaning against her father's desk, and wondered what had happened to him. She shook her head. "What a way to ask for a date, John. You're going to have to learn how to talk to girls. Do you want me to teach you?" she cooed over her shoulder.

"Oh, I don't know about that," John shrugged, on his way out the door. "I think I'm doing okay."

Cathy ran down the hall, yelling after him, "What's that supposed to mean? John? John?"

He didn't answer, leaving her to wonder.

Chapter Sixteen

Two weeks later, on the last day of school, Cathy and John went out again, this time to celebrate: report cards had been given out that day, and Cathy had managed to pass algebra with a B minus. "We did it!" she had ex-claimed when she met John after school. "We really did it!"

That evening they went out to the fanciest restaurant in town and then to a movie. Over dinner, Cathy tried teasing John just a little. "What's happened to you, John? You seem so different lately."

"I guess that's a compliment," he said, a twinkle in his eyes, "since you always hated the way I was before."

"I didn't hate you. I just didn't understand you very well. Actually, I still don't."

"Well, I guess I've learned something from you, Cathy." He looked at her slyly.

She grinned. "Really? You learned some-

126

thing from me? I thought you knew everything."

"Not quite ... I'm just a beginner when it comes to romance, you know."

Cathy smiled at him, excitement quivering insider her. "Maybe I can still teach you to dance," she suggested. "Do you want to learn?"

He grimaced. "I told you I can't dance. I don't want to make a fool of myself."

"Who's going to let you do that? Are you afraid of making mistakes?" she challenged.

"Well, no—I guess not." He searched for words to explain himself. "I'm just not the dancing type, Cathy. Maybe that part of your life should remain separate from me."

"What for?" demanded Cathy. "What's wrong with a good dance and party once in awhile?"

"I'm not a party person. I like quieter things."

"Ugh. Like chess? Practicing Spanish?" she taunted.

"Cathy," John said gently, "why don't we discuss this later, okay?"

"All right," she agreed sighing.

Later, at the movie, another comedy, Cathy really enjoyed watching John laugh. At certain parts of the movie, tears ran down his face, and she became more entranced in him than in the movie.

At one point, John's arm stole around the back of Cathy's chair, his hand close to her shoulder. Cathy held her breath. Most boys were so anxious to get their arm around you in a dark theater, but not John. His arm lingered on the seat back, and his hand brushed her arm lightly, then moved away.

Cathy was a little disappointed. She wanted him to run his fingers through her hair or squeeze her shoulder. Why was he still holding back?

Rarely did she long for affection or attention. But John's behavior toward her was so puzzling, so different, she couldn't be sure of his true feelings. And, Cathy realized, she was slightly panic-stricken to find that John was the first and only boy she had ever felt vaguely serious about. She had vowed never to feel this way about anyone. She didn't want to fall for John. Why couldn't he simply be like other boys? Why did he have to have so much power over her feelings?

Cathy couldn't bear to have the evening come to an end. It seemed like the most important night of her life, and she wanted it to last a little longer.

"Come on in for a little while," she said. "I think there's some ice cream in the fridge. Let's stuff ourselves."

As they sat on the living room couch, eating their ice cream, John became suddenly shy again. He was startled when Cathy jumped up, put a record on the stereo, and said, "Okay, Crowley, this is it. It's about time I taught you how to dance."

He eyed her warily.

"No, really, I won't do anything. I promise. I just—"She held her slim arms out to him, and he took her hands cautiously, glancing at the pearl ring she wore on her index finger.

"Nice ring," he said, clearing his throat.

Cathy tried to whirl him around, but he stood rooted to the floor. "John, why don't you move? You're like a tree."

"Upright," he stated solemnly.

"Well, okay, but that doesn't help when you're learning to dance. Now come on. I don't know how to lead, I only know how to follow." Her voice dropped to a husky whisper because she didn't want to disturb her parents.

She led John around the floor, chanting, "one-two-three-four, one-two-three-four." John shuffled, stepped on her feet, muttered several apologies, but Cathy persisted, insisting he was doing great.

Cathy thought she felt John's arms tighten against her back (was she imagining it?), and she closed her eyes, allowing the music to move the two of them across the floor, sliding gently in and out of rhythm as John lost his footing, then quickly regained it. She felt his breath against her ear, sending delicious tingles down the back of her neck.

John was holding her close for the first time, and it was just as wonderful as she had dreamed it would be. She knew now she would never grow tired of John Crowley. The boy she had once thought was so boring would never bore her, she realized.

John held her at arm's length and looked at her intently.

"What did you think of me the first time we met?" Cathy asked.

He answered right away. "I thought, 'How in the world am I going to keep my mind on algebra. She's the prettiest girl I've ever met.'"

Cathy giggled and buried her head in the hollow of his shoulder. "Do you know what I thought of you?"

"I can imagine." He winced.

"I thought, 'I'll never be able to loosen this guy up.'"

"I think you mentioned that once." John laughed, drawing her to him. "You sure made it hard for me to keep my mind on the job. And I really did want to help you, you know. You were so darn relentless—and irresistible—you drove me crazy."

"Irresistible? You sure managed to resist me long enough."

"That was for your own good," he teased. "What do you think of me now?"

"I think . . . " Cathy paused, wondering, *can I say what I really feel for him without being hurt?* Then, gazing into his sincere, expectant face, she knew she could trust him. "I think you're the only person, besides my family, that is, that I've ever really cared about."

There, she'd said it—she was trembling.

John stared at her in surprise. "Really? Are you being truthful, Cathy? I mean, you've dated so many popular boys, and I'm just—"

"I'm being truthful, cross my heart." Numbly she traced her finger over her heart. "I've never wanted to like anyone too much."

"And you do now. Is that what I hear you saying?"

She nodded, feeling as if she had just spilled the entire contents of her heart before him, ready to be mopped up any way he pleased.

"Well, I'll admit that I thought caring for you was completely hopeless." John smiled as he held her. "I thought you'd never like me, and I was crazy about you. I've never really looked at girls much before—I mean, I've always been sort of afraid to get involved, myself. Having a girlfriend also seemed so—complicated, especially with the way things are at home for me."

Cathy was about to ask him how he could possibly think she didn't care for him, after all she'd done to get him to notice her, but he was looking directly into her eyes and saying, "I guess we are alike in some ways, Cathy, that we never even suspected."

"You'd never guess that to look at us, John. We're about as mismatched as Mutt and Jeff."

"More like yellow phosphorus and water, actually."

"John! What in the world is *that* supposed to mean?"

"The phosphorus ignites when it hits water," he said, kisses punctuating his words.

"You mean, we're fireworks?"

"Something like that," he murmured, his lips moving over hers so softly and gently that Cathy forgot anything else she might say.

We hope you enjoyed reading this book. If you would like to receive further information about titles available in the Bantam series, just write to the address below, with your name and address: Kim Prior, Bantam Books, 61–63 Uxbridge Road, Ealing, London W5 5SA.

If you live in Australia or New Zealand and would like more information about the series, please write to:

Sally Porter
Transworld Publishers
(Australia) Pty Ltd.
15-23 Helles Avenue
Moorebank
N.S.W. 2170
AUSTRALIA

Kiri Martin
Transworld Publishers (NZ) Ltd
Cnr. Moselle and Waipareira
Avenues
Henderson
Auckland
NEW ZEALAND

All Bantam Young Adult books are available at your bookshop or newsagent, or can be ordered from the following address: Corgi/Bantam Books, Cash Sales Department, PO Box 11, Falmouth, Cornwall, TR10 9EN.

Please list the title(s) you would like, and send together with a cheque or postal order. You should allow for the cost of the book(s) plus postage and packing charges as follows:

All orders up to a total of £5.00: 50p
All orders in excess of £5.00: Free

Please note that payment must be made in pounds sterling; other currencies are unacceptable.

(The above applies to readers in the UK and Republic of Ireland only)

B.F.P.O. customers, please allow for the cost of the book(s) plus the following for postage and packing: 60p for the first book, 25p for the second book and 15p per copy for the next 7 books, thereafter 9p per book.

Overseas customers, please allow £1.25 for postage and packing for the first book, 75p for the second book, and 28p for each subsequent title ordered.

Thank you!

Sweet Dreams are fresh, fun and exciting – alive with the flavour of the contemporary teen scene – the joy and doubt of *first love*. If you've missed any Sweet Dreams titles, then you're missing out on *your* kind of stories, written about people like *you*!

With more than 100 titles in print, look out for titles you have missed!